THE GRUB-AND-STAKERS
HOUSE A HAUNT

ADULT MYSTERY FICTION
by Alisa Craig *and* Charlotte MacLeod

Madoc Rhys Series

A Pint of Murder
Murder Goes Mumming
A Dismal Thing to Do
*Trouble in the Brasses
The Wrong Rite

Grub-and-Stakers Series

The Grub-and-Stakers Move a Mountain
The Grub-and-Stakers Quilt a Bee
*The Grub-and-Stakers Pinch a Poke
The Grub-and-Stakers Spin a Yarn

Nonseries

The Terrible Tide

Peter Shandy Series

Rest You Merry
The Luck Runs Out
Wrack and Rune
Something the Cat Dragged In
The Curse of the Giant Hogweed
*The Corpse in Oozak's Pond
Vane Pursuit
An Owl Too Many

Sarah Kelling Series

The Family Vault
The Withdrawing Room
The Palace Guard
The Bilbao Looking Glass
The Convivial Codfish
The Plain Old Man
The Recycled Citizen
*The Silver Ghost
*The Gladstone Bag

Anthologies

Grab Bag
Mistletoe Mysteries
Christmas Stalkings

*American Mystery Award Winner

THE GRUB-AND-STAKERS HOUSE A HAUNT

Charlotte MacLeod writing as
ALISA CRAIG

WILLIAM MORROW AND COMPANY, INC.
New York

Library of Congress Cataloging-in-Publication Data

MacLeod, Charlotte.
    The grub-and-stakers house a haunt / by Charlotte MacLeod writing as Alisa Craig.
        p.   cm.
    ISBN 0-688-08644-6
    I. Title.   II. Title: Grub-and-stakers house a haunt.
PS3563.A31865G68   1993
813'.54—dc20   92-30534
                                                                    CIP

Printed in the United States of America

First Edition

1 2 3 4 5 6 7 8 9 10

BOOK DESIGN BY LISA STOKES

For Joan Hess

CHAPTER
1

*W*idows were scarce in Lobelia Falls, Ontario. Mrs. Zilla Trott might therefore have been regarded as something of a rarity, not that she couldn't have made it into the rarity class on her own merits. Tonight, sensibly dressed for a brisk October evening in leather scuffs, heavy wool socks, a long red flannel nightgown, a pink crocheted bed jacket, and a matching cap that sat jauntily on her abundant, close-cropped gray hair, she had added an old blue sweater of her late husband's to her ensemble and stepped out into the back yard to salute the harvest moon. Her cat, Nemea, had followed dutifully at Zilla's well-protected heels. Their brief moonwalk completed, Nemea had followed Zilla back into the kitchen without demur, hiss, spit, or catly cuss. At the moment, Nemea was sitting on the drainboard watching Zilla put her soybeans to sprout, and Zilla was worried.

"What's got into you tonight, Nemea? Why didn't you stay out awhile and go helling around with the rest of the cats, eh? I hope you're not coming down with something."

Nemea certainly didn't look to be ailing. She'd been named, not inappropriately, for the Nemean Lion. A fine strapping figure of a feline, she was bigger than most cats unless you counted lynxes and pumas, which even the most ardent cat lovers are often reluctant to do. Nemea's eyes were huge and green, they bore an inscrutable glint that had cowed many dogs and not a few humans. Her fur was a rich copper-gold color with streaks of strawberry roan. Thanks to all the wheat germ and yogurt with which Zilla supplemented Nemea's carefully balanced diet, and possibly also to the odd mouse or chipmunk she added on her own hook, the magnificent animal's pelt fairly glistened.

She was gleaming now in the lamplight. Her eyes were bright as emeralds, her pink nose was moist, her fine stand of whiskers showed not the barest hint of a droop. Yet Nemea couldn't fool her keen-eyed mistress. She was not a happy cat.

"I guess likely what I'd better do is make us both a nice cup of camomile tea."

Zilla put a lot of faith in camomile; she grew her own, of course. She filled the kettle, little recking what a handsome picture she made with the lamplight picking out coppery reflections on the high-bridged nose that revealed her part Cree heritage. She put another stick in the wood stove, for the night was chill and she wanted the fire to hold over till morning. She was just setting the kettle on the front lid when she heard from behind her a rather tentative "Boo!"

People didn't lock their doors much in Lobelia Falls, Zilla naturally assumed this must be one of the neighbor's kids practicing up for Halloween. She whirled around, all set to fling up her hands and exclaim, "My stars and garters!" as protocol demanded. However, her ensuing amazement was totally unfeigned.

There on her well-scrubbed linoleum stood an elderly man whom Zilla had never laid eyes on before in all her born days and could have done nicely without now. His gray mustache was even more striking than Nemea's, but that was the only impressive thing about him. His attire could best be described as rough: his baggy dark-gray trouser legs were stuffed into scuffed old boots with dirt caked on them, his gray flannel shirt had about as much class as a worn-out mop. The dark rag tied around his neck wouldn't have been fit to wipe out a coal bin with, and the billycock felt hat on his grizzled head was an out-and-out disgrace. Zilla's hand snaked out and grabbed the poker from beside the stove.

"Boo yourself, you dirty old goat! What's the big idea, barging in here unasked and scaring the daylights out of a defenseless widow? Not to mention her cat." Nemea had her back up and her tail bushed out, she was spitting a blue streak and Zilla didn't blame her. "You just turn around and waltz yourself out of my kitchen before I lam you one with this poker."

"That's a hell of a way to talk to company," grunted the interloper. "Ain't you even wonderin' who I am?"

"Not particularly. You don't look like any relative I'd care to own, that's for sure. Unless you're that no-good bum Aunt Jessamine got herself tied to back in nineteen forty-two. I thought you'd died of hobnail liver ages ago. I can't remember your name."

"Don't make no never mind. I ain't him an' never was. I'd o' known better than to get myself roped in by any she-devil of a woman."

"Huh! What makes you think any woman in her right mind would want you? What are you here for anyway? There's nothing in the house worth stealing except my family Bible and I expect that's the last thing you'd want. If you're after a handout, I'll give you some fricassee of tofu and a tumbler of buttermilk but you'll have to eat it out in the woodshed. And you'd darn well better not smoke, or I'll turn the hose on you."

"Cripes, you're a mean one, you an' that redheaded

mountain lion you got there. I been nose to nose with a chargin' grizzly bear, an' that bugger was some ugly! But it couldn't hold a candle to you two."

Even so, the man stepped forward. Zilla raised the poker. "You come one step closer, mister, and I'll lay you out flat as a barn door."

The gray whiskers swept upward. The old goat was grinning at her. "Go ahead, sister, hit me. I dare you." He took the forbidden step.

Healthful diet, hard work, ample exercise, and lots of practice at the archery butts as a member of the Grub-and-Stake Gardening and Roving Club had kept Zilla Trott in the finest of fettle. Her strength was as the strength of ten on account of all those bean sprouts, she whanged with will and purpose. Great, then, was Zilla's astonishment when the stranger just stood there and took the blow. Greater still was her dismay when the poker encountered no obstacle except her own right shin.

"Ouch! You moved, you coward."

"Do it again," the man offered magnanimously. "Thrash away as much as you've a mind to. How 'bout tryin' a backhander this time? Take a good holt on my chin whiskers so's I can't turn my head away."

Exasperated, Zilla made a grab for the ratty gray beard. Her hand encountered nothing. She swung the poker sideways and again hit nothing.

"Well, I'll be gum-swizzled! What is this, anyway? Am I having a nightmare?"

"Nope. Take a look at your cat. She knows."

Yes, Nemea knew. Suddenly, so did Zilla. "Well, dip me for a sheep! I thought ghosts were supposed to be gray and fuzzy."

"I'm gray an' fuzzy, ain't I?"

"Come to think of it, you are. Wait till I tell Minerva! How long have you been haunting me?"

"Oh, I dunno. Us ghosts don't pay no mind to time. I

been out in the woodshed mostly, just kind o' moochin' around an' gettin' the feel of bein' a haunt. I forgot where I was before that. Moulderin' away in some lonesome graveyard, I s'pose. How do I look?"

"Not too bad, considering." Zilla wasn't exactly warming up to her unexpected visitant, but she was beginning to feel a bit embarrassed about the poker. A hostess did have certain responsibilities, after all. "I don't suppose there's any use offering you a cup of camomile tea?"

"Well, I s'pose you might try, though I'm not sure I got any place to put it. Go ahead an' have yours, I'll just hang around an' watch. Cat gets a snort too, does she?"

"Oh, yes. Nemea likes a little cream in hers, though. There you are, puss, don't slop it all over the counter. And for goodness' sake unfuzz your tail. He's all right, whoever he is. Do you happen to remember your name, mister?"

"Seems to me it might o' been Hector or Harvey. No, by gorry, it was Hiram! Hiram Jellyby, that was it. Funny how your memory improves once you get off the astral plane. Yup, that was me, Hiram Jellyby. I was a wagon driver by profession. Mules was my specialty. You got any openin's for a disembodied mule skinner around here nowadays?"

"Not in Lobelia Falls, no. Offhand I can't think where I last saw a mule team. I'm sorry, Mr. Jellyby, times change, you know. It's mostly trucks and tractors these days, though in my humble opinion we'd do a darn sight less polluting of the environment with more animals and fewer machines. Here, sit down and make yourself comfortable. If you can sit, that is."

"I'll give 'er a go an' see how she works. I ain't too up on this manifestin' wrinkle yet."

Zilla watched with almost motherly interest while her strange visitor endeavored to accommodate himself to the chair. At first Hiram showed a tendency to ooze down through the seat, but he gradually got the hang of it and looked quite natural sitting there with a cup of camomile tea steaming on the table in front of him. He couldn't raise the cup, of course, but he seemed somehow able to absorb the steam. Zilla was fascinated to see the level of tea in the cup begin to subside, millimeter by millimeter.

As a former mule-team driver, Hiram Jellyby would probably have preferred strong coffee, she thought. Maybe with a plate of beans. Or a doughnut. Zilla herself wouldn't touch a doughnut with a ten-foot pole, unless it happened to be one of Minerva Oakes's. Minerva made the best doughnuts in town, perhaps she'd be willing to donate one or two in the interests of psychical research.

Zilla wondered why she didn't feel more peculiar sitting here drinking tea with a ghost, particularly with the ectoplasm of somebody she'd never met in the flesh, and more particularly in her nightgown. Not that she wasn't decently covered, though she did hope none of her neighbors would notice the light still on in her kitchen and take a notion to drop by for a chat.

Then there was the Peeping Tom whom some of the people who lived over near the inn had complained about lately. Strange things had been happening around there ever since Andy McNaster, the former innkeeper, had dashed off to become a movie star. In Zilla's opinion, that new manager, Hedrick Snarf, was no more up to scratch than a cat in mittens. It was a rotten shame Lemuel Pilchard, Andy's former right-hand man, had had that terrible fall so soon after his boss left town. Lemuel was a crackerjack at innkeeping, but it wasn't a job that a person could do well all wrapped up in plaster.

Hiram Jellyby must have noticed, or perhaps divined by extrasensory perception, that his hostess's mind was wandering. He broke into her reverie with a quite reasonable question. "Speakin' of names, missus, you mind tellin' me yours?"

"Oh, I'm sorry. My name is Zilla Trott. Mrs. Michael Trott, to be precise, though I've been a widow for thirty years. My husband was lost at sea."

In point of fact, the late Mr. Trott had met his demise trying to run the rapids on Big Pussytoes in a borrowed kayak while under the influence of some mysterious potion that he and a few friends had cooked up in a borrowed washtub one Victoria Day weekend, but Zilla saw no reason why she couldn't gild the lily a bit, as Mike himself would have done. She was something of a romantic at heart though a person might not think so to look at her, particularly when she was on the warpath about one thing or another, as she frequently was.

It occurred to Zilla that Michael Trott might have taken the trouble to manifest himself in place of this mangy old coot. Perhaps he would, when he got around to it. Punctuality had never been Mike's obsession; Zilla had often told him he'd be late for his own funeral. In a way, her prediction had come true. Mike's body hadn't come ashore till more than a week after he'd been drowned, although his would-be rescuers had salvaged the kayak right away. They never did find the paddle; it was thought to have been claimed as salvage by a family of rather tough and rowdy beavers who lived downstream. Nobody had wanted to tackle a beaver on the question of prior rights, so the matter had been allowed to drop.

Well, that was all water over the rapids now. Unlike her friend Minerva, Zilla wasn't one to keep open house for every wayfaring stranger who wandered along. She was emphatically not keen on having an unkempt specter oozing through her furniture for any extended length of time. A person could hardly come straight out and say so, but she supposed it wouldn't hurt to hint around a little.

"Are you here on business, Mr. Jellyby, or just passing through?"

"Hell, Miz Trott, just call me Hiram. Damned if I know what I'm here for. Wait a minute, maybe I do. Yep, it's comin'! Bones, that's it. Bones."

"Any bones in particular, or just bones in general?"

"My bones, dad-gum it. They got to be buried decent so's I can rest in peace like it says on the tombstones. An' furthermore, they got to be avenged."

"That so? How were you planning to avenge them?"

"Cussed if I know, but I'll think of somethin'. First off the bat, somebody's got to locate 'em for me."

Zilla snorted. "Isn't that just like a man? Leave things around and don't remember where you put 'em. Why can't you find the bones yourself, for Pete's sake?"

"You're kind of a cantankerous old besom, ain't you, Zilla? Meanin' no offense, you understand. Don't ask me why I can't find 'em. All I know is what I read in the Akashic Record. It says there I was murdered."

"Well, that must have been a surprise. Who do you suppose murdered you?"

"Some ornery sidewinder in a black frock coat an' purple gaiters, to the best o' my recollection."

"Are you sure about the purple gaiters?"

It was Hiram's turn to snort. "How do you expect me to be sure of anything, with a wad o' gray fuzz where my brains used to be? Assumin' they ever was, which I ain't sure of neither. But it does strike me them gaiters was purple. Or maybe kind of purply blue."

"Or blue with purple polka dots?" Zilla didn't mean to be sarcastic but purple gaiters on a murderer were a bit hard to swallow coming from a mule driver's ghost in the dead of night. "Was the killer a man or a woman?"

"Man, I think. Could o' been a woman, now that you mention it. Some o' them dance hall girls was pretty tough babies."

"I can imagine. They'd also be more apt than a man to

wear purple gaiters, wouldn't you think? How did you die? Were you shot, stabbed, poisoned, strangled, or hit over the head with something heavy?"

"You left out drowned, smothered, an' blown up with dynamite."

"If you'd been blown up with dynamite," Zilla pointed out reasonably, "I shouldn't think there'd have been any bones left to find. Didn't the Akashic Record let on what happened, for Pete's sake?"

"Could of, I s'pose. I was so cussed mad I plumb forgot to look. All I could think of was gettin' my mitts on that bugger who done me in."

"But Hiram, didn't it occur to you that your murderer must also be dead by now? I don't know when they stopped driving mule teams around here but it must have been quite a while back. I'll have to ask Grandsire Coskoff. He's our oldest inhabitant in Lobelia Falls. Oldest living inhabitant, anyway," Zilla amended out of politeness. "Grandsire will know if anybody does. He was born in 1894, if my memory serves me."

"Huh. Just a kid, next to me."

"What year were you born?"

"I dunno, maybe it'll come to me. Who's out there?"

"Out where?" Zilla glanced nervously at the door that led to the woodshed. "I don't hear anything. Maybe I'd better go look."

"Maybe you better not, it's prob'ly a skunk. Anyways, as I started to say, the reason this bugger in the purple gaiters killed me was so that he, or she, or maybe it for all I know, could steal my treasure."

"What treasure, Hiram? Your Sunday teeth?"

"Don't get funny, woman. This was a real treasure, dad-burn it. Gold pieces, a whole trunk chock-full of 'em. I dug it up, me an' the mules. They was thirsty, see, an' they could smell water close under the sod, so they started diggin' with their hooves. Mules are a dern sight smarter than they're given credit for. People don't appreciate mules. Nor mule drivers neither."

The ghost lapsed into moody silence, Zilla wasn't standing for that. "Never mind the mules, get on to the treasure. How did you find it?"

"Well, like I was sayin', the mules found water but it was just sort o' seepin' up an' not collectin'. So I got a shovel out o' the wagon. Us mule drivers never traveled without a shovel 'cause we never knew when we'd have to dig ourselves out of a hole or bury a pardner that had died o' lead poisonin'. Or rotgut whiskey, as the case might o' been. Anyways, I begun scoopin' out a good, big water hole so's me an' the mules could all drink together."

"That was sociable of you."

"Oh, yeah, I used to be a real nice feller. Good lookin', too. You should o' knowed me back then, Zilla. So like I says, while I was diggin', the spade hit somethin' hard an' I seen that it was the corner of a box. So after me an' the mules had drunk our fill, I turned 'em loose to graze awhile an' just out o' curiosity I begun to dig out the box. I thought at first it was prob'ly a coffin but it turned out to be just a little thing, no bigger'n a crate o' canned peaches. Once I got the dirt scraped off, though, I seen it wasn't no crate but a fancy trunk, with bands of iron around it an' a big lock on the front."

"My stars, that must have been exciting."

"I'll say it was! The bands was all rusted out from bein' so near the water but the box was sound enough 'cause the wood was covered with waxed canvas. So I guv the lock a whack with the shovel an' it fell right off clean as a whistle. An' I opened the box, an' there was the treasure! An' me out there in the middle o' nowhere with no place to spend it an' nobody to brag to 'ceptin' a passel o' mules that didn't give a damn nohow."

CHAPTER
2

"So what did you do?" Zilla prompted.

"Seems to me I hoorawed around for a while an' poured me a snort o' red-eye to celebrate, but then I got to thinkin'. I was ferryin' in supplies for the Mounted Police barracks. I knew if them Mounties caught sight o' that there trunk in my wagon, they'd get nosy an' make me open it out o' general cussedness. You can't trust them Mounties one inch when it comes to law an' order. They don't give a hoot for nobody, they got to do the right thing irregardless of whose toes they step on. Sure as shootin', they'd know where them gold pieces was robbed from an' make me give 'em back to the rightful owner."

Hiram fumed a moment in silence, then went on. "So what I done was, I cooked myself up a mess o' beans an' bacon while I waited till the waterhole cleared, me an' the mules havin' muddied it up pretty good. Then I filled my water bottles an' guv the mules another good drink, then I took my shovel agin an' filled in the hole an' put back the sod as best I could so's you'd never o' knowed there was nothin' underneath. Then I made me a little wooden cross an' planted it right over where the box was layin', so's it would look like a grave, see. Nobody'd go diggin' up a grave, but I'd be able to find the right place when I come back to get the treasure. I even carved R.I.P Hiram on the crossboard. I thought that was a pretty good joke. Which just goes to show, don't it?"

"It was tempting Providence, you old fool. You should have known better."

"Why? What would you o' done?"

"Taken the gold to the Mountie barracks and turned it over, of course, like any decent, law-abiding citizen."

"Huh! Ask a dern fool question an' you get a dern fool answer. Can't trust a woman no more'n you can a Mountie. Always got some bee in their bonnets about doin' the right thing."

"Yes, Hiram, you've made your point." Zilla was trying not to yawn. "Get on with your story, can't you?"

"Ain't much more to tell. I delivered my goods an' got my pay, then I went over to the saloon an' downed a few shots o' rotgut 'cause it would o' looked funny if I wasn't rory-eyed like the rest. I didn't want to start 'em thinkin'. Then I turned the wagon around an' come back to collect my gold."

"Back here to Lobelia Falls, you mean?"

"Here or hereabouts. This used to be a nice respectable town, as I remember. These days I s'pose it's a regular Sodden an' Gomorrah."

"Well, you suppose wrong," Zilla replied tartly. "Do you remember any of the people?"

"Couple o' fellas named Hunniker from down in the States built theirselves a camp on top o' that big hill over yonder. Used to burn off a big tract every year an' plant rye on it."

"That's a nice surprise," said Zilla. "Grandsire Coskoff seems to think the Hunnikers lived on salt pork and whiskey."

Hiram Jellyby was amused. " 'Course they did. What

do you think they grew the rye for? Fattened a few pigs on the leavin's from the still an' sold what they couldn't eat or drink. I used to cart 'em over to Scottsbeck, them an' the jugs an' the carcasses. Nice enough fellas, talked like they had a mouthful o' fried potaters but I got so's I could understand most o' what they said, not that it amounted to much. Made theirselves a pretty good pile, then went back to where they come from. Left the rye field to the town an' took their still with 'em. Seems to me they was gone a while before that last trip o' mine. Twouldn't surprise me none if that field o' theirs is where I'm buried."

"It's a small world, isn't it." Zilla was half asleep by now.

Hiram, like the Ancient Mariner, wasn't about to relinquish his audience until his tale was told. "Wake up, woman, I'm still rememberin'. What I done was, I took my bearin's an' drew me a map o' where the trunk was buried. This was after I'd filled in over it an' riz my cross. When I got to the Mountie barracks I bummed an envelope off'n their clerk an' addressed it to my brother Bill, which I never had one, an' ast 'em to mail it for me in care o' the Scottsbeck post office. Scottsbeck used to be a fair-sized town then. You ever been to Scottsbeck?"

"Certainly. It's our biggest city in Lobelia County now. The post office is a brick building with fancy lanterns out front and I don't know how many people working inside."

"I want to know! I wonder if they still got my letter, waitin' for ol' Bill to pick it up."

"Considering the rate of speed at which the post office operates, I shouldn't be surprised," Zilla replied with an indignant sniff. "I could go and ask, I suppose. Or they might have passed the letter on to the Scottsbeck Historical Society. But you still haven't told me how you got murdered."

"Don't rush me, I'm comin' to it. Cripes, this is the first time I've talked to a human since I got my chips cashed in for me. At least you might let a ha'nt get in a little practice. Ain't hurtin' you none, am I?"

He was keeping her up long past her usual bedtime and Zilla was feeling the effects of her camomile tea. Moreover, she was getting stiff from so much sitting, but she supposed it would be an act of charity to let the long-mute shade ramble on a little longer. She put another stick of wood in the stove and settled back into her chair. "No, I'm all right. So you came back to where you'd left the gold. Then what happened?"

"Well, I guess I must o' shot my mouth off more'n I'd meant to that night in the saloon, 'cause when I got near the buryin' place, I realized some bugger on horseback was trailin' me. Wasn't no way I could o' lost 'im on the open prairie with me drivin' a four-mule team an' a cussed great big freight wagon. So I just kep' my shotgun handy in case he showed signs o' gettin' too frisky, an' pushed on. 'Twasn't unusual for a lone rider to stay near a team for comp'ny on the way an' protection in case somethin' happened."

"Like what, for instance?"'

"Outlaws, grizzly bears, bad licker, mean women, you never knew. Anyways, after a while the rider caught up to me. I reached for my shotgun, but all he done was gimme a yell an' a wave an' gallop on ahead. By then I was pretty close to where I'd left the trunk, so I stopped an' made camp, figgerin' to let 'im get a good ways ahead before I went for the gold. But I'd no sooner got the mules pegged out an' the beans in the fryin' pan when I'll be cussed an' be jiggered if the bugger didn't come gallopin' back."

"My stars and garters!" said Zilla. "What did you do?"

"Ast 'im to haul up an' have a bite. Wasn't nothin' else I could do. That was the code o' the prairies. Them as had, guv. So he says thanks an' dismounted an' hobbled 'is horse an' sauntered over. I threw a few more hunks o' bacon in the fryin' pan an' when I looked up from the campfire, I was starin' straight into the barrel of a cussed great big six-shooter.

" 'Mister,' says the stranger, 'whereat's this gold you was mouthin' off about last night in the saloon? '

" 'Mister,' I says right back to 'im, 'that's my business an' none o' yours.'

" 'Mister,' he says, 'I got six bullets in this here shootin' iron that says it's mine. You talk or I shoot.'

" 'Mister,' I says, 'you might's well go ahead an' pull that trigger,' I says, 'cause I ain't talkin.' "

"That was awfully brave." Personally, Zilla thought Hiram Jellyby had been awfully stupid, considering that the gold wasn't even his in the first place. But that was a man for you every time. "Weren't you scared?"

"Nah. I knew he didn't mean to kill me, 'cause then he wouldn't know where to find the trunk. I figgered I could get the drop on 'im one way or another once he started diggin'. But be danged an' be jeezled if the bugger didn't go ahead an' whang a bullet straight past my left ear."

"Don't tell me you weren't scared then?"

"You're dern tootin' I was, but I still wasn't talkin'. So then the stranger goes to whang 'is second bullet past my right ear an' just as he pulls the trigger, a horsefly big as a buzzard buzzes along an' takes a chomp out o' my neck. Without thinkin', I jerked my head sideways, you know how you do. The bullet got me spang in the middle of the forehead an' there I was, stretched out on the prairie dead as a doornail. By gorry, Zilla, how's that for rememberin'?"

"Very impressive, Hiram, especially when you're so out of practice."

"Yep, I see it all like as if it was yesterday. Me on the ground with a couple of angels zoomin' down to pray over me, or maybe they was horseflies. An' him standin' over me, cussin' a blue streak 'cause he'd done hisself out o' findin' the gold. Then seems like I was whishin' down this long tunnel with a light at the end of it an' a bunch o' my dead relatives lined up waitin' to shake hands an' tell me how surprised they was to see me. They'd all figgered that wherever they went, I'd wind up in the opposite direction. As for what's been happenin' between then an' now, it ain't come back to me yet. All I remember is standin' in front o' that Akashic Record, seein' my name writ down in letters o' golden fire an' findin' out I had unfinished business back where I'd shed my flesh an' bones. So here I sit an' here I stay till I'm avenged."

"I'm not so sure about the staying, Hiram," said Zilla. "The strain of so much remembering must have thinned you out, you're looking awfully foggy in the middle. Maybe you'd better go back to the woodshed and rest your ectoplasm for a while."

She didn't mean to sound inhospitable, but a jawcracking yawn that she couldn't suppress was hint enough even for a deceased muleteer. With a nod of acquiescence, farewell, or possibly both, Hiram Jellyby drifted slowly backward, still in a sitting position, and seeped through the woodshed door into the darkness. Nemea, who'd been crouched under the kitchen lamp all this time eyeing the ghost with unconcealed dislike, now leaped into Zilla's arms and huddled there. Together they went in through the parlor and upstairs to bed.

The camomile tea hadn't lost its power to soothe. Zilla slept soundly for whatever remained of the night and on through the early morning hours. So, apparently, did Nemea. It was well after eight o'clock when they roused themselves, and then only because the telephone was ringing. Zilla had correctly surmised before ever she'd picked up the phone that the caller would be Minerva Oakes. What she hadn't anticipated was her friend's knowing chuckle.

"Fine one you are to talk, Zilla Trott, after all the lectures you've given me about taking in strangers. Who've you got staying with you, anyway? That cousin from Alberta back again? Or did you invite the Peeping Tom in for a midnight cup of tea?"

Zilla wasn't a whit surprised that Minerva already knew she'd had unexpected company of the male persuasion last night. Hiram had sensed an alien presence outside, she remembered. He'd claimed it was a skunk, no doubt because he didn't want her going out there and depriving him of an audience. She supposed she couldn't blame him for that, considering how long it must have been since he'd had a chance to socialize with a live human being. Obviously some neighbor out walking the dog or going home from a meeting had noticed a light burning later than usual in Zilla Trott's kitchen window, peeked in, and seen a strange man sitting with her at the table, ostensibly drinking tea.

In a way, Zilla found this reassuring. So she hadn't been hallucinating at all, and neither had Nemea. Whoever the peeker was, he or she would have told somebody, who'd have told somebody else who'd have told Minerva and a few other people, who in turn would have told a few more. If there was anybody left who hadn't been told, that person would darned soon find out because this was what invariably happened in Lobelia Falls. Of course the facts tended to get a little bent and twisted at various points along the line. Maybe that wouldn't be such a bad thing in her case, considering the circumstances.

Anyway, Zilla wasn't about to explain over the phone, she essayed a chuckle. "Come on over and have some tea yourself; Nemea and I were just about to eat our breakfast. We're running late this morning."

Breakfast with Zilla was apt to be a chancy business since her cuisine was so relentlessly healthful, but Minerva accepted anyway. She was dithering on the doormat almost before Zilla and Nemea had got their faces washed. In her hand was a covered plate, and on the plate were four recently fried doughnuts.

"You must have been reading my mind," said Zilla. "I

was wondering last night whether I could talk you out of a doughnut or two."

"You were? That's a switch. Last time I offered you one, you leaped back as if I'd been trying to feed you rat poison. I just thought maybe your company would enjoy one with his sassafras tea and yogurt, or whatever you've got on the menu this morning. Isn't he up yet?"

"I don't know," said Zilla. "I suppose I could look in the woodshed, but I'd just as soon not."

"Why not?" Minerva demanded. "And why the woodshed? What's wrong with your spare bedroom?"

"Nothing. He could be up there, for all I know. He oozes."

"What do you mean, he oozes? Zilla, are you feeling all right? I knew all that wheat germ would get to you sooner or later."

"It's not the wheat germ. I don't know what it is, if you want the God's honest truth. Not my cousin from Alberta, that's for sure."

"Zilla! You don't mean you're—"

"Having a red-hot love affair with the man who reads the gas meter? Not hardly. Look, Minerva, you'd better sit down. Have a doughnut. I might even have one myself. Just let me see to the kettle."

Once she'd got the teapot under control, Zilla felt a trifle more in command of herself. She was able to fill the cups without slopping up the saucers, and took that as a good sign.

"Now listen, Minerva. This is very hard to explain, and I don't suppose you're going to believe it when I tell you. The thing of it is, I'm being haunted."

"By remorse? What for, Zilla? You've never done anything particularly awful that I can remember. Except maybe that time at the Preservation Society clambake when you beaned the county commissioner with a boiled lobster for wanting to take down all the trees along the turnpike. But he had it coming. You're not repenting that lobster, are you?"

"Of course not. I did feel a twinge of remorse at the time because I never got to eat the lobster, but that's nothing to grieve about. When I say I'm haunted, I mean I'm being haunted by a haunt. A ghost. A thing that goes bump in the night, only he hasn't so far, at least not to notice. I don't know where he came from or how he got here. He just sort of floated in last night while I was putting my soybeans to soak, and we got to talking."

"About what?" Minerva sounded skeptical, and no wonder. Zilla shook her head.

"Wait'll I finish my tea. I'm all at sixes and sevens this morning. He kept me up half the night till I sent him back to the woodshed, where he's apparently been hanging around for quite some time. I've probably walked right on through him a dozen times or more and never noticed. He thins out, you know. Or rather I don't suppose you do, but he does because I saw it happen last night. At first he looked as solid as you or I."

"Then how did you know he was a ghost?"

"Because I tried to lam him with the poker," Zilla confessed. "It split him straight down the middle and whacked me on the leg but he joined right back up and never turned a hair. And don't look at me like that, Minerva, I'm neither drunk nor crazy. He was here, standing by the sink, and when I offered him a cup of tea he sat down in that chair where you're sitting now. Took him a couple of stabs to get the hang of it, I have to admit. At first he just sank through the seat, but once he'd got his bearings, he made out fine. In fact he was still sitting when he oozed back through the woodshed door. In a sitting position, that is to say. The chair stayed where I'd put it, of course."

"If you say so, Zilla. Whose ghost was he, did he happen to mention?"

"Oh, yes. He couldn't think of it just at first, then he remembered. He's quite smart at remembering, though he doesn't seem to have had much practice. His name used to be Hiram Jellyby and he drove a four-mule team for some supply house over in Scottsbeck. I suppose it's gone by now. He knew about Lobelia Falls, he had some dealings with the Hunniker brothers who used to live up on the Enchanted Mountain before they went back to the south. He claims they raised pigs and rye, ran a still, and lived on pork and moonshine. They were among our early settlers, as I don't have to tell you. Eighteen sixty-three or thereabouts, wasn't that when they came?"

"I think so. Dodging the draft during some trouble down in the States, as I recall. Where did this Hiram Jellyby take his supplies?"

"To a Mounted Police barracks, he didn't say where. Somewhere north of here, I gathered."

"That would have had to be late eighteen seventy-three or after," said Minerva. "The Northwest Mounted Police, as it was then, didn't get started till August first of that year."

"It could have been almost any time within the next ten or fifteen years then, because the Hunnikers didn't pull out till eighteen eighty-eight, I think it was. There might have been records over at Scottsbeck by then. I can ask Hiram next time I see him, assuming that I do."

"You sound pretty calm at the prospect. Weren't you scared last night, Zilla? Did you actually sit here with a mule skinner's ghost and swap gossip the way we're doing now?"

"That's just what we did, and no, I wasn't. Hiram's a sociable cuss, in his way. Takes a little getting used to, of course. I set a cup of camomile tea in front of him and he—well, he didn't exactly drink it, but somehow or other that cup got emptied. And don't tell me I was seeing things. Nemea was right here on the table under the lamp, she watched him like a hawk the whole time. She didn't like him a bit."

Minerva nodded. "That's understandable. I doubt if I'd have liked him either. What did he come back for?"

"Revenge, he says. He'd just found out he'd been murdered. He claims the killer had on a black frock coat and purple gaiters."

"Do tell. You don't suppose it could have been one of those English high-church bishops?'"

"I hadn't thought of a bishop," Zilla confessed. "My guess is it was a dance-hall girl wearing purple tights and a man's coat. Not to run down my own sex, as I never have and never would, I don't have to tell you that, but some of those women must have been mighty hard cases."

"Had to be, I suppose, in their line of work. Did the murder happen in a saloon?"

"Not exactly. Hiram's story is that his mules had been digging for water and turned up a trunkful of gold pieces. Instead of taking the gold along to the Mountie barracks as he ought to have done, Hiram reburied the trunk, meaning to pick it up on his return trip. But he got drunk in a saloon up there before he started back and must have spilled the beans because this bishop, or whoever it was, followed him on horseback. Hiram says ol' Purple-Legs was firing past his ears, trying to scare him into telling where the gold was, when a horsefly bit him on the neck. He jerked away just at the wrong instant, and the bullet hit him in the head."

"So where's the murder?" snorted Minerva. "Sounds to me as if it was Hiram's own darned fault. Or the horsefly's fault, if you want to get picky. You'd better tell old Hiram to manifest himself a fly swatter and go work off his spleen at Jim Thompson's horse farm. You'll be getting yourself a bad name if you keep on hanging around all night with a mule skinner's ghost."

CHAPTER
3

Zilla Trott was not one to smirk as a rule, but she was smirking now. "I should worry about my name. How many widows my age get the chance of having their reputations ruined for consorting with strange men in their nightgowns? Too bad Hiram fades so easily, or I'd take him out and parade him down Queen Street. Not that he's much for looks, but what the heck? Who's that at the door?"

"Better not open it," Minerva cautioned. "You might let in another ghost."

"You still don't believe me, do you? Oh, nice, it's Dittany and Osbert, with the babies. Yes, Ethel, you can come in. Just don't go pestering Nemea, you know what she did to you last time. Osbert, I'm not sure that double carriage will go through the door."

"No matter, Zilla, we'll just pick up the kids and lug them in. Unless you'd rather come outdoors?"

"And have every ear in the neighborhood wagging out the windows?" Dittany Monk, nee Henbit, was petite, full of beans, and not one to waste any time getting to the point. "We knew you'd be yelling for Osbert as soon as you got a breathing space, so we thought we might as well buzz along and save you a holler."

She bent over the twin-sized baby carriage and scooped up the pink bundle that lay within. Osbert picked up the blue one. Ethel, a large, black, shaggy creature reputed to be a dog, although nobody really believed she was, watched nervously. Dittany was mildly annoyed at her solicitude.

"For Pete's sake, Ethel, don't be so bossy. I wish we'd never let her watch Peter Pan on the television. She's bound and determined to play Nana."

"We wouldn't mind if only she were a little handier at changing diapers," said the justifiably proud papa.

Osbert Monk looked almost too young to be the father of twins, though obviously he wasn't. He cut a personable figure withal, tall and slim, with a rampant cowlick in his fair hair and an intellectual though pleasant expression on his lightly freckled face. Well there might be, for Osbert was a widely read author of Western stories, greatly admired by the sagebrush intelligentsia for his erudition and literary style even if he did occasionally forget which was the mustang and which the maverick.

Osbert and Dittany had so often been called upon to address their combined acumen to various problems involving Lobelia Falls residents that it was only to be expected people would start bugging them about this latest development. Indeed, a number of somebodies had already done so.

"What we're really here for is to get away from the telephone," Dittany confessed as she loosened the tie of her daughter's sacque. "It's been ringing off the hook since half past six. Nobody dares to call you, Zilla; they're all scared of getting scalped. I'll bet your phone's been buzzing, though, Minerva."

"It was, till I took it off the hook. Before I even found the time to put in my partial plate, I'd had calls from Caroline Pitz, Therese Boulanger, and that woman who's staying at the inn trying to find her roots. What's her name? Belinda somebody?"

"No, Tryphosa, with a y," Dittany amended. "Tryphosa Melloe. I hope she digs up her darned old roots pretty soon and plants them someplace else. Trying to tell Minerva that her great-grandmother may have been a connection of the Henbits! No Henbit ever had a nose like a slide trombone."

"She could have got it from the other side of the family." Minerva was always ready to come down on the side of charity, often to the expressed annoyance of her friends and neighbors.

Dittany was not to be pacified. "Maybe she could, but why would she want to? To heck with Mrs. Melloe, what's this about you and a posse of desperadoes trying to dig up the loot from some old stagecoach robbery?"

"Dittany darling," Osbert corrected gently, "desperadoes don't come in posses. They're the bad guys, remember?"

"Oh, I'm sorry, dear. I keep forgetting. Anyway, let's skip the technicalities and get down to the loot. Where is it, Zilla?"

Mrs. Trott raised a warning hand. "Wait a second till we make sure nobody's listening at the keyhole. Too bad I didn't think to do that last night. Honest to Pete, a person can't open her mouth in this town without somebody leaning in over her tonsils for fear of missing a syllable. I'd just like to know who was snooping around here last night. Go take a look, will you, Minerva? You've already heard what I'm going to say."

"All right, but don't you go tacking on anything new till I get back."

"I'm not tacking on anything. I'm just telling it the way it happened. If you won't believe me, that's no skin off my nose."

"Zilla, why shouldn't Minerva believe you?" Dittany protested. "You're the most relentlessly truthful person in Lobelia Falls, not counting Roger Munson, and he only sticks to the facts because he doesn't have imagination enough to think up a convincing lie. Do get on with the story. Osbert's rustlers are about to snaffle a herd of elk, he has to get back and head 'em off at the pass. We only came because we thought the situation must be desperate. You don't want a gang over here digging up your parsnip patch, do you?"

"They wouldn't dare."

"Don't be too sure of that, Zilla," said Osbert. "You never know what people will do once somebody gets them worked up. Look at lynch mobs, for instance."

"I wouldn't look at a lynch mob if you paid me a million dollars on the spot. Anyway, Canadians have more sense. Some of 'em, anyway. Sit down, can't you? Want a cup of sassafras tea?"

"No, thanks, we just had breakfast a while ago. What's happened and where's that man you've got staying here?"

So Zilla had to go through the whole recitative again, this time to a more receptive audience. As a writer of fiction, Osbert was always willing to entertain the possibility of the improbable. As a native and lifelong resident of Lobelia Falls, Dittany was schooled by experience to believe anything about anybody. Only the twins, having been born not quite three months previously, showed little or no interest in Zilla's story.

"So there you are," she wound up. "Take it or leave it, but it looks to me as if the only way I'm going to get that old coot out of my woodshed is to dig up his bones and bury them properly."

"I expect you're right, although it seems to me the gold's more urgent than the coot," said Dittany. "If we don't find that cache of his pronto, we'll have this whole darn town dug up and reburied before you can say scat. No, Nemea, not you. You know how people are, Zilla, I don't have to tell you what a mess this could turn out to be. Didn't old Hiram give you any clue about the gold?"

"He told me he'd drawn a map up at the Mountie barracks and mailed it to himself in care of the Scottsbeck post office. I suppose we could drop over there and ask whether it's been delivered yet."

Osbert shrugged. "Why not? You read stories in the papers every now and then about some hundred-year-old letter that turns up in a drawer somebody finally got around to cleaning out. As far as the digging's concerned, why not turn it to good purpose? Let's spread a rumor about the field out beyond the Enchanted Mountain that the development commission said it would be okay to use for a community garden because it's part of the Hunniker Land Grant and belongs to the town."

"What we really want that land for is an old folks' housing project, though the Lord knows whether we'll ever get together money enough to build one," said Minerva. "But you're right about the community garden, Osbert. Why not? Digging there now would at least save us the cost of getting the land plowed and tilled for planting next spring. Somebody'll have to stick around and make everybody fill in their holes after they've messed the place up and not found anything, needless to say."

"I should darn well hope so," Zilla snorted. "How do we go about starting the rumor?"

"In this town?" said Dittany. "Nothing easier. We just rope off the area we want dug up and march out there with pickaxes and shovels over our shoulders and a smug look on our faces. On second thought, what if Hunnikers' Field should happen to be the right place and somebody dug up the chest of gold by accident, the way old Hiram's mules did? There might very well be an underground spring; it's a bit squishy in some places. Maybe we'd better get Polly James to dowse the field before we start our stampede."

"You'd better not let Pollicot James's mother hear you calling him that," Minerva cautioned.

"Why not? It's her own fault, saddling the kid with

her maiden name just because the Pollicots were supposed to be descended from dukes or earls or lesser seraphim or somebody. Mrs. James is always quick enough to point out other people's mistakes, she might have given a little thought to her own. I wonder how she ever let Polly take up anything so down-to-earth as dowsing, anyway?"

"Oh, dowsing isn't plebeian," said Minerva. "Being hipped on folklore is quite the thing these days. Remember, Zilla, the time Mrs. James offered to sing folk songs about flowers to the garden club? She brought along a two-string dulcimer and sat there strumming those same two strings and squealing 'Willow, willow, waly' for a solid hour and a quarter before Therese could get her turned off."

Zilla sighed. "I've spent a lot of time trying to forget that afternoon, Minerva Oakes, and I'll thank you not to remind me again. I suppose it wouldn't hurt to get the son to dowse, though, long as he doesn't have any funny ideas about being paid."

"We could tell him we're anxious to find water for the community garden and appeal to his sense of civic responsibility," Dittany suggested. "Mrs. James seems to be awfully big on civic responsibility, she's always spouting off about it in the *Scottsbeck Sentinel*. Maybe we could gently suggest that we'll send his picture to the paper. Of course the Jameses don't exactly live in Lobelia Falls, but Polly's over here all the time lately, asking Mr. Glunck dumb questions about the artifacts at the museum and having soulful chats with Arethusa."

"Which of them does the chatting?" asked Zilla.

"Polly does, naturally. Arethusa just sits there looking like a Burne Jones painting and letting him think she's listening. Little does he reck that she's actually entertaining lustful fantasies about snaffling all the pickled onions next time she invites herself to supper at our house."

The "little does he reck" came easily to Dittany's lips.

During her pre-Osbert period and even occasionally after her marriage while still in the pre-twin phase, she'd typed manuscripts for Osbert's aunt. Roguish Regency romance was Arethusa Monk's all-too-fertile field of fictional fabrication. Not only rich and famous, the authoress was also possessed of a magnificent head of jet-black hair and eyes like fathomless pools of mystery; hence she was always being fallen in love with by somebody or other. Since her own two loves were her work and her meals, she often failed to notice who belonged to whichever heart was being laid before her feet at any specific point in time.

Mrs. Pollicot James, as she liked to be known, seemed to be fairly important in provincial garden-club circles. Recently, she'd invited members of the Grub-and-Stake Gardening and Roving Club to tea at her more or less palatial house just over the line in Scottsbeck. This could have been merely a hands-across-the-border gesture, or it could have been a preliminary softening up in the hope of getting the Lobelia Falls group to do all the dog work at the upcoming spring flower show. It might also have had something to do with the fact that the Grub-and-Stakers had inherited a rundown Victorian house, turned it into the by now lavishly endowed and increasingly acclaimed Aralia Polyphema Architrave Museum, and thus boosted their organization to a level of civic responsibility that even Mrs. James would have been hard put to snoot.

Dittany had missed Mrs. James's tea on account of the twins, but of course she'd heard all about it. No Mr. James the elder had been present. He was said to have departed this earth some years ago and probably wouldn't have been caught dead at his wife's hen party anyway. Mr. James the younger, however, had been right there with bells on. Pollicot hadn't seemed to mind a bit being the only male present. He'd mingled freely with the company until Arethusa Monk had shown up rather late, firmly escorted by a somewhat tight-lipped Dot Coskoff and muttering darkly of abduction.

To any discerning female eye, it must have been clear that Arethusa had forgotten all about the tea until Dot showed up to collect her and that she had been forced to dress in an almighty rush. Usually a model of elegance, Arethusa had on this occasion displayed that sweet disorder in her dress whose effect Robert Herrick had so accurately assessed some three centuries previously. Thus also had been kindled a certain wantonness in the bosom of a middle-aged bachelor who'd been kept all his life under the heavy thumb and the eagle eye of a domineering mother.

Nor had the siren's allure worn off. Pollicot James was still lugging along his tributes of flowers and candy with monotonous regularity. For Arethusa to beguile him into an afternoon's worth of free water-witching ought to be a piece of cake. Dittany said so and her hearers agreed, all but the littlest two. Ditson Renfrew (named for Dittany's late father and Osbert's favorite literary hero) and Dittany Anne (named for her mother and Dittany Senior's favorite literary heroine) showed as yet no interest in the subtleties of local lives and events. They would come to it, no doubt, in the fullness of time. At the moment they were both busy waving their legs and examining their fingers, perhaps speculating on the desirability of getting one or more of these small but shapely digits into their respective mouths. Dittany studied them with a mother's pride and a mother's foreboding.

"Osbert, I think we'd better get these kids home before they start yelling. Okay, Zilla, we'll check out the post office and get Arethusa to work her wiles on Polly. Why don't you two get hold of some pegs and string and begin staking out the area we want dug up?"

"Someone had better see Mr. Glunck too," said Osbert. "There might be something useful in the museum files."

"I thought of asking Grandsire Coskoff whether he'd ever heard of a mule skinner named Hiram Jellyby getting shot out in Hunnikers' Field," said Zilla. "Grandsire wouldn't have known Hiram himself, I shouldn't think, unless he's been lying about his age all these years, but his father might have."

"That's a good idea," said Osbert. "Grandsire might also have heard talk about a payroll robbery that happened back before the turn of the century. It would be nice to know where the gold came from."

"It would be nice to know whether there ever was any gold in the first place." Minerva Oakes still wasn't buying that spectral mule skinner. "Before you try nailing Grandsire Coskoff about any big gold robbery, you'd better find out from Dot whether his hearing aid's back from the repair shop. You know what Grandsire's like when he gets going on something you don't want to listen to and can't hear you trying to shut him off."

"It might be interesting to get him in a room with Mrs. James and her two-string dulcimer some time and see who comes out ahead," said Dittany.

"Just so I'm not around the day you decide to try it. Dittany, you really are your mother's daughter. I just hope Annie here doesn't take after Clorinda's side of the family." Minerva pushed back her chair and buttoned her cardigan. "All right, then, Zilla, I'll go home and change my shoes and get that big ball of heavy twine we use to mark the trails on the Enchanted Mountain."

"Then I'll bring my hatchet and an armload of kindling wood that we can chop up for pegs," her friend agreed. "I suppose we might as well each carry a shovel as well. Not that we'll need 'em, but just to start the ball rolling."

"Good thinking, ladies." Osbert collected his offspring, one under each arm, and went to push the outsize baby carriage out of the way before somebody stumbled over it. Ethel followed close at his heels, emitting naggish whines and whoofles, somewhat to Osbert's annoyance, though he didn't complain out loud because he knew that Ethel meant well.

The Monks didn't live very far from Zilla; indeed, it was next to impossible for anybody to live any great distance from anybody else in Lobelia Falls. They did take rather a long time getting home, though, because they kept being intercepted by sundry fellow citizens wanting to know what was up. Dittany, skilled in the intricate diplomacy of her native heath, told the simple truth about Zilla's desire to get a start on readying the soil for next year's community garden. She told this truth with just enough extra earnestness to convince her hearers that she was stringing them along for dark and devious reasons.

Osbert was subtler still. He merely smiled vaguely at all interrogations and didn't say much of anything, thus making his interrogators assume he was trying to give the impression that his mind was drifting off to imaginary arroyos, as it so often did, whereas in fact he must be thinking about something far closer to hand that he wasn't about to mention.

By the time they did at last reach home and look out their kitchen window, which commanded a clear view of the Enchanted Mountain (which was, to tell the truth, only a pretty high hill), the Monks were gratified to spy a trickle of furtive figures already sneaking around its base toward the field that had thus far always been thought of as the more insignificant part of the Hunniker Land Grant. Each of them shouldered a shovel, a mattock, or a spading fork. Some of them carried all three.

"Goody," Dittany gloated, "they're already snapping at the bait. That was brilliant of you, dear. Now that you've taken care of your civic responsibility for the day, how'd you like to stay here with the kids and round up your elk while I beard Arethusa about Polly James?"

"If you're sure you wouldn't mind, darling." Any excuse to dodge a meeting with his Aunt Arethusa was welcome to Osbert. "I really should get down to work, now that I have a family to support."

"Indeed you do, and it won't be long before the twins will have outgrown their booties and be clamoring for Reeboks. Doesn't it break your heart, dear, how fast they grow up?"

Osbert clasped his wife to his bosom and began exploring with his lips the little dimple beside her mouth. "Awful, sweetheart. We'll soon be facing an empty nest. What shall we do without our wee ones racing their ponies up and down the stairs?"

"Never mind, darling, we'll still have each other. And Annie and Rennie will be coming home for the holidays with their own sets of twins. Just think how this old house will ring with merriment as we sit in our rocking chairs and listen to the patter of our grandkiddies' feet. Maybe we ought to buy another rocking chair and start breaking it in."

"Couldn't we wait awhile?" Osbert demurred. "Frankly, rocking chairs always make me feel as if I'm going to be seasick, though I expect you'll despise me as a weakling for saying so."

"Pooh! I'll bet you could make a pride of African lions look like a litter of kittens if you took the notion. Only I'd as soon you didn't till the twins are a little older. Go ahead with your elk, darling. I'd better whiz over to Arethusa's before Polly James shows up without his divining rod and we're stuck for another day."

CHAPTER
4

*P*eople who didn't know Arethusa and Osbert Monk very well naturally supposed that two writers of the same family, living so close together, would spend a good many pleasant hours together talking shop about apostrophe, hyperbole, synecdoche, and other mysteries of their profession. In fact, the aunt and the nephew seldom talked amicably for long about anything at all. The only writing-related subject they fully agreed on was that typewriters were better than word processors.

Typewriters gave instant gratification. You poked the keys, you looked at your paper, and there was a word. It might be misspelled, it might have got garbled in the typing, it might even be the wrong word; but there it was, by golly, and you didn't need to fry your eyeballs on a dinky little screen and go through a lot of technical gyrations that probably wouldn't have worked anyway to get the word into your clutches and gloat over it.

Furthermore, typewriters clicked. When you were sitting all alone with a piece of blank paper and an even blanker mind, that familiar click could be welcome company, like a cricket on the hearth. Before you knew it, one click would have led to another and there you'd be, clicking off metaphor and simile right and left, switching painlessly from passive verb to active verb, from proper noun to mildly improper noun, popping quaint images straight from your subconscious to your fingers, lured forth by the magical rhythm of the click.

While Osbert's faithful old Remington standard often clicked at a pace that suggested a herd of longhorns in full stampede, Arethusa's svelte rose-colored electric was more inclined to lilt along at approximately the tempo of a Viennese waltz or mazurka, occasionally slowing to a minuet or even a pavane, speeding up to a schottische or galop in the more hair-raising moments. Arethusa was clicking along in three-quarter time this morning, she wouldn't have heard Dittany knock, therefore Dittany didn't bother to do so.

"Hola, Arethusa!"

Arethusa heard that all right, she jumped about six inches off her chair and left off in mid-synecdoche. "Egad, woman, hast no respect for a writer's nerves? What do you mean, hola?"

"I don't know," Dittany confessed, "but I thought you might. Isn't that what Sir Percy says to Lady Ermintrude?"

"In a pig's eye he does. He says, 'Good eventide, my fairest one.' "

"Arethusa, that's ridiculous. Nobody in the world ever said, 'Good eventide, my fairest one.' "

"Wouldst give me the lie, churless? Look at this, it says so right here." Arethusa waved a sheet of typescript, somewhat frayed at the top. Her feline familiar, Rudolph Rassendyll, liked to catnap in the basket where she was wont to toss her pages as they came dancing from her typewriter, and Rudolph was a restless sleeper. "Stap me, you wouldn't flout documentary evidence, would you?"

"Come to think of it, I wouldn't," Dittany conceded.

"Not at the moment, anyhow. Arethusa, I'll make a bargain with you. I grant you the eventide and you do me a small favor in a noble cause."

"How noble? And how small?"

"All you have to do is bat your eyelashes at Polly James when he comes slavering at your feet and persuade him to dowse for water on the Hunniker boys' back forty."

"A beautiful thought, in sooth. The noble cause being to get him off my back for a few hours so that I can finish my chapter, needless to say. Remind me to leave you my dining table with the gilded crocodiles in my will. Not that I expect to predecease you, since having to put up with that rumscullion nephew of mine will no doubt drive you to an early grave, but the gesture will indicate the depth of my gratitude. How soon do you want the field dowsed?"

"The sooner the better. This afternoon, for preference. Are you expecting Polly here today?"

"No, but that doesn't mean he won't come." The reigning queen of roguish Regency romance heaved a mighty sigh. "Ah, welladay! Why did I have to be cursed with fathomless pools of inscrutability instead of plain old eyeballs like everybody else?"

"Some people just don't get the breaks, Arethusa. Well, maybe one day your prince will bug off and leave you in peace. In the meantime, why don't you give him a buzz and ask him to toddle on over with his divining rod?"

"Pollicot's mother doesn't approve of women calling him up."

"Figo for his mother. Polly's a big boy now. Tell him it's a case of civic responsibility."

"Is it, i' faith?"

"Certainly it is. We're preparing the ground for a community garden as part of our project to assist the disadvantaged."

"What disadvantaged? Nobody in Lobelia Falls is any

less advantaged than the rest of us. Generally speaking," Arethusa was forced to admit, considering the size and frequency of her and Osbert's royalty checks as compared to the average net income of the nonwriters in town. If these latter had been writers, most of them would be a darned sight poorer than they were now, as Dittany took pains to point out.

"We're the lucky ones. But what about all those people around the country who were thrown out of work when the Piltdown Mill closed? What about the old folks trying to scrape along on their pensions?"

"What about that big chunk of money that was supposed to have been raised to start a low-rent housing project over in Upper Scottsbeck?" Arethusa could show astonishing flashes of practicality now and then, especially where money was concerned.

"That's what everybody else is wondering," Dittany snarled. "You might ask Mrs. James. She was among the sponsors of the fund drive, if memory serves me correctly. Anyway, we do want to get that garden plot ready for spring planting so that we'll at least have fresh vegetables to hand out to people who need them. Tell Polly we're trying to find water for the garden in Hunnikers' Field."

"He doesn't like to be called Polly."

"Then call him whatever he does like to be called. Only for Pete's sake call him right now or first thing you know he'll be breezing in here all togged out like a hog going to war, wanting to drag you off to some fancy restaurant for lunch."

"Come to think of it, you're probably right."

An anticipatory smile began to play about Arethusa's ruby lips, not that they were particularly rubeous at the moment because she hadn't put on her lipstick yet. In fact, she hadn't put on anything except a fuzzy pink bathrobe over her nightgown and bedroom slippers on her bare feet, since she preferred to work as unfettered as was consistent with common decency and the vicissitudes of the local climate.

"If he wants to take you to lunch, that means you'll have to get dressed," Dittany cautioned.

"But if Pollicot agrees to dowse the field, he'll expect me to go and watch," Arethusa fretted.

"Tell him there'll be a whole crowd there taking pictures for the papers while you stay home and prepare a nice high tea for after he's finished. That will leave you almost the whole afternoon to yourself."

"Unless he happens to find the spring right off the bat."

"He won't." Dittany spoke with confidence. Zilla would make sure he didn't. A dowser trudging back and forth all afternoon would be quite a draw for the pick-and-shovel brigade. Arethusa, however, was not yet ready to acquiesce.

"That still means I'll have to make the tea."

"So what?" said Dittany. "By then you'll be wanting some yourself."

"True enough, ecod. All right then, since it's in the interests of civic responsibility. You'll bring the hot scones in plenty of time, I trust."

"I have a better idea. Why don't I mix them right here while you make your phone call? I'll leave them in the fridge unbaked, then all you'll have to do is slip the pan into the oven as soon as he shows up. That way you can tell him quite truthfully that you've baked the scones yourself."

"So I can. Mix on, Macduff, and don't be stingy with the currants."

Arethusa reached for the telephone, Dittany left her to work her siren wiles. Cooking in somebody else's kitchen was not young Mrs. Monk's idea of fun, particularly in a kitchen as spotless as Arethusa's. But the spotlessness was only because the room didn't get used much, Arethusa being far more apt to invite herself over to Dittany's when she wasn't being squired elsewhere by one swain or another. Anyway, a deal was a deal. Dittany mixed, stirred, patted, cut the dough in wedges, and arranged the scones on a greased baking sheet. She covered the pan with a damp tea towel and set it in the refrigerator till baking time, and resisted a mean and sneaky urge to leave the mixing bowl unwashed.

By this time, Arethusa had got through to Pollicot James. She reported that he was already speeding fieldward with his dowsing rod on the car seat beside him, ready to be whipped out of its monogrammed leather case and primed to dip like a falling arrow should the crucial spot be reached. There was nothing more to be done here, Dittany was free to tackle the next leg of her mission.

It had occurred to her while measuring the baking powder that she was going to feel awfully silly barging into the Scottsbeck post office and asking for a letter that ought to have been delivered approximately a century ago. She'd decided it would make more sense to exercise the authority of her position as a trustee of the Architrave and send Mr. Glunck instead. Coming from the curator, a mild inquiry as to whether any antique mail might be hanging around still waiting to be picked up would sound comparatively sane. This was assuming Mr. Glunck didn't already have the crucial document stashed away in the museum's by now capacious archives. Dittany wouldn't put it past him. Despite his unassuming manner, Mr. Glunck was a real go-getter.

A few minutes' brisk walk brought her to the museum. The chrysanthemums around the sign out front were still doing nicely, she noticed, and the brass plaque on the door was freshly shined. Mr. Glunck was sitting at his desk, happily authenticating an artifact. Dittany knocked twice at his open office door as protocol demanded and went on inside without waiting to be asked. Not that he wouldn't have invited her if she'd waited; Mr. Glunck had a soft spot for Dittany. Most people did, at least some of the time.

Characteristically, she got straight to business even though Mr. Glunck would have preferred to tell her first about his new artifact. "Mr. Glunck, would we happen to have a letter in the files somewhere around a hundred years old, addressed to one Hiram Jellyby and containing a roughly drawn map that shows where a trunkful of gold pieces is buried?"

"Why, no," said Mr. Glunck after a moment's cogitation, "I don't recall that we do. Of course there's that photograph of Mr. Jellyby with his four-mule team."

"There's *what?*"

"Yes, indeed, Mrs. Monk, a perfectly splendid photograph, taken by your own husband's great-great-grandfather. Eliphalet Monk was, as you may not have been aware, a true artist of the lens. He spent the best years of his life with his hand on a squeeze bulb and his head inside a black velvet bag. Thanks to the generosity of our chairman of trustees, we have a fine collection of Eliphalet's work. Miss Arethusa Monk is, of course, Eliphalet's great-granddaughter; I'm sure I didn't have to tell you that."

Actually, he didn't. Dittany would have been quite capable of figuring out the connection for herself, had she not been preoccupied in regretting that she hadn't told Arethusa about Zilla's new boarder. Arethusa might have remembered the photograph. More likely, she mightn't. Nor would Arethusa have remembered not to go around shooting her mouth off about why the photograph had suddenly become important.

There were people in town who already considered Zilla Trott somewhat eccentric. In fact Dittany couldn't think offhand of many outside her immediate circle who didn't. Zilla's tale of a muleteer's ghost oozing through her woodshed wall would probably not fail to convince. What it would convince most Lobelia Falls residents of, however, was that Mrs. Trott had oozed herself clear around the bend and somebody had better slide over to that allegedly haunted woodshed and pinch Zilla's hatchet in the interests of civic responsibility.

But with photographic proof of the muleteer's former existence, the outlook would be less dismal. Asking Mr. Glunck for the photograph of Hiram and his mules would have been superfluous, the curator was already rooting through the archives like a beagle after a badger. In a matter of moments, he had taken the stiffly matted artifact out of its acid-free envelope, turned on his gooseneck desk lamp, and handed Dittany his own personal magnifying glass so she wouldn't miss any of the nuances.

"Eliphalet Monk was one of Canada's pioneers in the use of the platinum printing process, you know, Mrs. Monk. Or perhaps you don't, but he certainly was. Yes sirree, Bob! When it came to platinum prints, old Eliphalet was right up there with the best of them. Actually he was right up there by himself a good deal of the time because there were darned few photographers around who had both the inclination and the money to buy the platinum. You don't see many photographers making platinum prints these days. At least I don't, and it's a darned shame, if you'll pardon my language. There's a special virtuosity to platinum printing. You just don't get the same effect with all these newfangled chemicals. Masterful, isn't it? Just look at that depth of focus."

"I'm looking."

Moreover, Dittany was thrilled by what she saw. Not that Hiram Jellyby would ever have been shot for his beauty, but Eliphalet's depiction of him was truly superb. Every wart and wrinkle, every bristle of the muleteer's beard showed up with amazing clarity. She could count the pebbles in the dirt road, she could even see the eyelashes on the mules. "Are you positive this man is Hiram Jellyby?" she asked.

"As positive as anyone can be. That's another great thing about Eliphalet Monk, he was very careful about labeling his work. It's right on the back of the mount. Allow me."

With reverent care, Mr. Glunck turned the photograph over and pointed to the yellowed label attached to the equally yellowed mount. In clear Spencerian script was written: "Hiram Jellyby of Scottsbeck, en route with his mule team to the NWMP barracks with supplies. Taken at Lobelia Falls October 2, 1889."

"This is wonderful!"

Dittany meant that this would be a wonderful way for Zilla to tell whether her ghost was really Hiram Jellyby or some spectral interloper trying to trade on Hiram's former reputation. Mr. Glunck, however, assumed understandably that she was talking about the platinum printing process.

"Absolutely masterful! I've been thinking, Mrs. Monk, that we really ought to set up an exhibition of Eliphalet's work. What would you say to our packing away the Thorbisher-Freep Collection—only temporarily, of course —and utilizing the display cases to show the photographs?"

Dittany was not at all surprised by the curator's suggestion. She'd suspected all along that Mr. Glunck had welcomed the Thorbisher-Freep acquisition not for the theatrical memorabilia but for the handsome glass-topped cases that housed the collection. She didn't blame him a bit.

"I'd say let's. These photographs would certainly be more appropriate as records of Canadian life in the early Lobelia Falls period than those ruffled pantalettes Claude Rains was alleged to have worn when he played Little Nell as a child actor, wouldn't they?"

"Definitely. But do you think the other trustees will concur?"

"I'll tell you what, Mr. Glunck, I'll take this photograph with me right now and show it to them. Once they get an eyeful of all this virtuosity, they'll be onto your idea like a flock of hawks on a henyard."

"But couldn't we call a meeting here in my office, Mrs. Monk? I know I'm an awful Nervous Nellie, but I do hate to see an artifact taken out of the museum."

"Mr. Glunck, this particular artifact must have kicked around Arethusa's attic for half a century or more without coming to any harm. We can't call a meeting this week and maybe not next because most of the trustees are up to their eyeballs in our community garden project. If I just go and show them this photograph, I'll have your answer on the display cases by the end of the day. Would you happen to have a clear plastic envelope to keep their fingerprints off the mat?"

Knowing it was useless to try to talk Trustee Monk out of anything she'd set her mind on and seeing the force of her argument, not to mention the prospect of getting to use the Thorbisher-Freep display cases in a truly meaningful way, Mr. Glunck had no course but to acquiesce. So he did.

CHAPTER
5

"*T*hat's him all right. So I wasn't having a pipe dream after all."

Zilla was studying the photograph, shaking her head in amazement. "That's exactly how Hiram Jellyby was dressed when I saw him. Gives a person a funny feeling. I must say that's a fine-looking team of mules, though I'm just as well pleased he didn't bring 'em along last night."

"You're sure he didn't leave them in the woodshed?" said Dittany.

"How the heck can I be sure of anything? I don't know but what I'd just as soon have had the mules instead of Hiram. They're a darned sight better-looking, that's for sure. And I'll tell him so to his face if he shows up again yammering about his cussed old bones. Here, you'd better take this. I'm getting muddy fingerprints all over the mount."

"No, you're not, they're only on the plastic. Mr. Glunck wouldn't mind a few smudges anyway, you've just authenticated an artifact for him. What do you think of the platinum printing process?"

"Oh, what do I care about a bunch of old photographs?

Tell Mr. Glunck he can do as he pleases, for all I care. Dittany, you're not going to blab to the rest of the trustees about Hiram, are you?"

"Well, his name's written on the back, but I won't tell them he's the one you've been hitting the camomile with. Only you'd better let Minerva know so that she'll quit suspecting you've addled your brains eating too much tofu. Where is Minerva, by the way? I took it for granted she'd be out here with you."

"She was, but she had to go. That Melloe woman came along and reminded her this was the day they'd set to go over their family trees together, and you know Minerva. She didn't have the heart to tell that old besom to go climb her own branch and stick there. Just as well she had to quit digging, I suppose; Minerva's rheumatics have been acting up on her again since the weather changed. I told her to drink lots of sweet cider, but she claims it gives her the gripes."

"What a shame. I must say, though, I find it rather pushy of Mrs. Melloe, tracking Minerva clear out here."

"Of course it was pushy. Tell me one thing about Mrs. Melloe that isn't pushy. You going to dig awhile, or just hang around and get in the way?"

"I'm going to show this photograph to the rest of the board, then take it back to Mr. Glunck before he gets in too much of a swivet. After that, I'm going home and take care of my babies. Osbert's been stuck with them ever since we left your house. Who else is here?"

"Therese, of course."

That figured. As president of the Grub-and-Stake Gardening and Roving Club and ex-officio member of the museum's board of trustees, Therese felt it her duty to make at least a token appearance at any event in which club members were taking a hand, or a voice, or a shovel, as the case might be. Dot Coskoff, as treasurer, was probably here, too. Hazel Munson almost certainly wasn't. This was her day to get her hair done, and Hazel wasn't one to deviate from her schedule except in emergencies.

No matter, Dittany could catch Hazel under the dryer on her way back downtown to give Mr. Glunck back his artifact. She interrupted Therese and Dot long enough to give them a quick briefing on the platinum printing process and Mr. Glunck's hopes for the Thorbisher-Freep display cases. They agreed it was a far, far better thing their curator was planning to do, and suggested that Dittany send Osbert out to lend a hand with the digging, since he wasn't doing anything but sitting around the house making up tall stories.

"And putting Pablum in his children's mouths," Dittany added somewhat snappishly. "Just because my husband doesn't tootle off to an office every morning, that doesn't mean he's free to drop his typewriter at a moment's notice and take a hand in any jolly game that happens to tickle his fancy. He can't come because he's minding the kids and rustling some elk."

"He'd come fast enough if Sergeant MacVicar asked him to." Dot's tone was a trifle acrimonious also, perhaps because she'd got a speck of dirt in her eye.

"Don't rub it, Dot. Pull on your eyelashes and blink. Osbert's situation with Sergeant MacVicar is quite different. He has to go once he's been deputized."

"He doesn't have to keep letting himself get deputized, though."

"Certainly he does, it's his civic responsibility. Speaking of which, hasn't Pollicot James hove into sight yet? Arethusa deputized him to come out and dowse us some water so we'll be able to take care of the garden without breaking our backs."

"Fancy that!" cried Therese. "Isn't it amazing how efficient Arethusa can be once she puts her mind to a project. Who but she would have thought of dowsing? I wonder if it really works. And she's actually persuaded

Pollicot James to join us? Wouldn't it be lovely if she could get him to map out all the town water mains?"

Neither Therese nor any of her clubmates liked to speak harshly of the late John Architrave now that they'd inherited his property, but even his former cronies down at the fire station could not deny that John's name ranked high on Lobelia Falls's roster of all-time knuckleheads. As hereditary chief of the town's water department, John had been just shrewd enough to refrain from letting anybody else know where he and his father had laid the mains, thus assuring himself a lifetime job. Perhaps he'd meant to reveal the secret on his deathbed, but that had died with him quite suddenly one day on the Enchanted Mountain. Great had been the local frustration ever since; what a relief it could be for the town if Pollicot James's dowsing really worked.

And here came Pollicot now, in a dashing red sports coupe with a good deal of shiny chrome trimming designed, no doubt, for the bachelor-about-town and paid for, Dittany assumed, by his doting mama. She further assumed that, as Arethusa's relative by marriage and actual instigator of his coming, it was up to her to do the honors, such as they might be.

"Mr. James?" She wasn't about to risk calling him Polly by accident and have him flounce off in a huff. "I'm Dittany Henbit Monk, Arethusa's niece-in-law. She wanted me to thank you for coming and explain what we're doing here. Not that there's much to explain, really. I expect you've already heard that we're getting the ground ready for next spring, when we intend to plant a big community garden and raise food for the underprivileged of Lobelia County. We've been told there used to be an underground spring around here somewhere and we're hoping you can find it for us so that we don't have to spend all next summer doing rain dances or trucking in water. Oh, and would you mind letting our club's president, Therese Boulanger, take some pictures of you in action?"

Therese had her camera slung around her neck, of course, Dittany had known she would. Therese deemed it a president's duty to make sure all the doings of the club she headed were properly immortalized for posterity. This was a very good thing, since they'd never have been able to get a real newspaper photographer over here on such short notice, even assuming they'd got around to asking for one.

Having graciously conceded Therese permission to shoot at will, Pollicot carefully removed his tweed shooting jacket and laid it on the seat of his car, leaving himself suitably clad in a heather-mixture shetland pullover, a soft tweed hat, and gray flannels tucked into the tops of olive-green Wellington boots such as any landed squire might properly wear whilst demonstrating his civic responsibility by means of a divining rod.

The rod itself, when he'd extracted it from its suede-lined leather case and twiddled it into shape for business, was seen to be no mere forked hazel twig but a fairly complicated affair of assorted metals. Brass, copper, and a few snippets from an old zinc-lined bathtub, Dittany decided; though of course she was only guessing about the bathtub. Anyway, Mr. James grasped its two handles, if that was what they were supposed to be called, in a light but purposeful grip and scanned the by now pockmarked terrain with a keen and practiced eye. Therese nodded approval and took his picture.

Obviously there wasn't much sense in dowsing where the soil had already been dug—and the dowser might well have been wondering why some of the diggers were excavating trenches in which a person could bury a cow standing up if the purpose was merely to plant vegetables—but Pollicot James didn't say anything. He merely held the divining rod out in front of him at waist level, eyes straight ahead, chin up, mouth firm but not disagreeably tight, until he was sure Therese had quit snapping her shutter. Then, with deliberate, almost stately tread, he began to pace.

He paced directly across, starting from the nearward string that Zilla and Minerva had strung to define the garden area. When he reached the opposite string, he performed a smart quarter-wheel right, stepped one pace ahead of where he'd last stridden, executed another quarter-wheel right so that he was facing his original point of departure, and began pacing back across the field without once losing his stride.

Dittany knew she ought to be at the beauty shop luring Hazel out from under the dryer for a quick consultation, or breaking in on Minerva and her genealogy-minded incubus, or trying to pry Arethusa loose from the eighteenth century long enough to send Mr. Glunck a yea or a nay, or even going home to cuddle the twins and speak words of cheer and comfort to her elk-bedeviled spouse. But there was an odd fascination about Pollicot James's measured tread. She'd known it was possible to tread a measure, but this was the first chance she'd ever had to watch somebody treading measuredly who wasn't in a marching band or a Decoration Day parade.

Pollicot James was a tall man. His long legs appeared, as far as Dittany could judge, to be treading at the rate of precisely one meter per stride. Zilla and Minerva hadn't gauged their measurements all that accurately, he didn't always come out just right at the end of a row. However, he took these minor annoyances appropriately in stride and kept on going: eyes front, hands at belt level, rod pointing straight ahead. The suspense was building almost to the point of agony, even the most zealous diggers had paused to watch this human automaton march over and back and over again. And still the tip of his rod hadn't so much as quivered.

But wait! Now! Sudden as a hiccup, the tip plunged, and stayed. With one accord, the shovel brigade dashed to where the dowser was standing, each determined to be first to uncover the spring. The rush could have become a melee, but Pollicot merely held his pose just long enough for Therese to snap her shutter twice, then stuck his divining rod into the top of his boot and politely asked his nearest onlooker, who was Zilla, for the loan of her spade.

With an expertise that belied the slight foppishness of his attire, Pollicot set the point of Zilla's spade in the earth directly at the spot toward which his rod had pointed, poised a rubber-booted foot on the top of the spade, and pushed. He turned the sod that the spade had loosened, a faint smile began to play about his lips, he thrust again, and again. At the fourth thrust, water began to trickle slowly into the hole that the spade had left.

Now was the time for a wild "Huzzah!" Had Arethusa been present, they'd probably have got one. As it was, Pollicot had to settle for a "Wow!", a "Hey!" and a "What do you know about that?" along with an assortment of grunts and murmurs, Canadians, by and large, being zealous guardians of their reputation for playing it cool. Therese did go so far as to snap his picture again.

"Well, eh, isn't this nice?" was Zilla's contribution to the furore. "Thanks a lot, Mr. James, we're greatly obliged to you."

"On behalf of the disadvantaged citizens of Lobelia County and environs," Dittany added smartly before some lamebrain could start gabbling about buried treasure. "You'd better zip on over to Arethusa 's and get washed up for tea, Mr. James. I'll ride with you if you don't mind. I have to talk with her for about thirty seconds on a matter of museum business, then she's going to bake you some scones. With currants."

"Currants?"

A moue of distaste flickered for barely a trice across Pollicot's normally bland countenance. Aha, thought Dittany, a potential rift in the lute. Once Arethusa had got Pollicot to map the water mains and decided she couldn't stand having him underfoot any longer, she had only to start putting currants into everything she fed him. Arethusa herself wouldn't find the ruse any sacrifice, she could eat currants till the cows came home.

But currants were hardly germane to the present issue. What counted here and now was that Hiram Jellyby's spring had been found. Now if Zilla could only keep all those treasure seekers from digging too close to where the gold must be! Dittany hadn't thought of the possible ramifications, but she'd darned well better think of them now. Arethusa would have to manage entirely on her own.

Abruptly, she said to Pollicot, "I'm sorry, Mr. James, I've just thought of something, I need to stop at my house. You won't mind going on to Arethusa 's without me, will you? Just drop me at the corner of Applewood Avenue."

"That's quite all right, Mrs. Monk, I don't mind a bit."

No doubt he meant it, currants or no currants. He even offered to drive Dittany straight to her door but she said, "Never mind, it's the first house in," and jumped out before he could go around and open the car door for her, as he assuredly would have done if she'd given him half a chance.

By the time Pollicot got rolling again, Dittany was already home and sounding the alarm. "Osbert, you'd better get out there."

"Out where, darling?" Osbert had obviously been spending some quality time with his family, there were empty nursing bottles on the kitchen table and a twin on his lap. "What's happening?"

"Look at this." She thrust the platinum print under his nose. "That's Hiram Jellyby, it says so on the back. And Zilla says so too. So he really did exist. So does the spring, Polly James just dowsed it. And we've got a slew of people out there digging and I'm not sure Zilla can keep them away from the spring, and I think this is a case for Deputy Monk."

"Darling, you do? Then here, take Annie. Rennie's

asleep in his crib. He was awake when she was asleep and then he went to sleep and she woke up and you don't mind, do you, dear? Maybe you'd better call the sergeant."

"I'm not sure whether—" Dittany was beginning, but Osbert was already out the door and making excellent time down Cat Alley. He was probably right, at that. This could well be a two-man job if the wrong person happened to dig up that boxful of gold. She gave Annie a kiss and picked up the telephone.

Crime couldn't be very rife in Lobelia Falls just now, Sergeant MacVicar sounded as if he might have been taking a little snooze in his chair. He woke up fast enough, though, when he heard who was on the line.

"Ah, Dittany lass. How are the wee bairns?"

"Fine. Listen. Osbert's off to the community garden and he said I'd better call you, just in case."

"Oh, aye? In case of what?"

"In case the wrong person digs up the gold. Pollicot James just dowsed the spring and we have documentary evidence that Hiram Jellyby existed."

"Have you indeed?"

"He was alive and driving mules on October 2, 1889," Dittany replied impatiently. It was not like Sergeant MacVicar to be so obtuse. "Sergeant, don't you think you'd better quit making idle conversation and get over there before people start banging Osbert with their shovels? I'd go back myself if I had anybody to leave the twins with."

"Aye."

The line went dead, the sergeant was on his way. Dittany relaxed and wondered why she'd developed a craving for cookies. Then she realized that, what with one thing and another, she'd never got around to eating any lunch and that somehow the time had worked itself around to half past three. Maybe a small cheese sandwich would tide her over till suppertime.

Now she was going to worry about whether Osbert

would wind up having to sit out there all night guarding the spring. Or had she better worry instead about whether Osbert was already digging up the gold and setting off a riot? First, the sandwich. She'd got Annie snuggled down and was cutting bread and cheese for herself when not one but two MacVicars knocked and came into the kitchen.

"Officer Bob's minding the desk," said Margaret MacVicar. "I'm going to stay here with the twins while you take Donald out to Hunnikers' Field and tell him what's going on. Are they fed and changed?"

"Yes, Osbert fed them. Rennie's asleep and I just put Annie in her basket. Maybe you ought to go with the sergeant instead of me. We've never left the babies with anybody before."

Margaret MacVicar was an eminently sensible woman. "Dittany, I have raised three sons and babysat seven grandchildren. I know all about babies. I know nothing about this latest mess you're dragging Donald into. Go."

CHAPTER
6

*T*here was so far no sign of a riot or even a melee in Hunnikers' Field. Most of those who'd come to find hidden treasure were still digging in the wrong places. Only a few were standing around watching Osbert enlarge the hole that Pollicot James had begun and these were behaving themselves, partly because they were generally nice people and partly because Zilla was standing guard with her hatchet.

Excitement was not altogether lacking, however. Water was seeping into the hole, enough to fill a teakettle, then enough to splash in, then enough to provide drinks for a team of thirsty mules. Surely this must be the spring where Hiram Jellyby had discovered the gold that had got him into such a pickle with the Akashic Record. Dittany could feel it in her bones.

Which reminded her, nobody had dug up Hiram's bones yet, although one diligent delver had found what appeared to be part of a buffalo skull and another had unearthed a tin pannikin that was long past any earthly use, unless Therese might have a spot for it in one of her artistic flower arrangements. But Osbert wasn't finding anything except water. Maybe Dittany's bones were playing her false. Maybe this wasn't the place at all. Maybe this spring was just one of many. Her stomach was beginning to knot itself up again, the way it had a little while ago when she'd been waiting for the dowsing rod to dip.

Then suddenly Osbert quit shoveling dirt from the waterhole and began feeling around gingerly with the tip of his borrowed spade. "I think I've hit something."

The words came out in a kind of prayerful whisper. He bent down and began scraping the dirt away a bit at a time until he could catch sight of whatever it was that the shovel had struck.

It was a box, an old box from the look of it, covered in canvas that might once have been white but was now the color of mud. Not a particularly large box, perhaps about the size of a crate of canned peaches. Zilla kicked off her shoes, jumped down into the water hole, and began using her hatchet blade as a scraper to free the lid while Osbert worked to loosen the dirt around the other side.

People were beginning to notice what was going on, to drop their picks and shovels and rush to the scene of the action, to be caught by Sergeant MacVicar's basilisk eye and fall back meekly to a respectful distance. Zilla was flinging out the dirt in a steady stream, clearly itching to get her hands on the box. Once the top was free, she lost patience and tugged at the lid. It wouldn't budge.

"What's got into the thing? It can't be locked. Hir—" She caught herself just in time. "Here, Osbert, you try."

"Zilla, I'm not sure this is—" Osbert too made a quick recovery. "Whether this is locked or just stuck. Lend me your hatchet, will you?"

Using the tail of his shirt, to Dittany's chagrin, he rubbed at the spot from which, according to Hiram Jellyby's tale as repeated by Zilla, the lock ought to have been knocked off a century ago. The lock was however still in place, not rusty, just tarnished; not broken, but whole. Osbert was good at locks; he whipped out his trusty Boy

Scout knife and jimmied this one with only a small amount of difficulty and that little due mainly to the dirt that had been clogging the keyhole.

Even as he released the catch, however, Osbert was puzzling. Here was a curious anomaly. The box, which was actually a small trunk, had turned up just where Hiram had said it was. It was the proper size as far as a person could tell who hadn't been around long enough to know the exact dimensions of the crates that canned peaches had come in a century ago. It had the right kind of cover, but the cover was in oddly good repair considering its presumed century-long proximity to the spring. The iron bands Hiram had mentioned were not present, Osbert could see no sign that they ever had been. On the other hand, there were ornamental brass doodads at the corners—*doodads* was probably not the correct term for them, but it was the best one Osbert could think of in the confusion of the moment—that Hiram hadn't mentioned at all.

But this was no time for pondering. An inexperienced ghost couldn't be expected to remember details with any great degree of accuracy and the cries of "Open it" were mounting to a crescendo. Osbert moved back and, with as courtly a bow as he could manage without falling into the water hole, gave Zilla the honor of raising the lid.

The hinges still held and still worked, albeit a trifle stiffly as was only to be expected. There was a mass holding of breath among the onlookers as she pushed the lid back, and a mass whooshing of exhales as she reached in to dislodge the crumple of brown canvas that hid whatever might be lying inside. Instinctively, everybody took a giant step forward, nor did Sergeant MacVicar glare at anyone for having done so. His eyes, like all the others', were on the box.

And well they might have been. The box was packed solid, not with antique gold pieces but with heavy sacks covered in clear plastic. And inside the sealed sacks were small packets, many of them, each sealed up in its own little Zip-locked plastic bag. And inside each little bag was a neat stack some three inches thick. And these stacks appeared to be made up entirely of crisp, clean, Canadian one-hundred-dollar bills.

"Well, flip me for a pancake!"

Zilla Trott had clearly voiced the mood of the gathering. They were flipping, too; there was no holding them back. To crowd around and goggle was the only reasonable thing to do. Even Sergeant MacVicar goggled, but only for a second. Then he said crisply, "Deputy Monk, wad ye kindly shut yon box?"

"But we want to see how much is in it," wailed Dot Coskoff.

As treasurer for the garden club, for its museum, and potentially for its community garden, Dot of all people had a right to ask, but the sergeant was adamant. "Mrs. Coskoff, there is a grave doot in my mind as to whether yon box was buried here for any legitimate reason. And belike in yours as weel. Am I no' correct?"

When Sergeant MacVicar started calling people by their last names and talking broad Scots, those who knew him did not gainsay him. "I suppose so," Dot admitted. "I can't imagine who in his right mind would bury a trunkful of money out here in the middle of nowhere just for the fun of it. Unless it's counterfeit, and the person was scared to keep it around the house."

"Aye, but to get rid of counterfeit money, a pairson needs only a lighted match. A likelier reason, to my mind, is that this is real money that has been stolen, that the thief who buried it here has gone into hiding or else to jail, and intends to come back and excavate his loot when it becomes feasible to do so. That is why I dinna want anybody, including myself, handling these packages. There may be fingerprints that could help to convict yon hypothetical evildoer."

"Well, yes, I can see your point," Dot admitted. "But how would the crook have found the money again? The spot was all grown over, it looked the same as the rest of the field, and there was no sort of marker. Unless the crook was a dowser too," she added doubtfully.

Sergeant MacVicar shook his head. "I misdoot his intention had been to use a metal detector. This would account for a receptacle so lavishly trimmed with brass."

"But why bury the trunk so close to the spring? Wouldn't he have been afraid the water might get in and spoil the money?"

"Evidently not. The bundles are well sealed, and that canvas covering on the trunk has nae doot been heavily waterproofed. All in all, this was an ideal spot for the clandestine concealment of stolen currency. I wad remind you that, whilst Hunnikers' Field seems isolated, it is in fact close to the highway that runs behind the Enchanted Mountain and is little populated for some fair distance, hence a good and easy place for a fleeing criminal to park his getaway vehicle undetected after dark and dig out a hiding place for his ill-gotten booty. He wad dootless hae prodded around with a rod or other implement, looking for a relatively soft spot to dig, and found it here where the underground water had kept the soil loose. If he was careful about cutting the sod and rolling it back over the spot after the box was buried, his chance of detection by any casual stroller wad hae been small."

"Yes, of course. And nobody ever comes out here much anyway, except when Jim Thompson cuts the hay, and he wouldn't notice anything that didn't interfere with the baler. So what are you going to do with the trunk? The bank's closed for the day by now, though I expect they'd open up for you."

"Aye, but I intend to take yon trunk to the Mounted Police, they may have some leads as to where the money came from. They will surely be able to detect any fingerprints on the plastic, as well as to determine whether the bills are indeed genuine or bogus."

"I should think there must be fingerprints," said Dittany, who'd been uncharacteristically silent thus far. "Can you imagine anybody packing up this many bills without having to lick his thumb now and then?"

From force of habit, Sergeant MacVicar gave her his wee-fatherless-bairn smile. "A point to consider, Dittany lass. Deputy Monk, the two of us should be able to carry the trunk between us easily enough."

"I'll help," offered one of the diggers, who happened to be Dot Coskoff's husband, Bill. "I've got my car right over there beside the road. I can run you all the way to RCMP headquarters, if you like."

"And not come back for two or three hours," snorted Dot. "I hope everybody else isn't going to skitter off now that there's no more buried treasure to dig for."

"As do I." Sergeant MacVicar gave the onlookers an extremely Scottish look and they all slunk back to where they'd dropped their gardening tools.

Osbert exchanged a glance with Zilla before saying, "Since Bill's going to take you, Sergeant, I guess you won't need me, eh. I'll walk Dittany home, then maybe come back and work some more on the water hole. It ought to be quite a lot deeper if people are going to pump out water for the garden. Happy deputizing, Bill."

"Zilla, why don't you come along and have a cup of tea with us?" said Dittany, easily divining what was afoot. "We need to talk to Minerva about that exhibition Mr. Glunck wants to set up. And to Arethusa also, if she's through stuffing scones into Polly James by now. Though I suppose we ought to quit calling him Polly now that he's dowsed us our spring."

"It's the least we can do," Zilla agreed. "Another thing we really ought to do is find out whether the water department will cough up a hunk of drainpipe or something to keep the dirt from trickling back into the hole and clogging the pump. Once we get a pump, that is. Don't any of the rest of you do any more digging here till we find out how the water department wants it done."

"Furthermore, it might not be safe," said Dot. "We don't want anybody caved in on."

"Except one or two I won't mention," Zilla amended with a menacing glance at a couple of teenagers who were acting the way teenagers all too often do. "All right then, Dittany, let's go. Anybody who wants to come back and dig some more tomorrow will be more than welcome."

Joyous shouts of acquiescence were conspicuously lacking, people were already casting wistful glances at their cars or their companions. "I'll bet you any money there won't be a soul left here twenty minutes from now," Zilla grunted as soon as she and the Monks were well away from the garden area.

"Of course there won't," Dittany agreed. "You and Osbert played that scene quite nicely. Zilla, you don't really believe Hiram managed somehow to change his gold into currency?"

"Well, he'd have had to, I expect, if he'd been planning to spend any. Gold pieces aren't legal tender any more, are they? Frankly, I don't know whether I believe in that gold or not. There was the spring and there was the trunkful of money. Not quite the way Hiram described it to me but, darn it all, what's a person to think? It seems awfully far-fetched that two similar trunks could have been buried near the same spring, but I suppose it won't kill us to look. Though we'd better wait till after dark, just in case."

"It'll be dark anyway pretty soon," said Osbert. "I'm just hoping we don't get a bunch of sightseers out here messing around, falling in holes and breaking their legs and blaming it on us."

"No fear," said Dittany. "This is hoedown night at the high school, there's a bean supper and social at the United

Church, the Madrigal Society's meeting at the Burberrys', and of course they'll be holding the usual Saturday night euchre tournament down at the fire station. Who's going to have time for sightseeing? Oh, gosh, Hazel Munson must be out from under the dryer by now. I'd meant to catch her at the Twirl and Curl and show her Hiram's photograph. I told Mr. Glunck I'd get back to him about the display cases before the museum closes."

"Hazel will be home by now, then," said Zilla. "Call her up and invite her for tea."

"We're awfully low on molasses cookies. The twins take up so much of my time that I don't get around to baking the way I used to."

"I could bring you some tofu."

"No you couldn't, Osbert won't eat tofu. He says it's just a lot of squish."

"Well, he'd better learn to like it before his arteries start backing up on him."

"Osbert's arteries are clear as a bell. Aren't they, darling?"

"Yes, darling. I keep hearing this little tinkle, tinkle, tinkle as the blood burbles merrily on its way like Tennyson's brook. I think it was Tennyson's. Somebody's brook, anyway. Speaking of brooks, I wonder whether our water hole out there might actually be not just a spring but part of an underground stream."

"Osbert!" groaned Zilla. "You mean Hiram's gold might be someplace else along the route and we've got to go back and dig up the whole darn field till we come to it?"

"But if the spring's a brook, how come the dowsing rod didn't keep dipping every time Polly James crossed over?" Dittany argued.

"I don't know, dear. It seems to me I've read someplace that you can dowse for metal as well as for water. Maybe Polly's rod has an affinity for fancy brass trimmings."

"I'll bet it does! I noticed part of it was brass. What if we got Polly back out there and had him hang a gold ring on the end?"

"How about a gold tooth?" snarled Zilla. "I think the less we go shooting our mouths off about gold, the less trouble we'll likely run into. Furthermore, that bird rubs me the wrong way, I can't quite say why. His chin's got a funny set to it."

"Really? Now, that I hadn't noticed. I must study Therese's photos when they come out."

"Provided they do."

"Of course they will. Therese couldn't do anything wrong unless she took a course on how to be stupid in ten easy lessons. I hope Margaret MacVicar's not mad that we stayed away so long, at least we'll have something to tell her. Where in heck do you suppose all those bunches of paper money came from?"

CHAPTER
7

"*T*hey might have been the payroll for the mine," Osbert suggested.

"No, dear," Dittany explained gently. "The stagecoaches quit running quite some time ago. Hiram's gold could have been the payroll for the mine, assuming any mines were in business around here then. These days, miners probably just get paychecks out of a computer. Too bad, but there it is."

"Dad-blang it, why couldn't people have left the wide open spaces the way Zane Grey invented them? All right then, if you're going to be picky, I suppose the money must have come from a bank. Or maybe a supermarket. Supermarkets take in scads of cash."

"So they do, darling, and much of it ours. Zilla, can you remember any major supermarket heists around here in the past few years?"

"No, but there was that awful bank robbery somewhere down toward Hamilton, or maybe Windsor. I forget. Anyway, a lot of money was taken and the man who ran the bank was kidnapped and murdered. To the best of my knowledge, the money's never been found and neither have the robbers. Six or eight years ago, that must have been. I don't remember the details."

"I'll bet Sergeant MacVicar does, though. That could be why he was in such a swivet to talk to the Mounties, they keep records on all that stuff. Now he's going to be late getting back for supper. Poor Margaret! And she's been so sweet about keeping the twins for us."

"Oh, Dittany, stop dithering about the twins," Zilla snapped. "Margaret MacVicar must be used to late suppers, the sergeant's been on plenty worse errands than this one. He'll be all right. Long as nobody hijacks Bill Coskoff's car."

"You're such a comfort, Zilla. Why should they? They don't know what he's got stashed in his trunk."

"They who?"

"Whoever might if they did," Osbert interjected reasonably. "Tell us more about that bank robbery, Zilla, I don't recall anything about it. Do you, Dittany?"

"No, I expect there was something more interesting going on here in town at the time. There usually is."

That was likely enough. Lobelia Falls folk didn't bother much as a rule about what was happening elsewhere. They had all they could do just trying to keep up with each other.

"I only remember because my mother had an uncle who used to be a head teller in a bank," Zilla half apologized. "We stopped to visit him at work once and he gave me a silver dollar. Out of his own pocket, naturally, not the bank's, but kids remember those things. It was the first one I'd ever had, I don't suppose I was more than seven or eight at the time. Anyway, as I recall, this banker in Hamilton or wherever was working late one night, foreclosing on mortgages or whatever they do. He was all alone in the building except for the night watchman, who was out back making tea when a bunch of robbers, or maybe it was only one robber, snuck in somehow and knocked him down on the floor and tied him up, and stuffed something in his mouth so he couldn't yell to warn the banker."

"Standard procedure," said Osbert. "I always gag the watchman, myself. At least my villains do. So then what?"

"So then the robber bullied the banker into opening the vault and loading all the money into a sack he'd brought with him. The watchman couldn't see this happening, being still tied up in the back room, but he could hear the robber bossing the banker around and threatening to shoot off his toes if he didn't step lively. And then the robber came tearing out past where the watchman was lying, with this big sackful of money over his shoulder. After that, by gum, he went back and got the banker and carried him out too."

"The ornery sidewinder! That's not standard procedure. I always just tie the banker to his chair, myself."

"Well, I'm telling you what this other one did," Zilla insisted. "He stepped right over the watchman, staggering a little as you might expect because the banker was no lightweight, but making pretty good time, considering."

"Gosh! Did the watchman see his face?"

"No. He had on a black hat pulled down over his forehead, and a black scarf tied over his face, you know how they do, and dark glasses on. And gloves. Black, I suppose, not that it matters. The watchman said the robber looked to be about seven feet tall, but that was only natural considering that he was down on the floor looking up. He said the banker seemed to be unconscious but wasn't dripping blood or anything. The police decided he'd most likely been slugged over the head with the robber's gun butt so that he wouldn't make a fuss about being lugged off."

"But why take the banker away at all?" said Dittany. "The robber couldn't have needed a hostage if there was nobody around to stop him from getting away with the money."

"No," said Zilla, "that was the interesting part. What the robber seems to have had in mind was to hold the banker for ransom. Late that same night, he called up the banker's wife, who'd just got in from the opera, I think it was, and told her he wanted some outlandish ransom or she'd never see her husband alive again. The wife was pretty well heeled in her own right, as I recall. But you know how those rich people are with their money, she jumped to the conclusion that her husband had been out tying one on with the boys and this was just one of his cronies trying to be funny. So she told the kidnapper to stuff it in his ear, or words to that effect, and went to bed expecting the old man to roll in sooner or later. But the banker never came home. That next afternoon, she got a package with his left little finger in it and the signet ring bearing his ancestral crest that he always wore, still on the finger."

"Oh my gosh!"

"Yes, it shows the folly of jumping to conclusions, doesn't it? There was also a note in the package, telling the wife she needn't worry about her husband coming back because she was now a widow. She held a nice memorial service for the finger after she'd kept it in the fridge for a while in hopes the rest of him might show up, but the police never found so much as a hair from his mustache. Nor the money, nor the robber. I don't know what became of the widow but I certainly do hope she'll know better next time. You don't really want me to stay for tea, do you, Dittany?"

"Sure we do, unless you've got something more interesting on the fire."

"Well, to tell you the honest truth, I'm sort of curious to see whether Hiram shows up again before we go digging after that other trunk."

"If he does, be sure to tell him you've seen the platinum print of him and the mules. He'll be pleased, I should think. Give us a ring after supper and let Osbert know if the expedition's still on."

"Right you are. 'Bye then."

They went their separate ways. When the Monks got home, they found Margaret in the rocking chair with a twin on each arm. She looked a trifle disappointed to see them but agreed willingly to stay to tea once they'd explained why her husband would be late for supper.

"Thank you, I may as well. Goodness knows when he'll be along. I don't know why disaster always seem to strike at suppertime. Not that finding a trunkful of hundred-dollar bills can exactly be counted a disaster, I don't suppose. And Donald has no idea where the money came from?"

"If he does, he didn't say," Dittany replied. "Zilla was telling us about a banker who was robbed and kidnapped some years back, and all they ever found of him was a finger that the robber sent back out of spite because the wife wouldn't pay the ransom."

"I remember that case, Donald was very interested in it. The assistant manager had to be operated on for a hernia a while after the banker disappeared and came under heavy investigation, but it was never proved that he got it lifting the money. He'd just been married, I believe; his wife swore up and down that he'd ruptured himself trying to move one of those great big old-fashioned golden-oak hat racks with a boot box and a plate glass mirror and a lot of deer feet sticking out to hang hats on, which had been given them for a wedding present."

"That sounds reasonable enough," said Dittany. "Those things weigh a ton, as everybody knows who's been unfortunate enough to inherit one."

"I know," said Margaret. "I quaked in my shoes when my mother's Aunt Gertrude died for fear she'd will hers to me, but luckily she'd left it to her husband's nephew Percival, who used to board with them before he got married. I don't know what effect those deer feet may have had on Percival's marriage, I haven't laid eyes on him since Aunt Gertrude's funeral. The twins have been good as gold the whole time, bless their little hearts. Look at those big blue eyes. I think Annie favors your mother a bit, Dittany. When's Clorinda coming back?"

The conversation drifted into familiar paths, the time passed agreeably. Dittany had got up to refill the teapot when she suddenly froze with the kettle in her hand. "Darn it, I forgot! I'm supposed to see Hazel, Arethusa, and Minerva about whether they'll approve an exhibition of photographs Mr. Glunck wants to put in the Thorbisher-Freep display cases."

"Any change would be an improvement, in my opinion," said Margaret. "Can't you simply call them up and ask them?"

"Good thought."

Dittany phoned Hazel Munson first. Hazel said she didn't give two hoots and a holler what Mr. Glunck put in his darned old cases, nor did she want to hear about the platinum printing process because her custard sauce was about to curdle.

Pollicot James must have been starting to curdle too. Arethusa was almost frantic with eagerness to express her contrition at having forgotten the important trustees' meeting scheduled for ten minutes ago; she'd be along as soon as she'd had a chance to speed her parting guest and set the cream back in the fridge.

After those two, Dittany was a trifle nervous about calling Minerva Oakes, and well she might have been. It turned out that Mrs. Melloe was still there and particularly eager to meet Dittany Henbit Monk. Mrs. Melloe had found new reason to believe that she might be connected to the Henbits on her mother's side, and wondered if she might just pop over for a few brief moments.

"Not on your life," yowled Dittany. "Minerva, I do not want Mrs. Melloe over here at any time, particularly not now. I want you to come and look at a photograph of Hiram Jellyby that Mr. Glunck dug out of the museum files and I have to take back to him pronto before he falls into a swivet. Tell Mrs. Melloe you've got to attend an emergency trustees' meeting. She can phone me in the morning."

"She's going to Toronto in the morning."

"Good. Hurry up, Minerva, we need you."

"I can't just leave Mrs. Melloe sitting here."

"Then tell her to go away. Oh, darn it! Tell her to go have her supper at the inn and I'll see her this evening after I get the twins to bed."

"You tell her."

"For the cat's sake, Minerva! Why do you waste so much time being nice to pushy people?"

"Dittany"—Margaret MacVicar had been listening to Dittany's half of the conversation with wry amusement— "if you'd like to run over and show Minerva that photograph, I'd be more than happy to sit here with Osbert and give the babies their supper. Truly, I don't mind a bit."

Since Margaret so very obviously didn't, Dittany snatched up the platinum print and ran. It was almost dark out by now, but that didn't matter; she knew her way blindfolded. Minerva was looking a trifle pinched around the mouth, as served her right for letting herself be imposed upon by large ladies with jutting chins and artifact-strewn bosoms.

In addition to a triple necklace of gold beads, Mrs. Melloe was wearing a gold chain with a single eyeglass hanging from it, another gold chain bearing a gold hunter watch, a third gold chain with a little gold pencil, and a large gold brooch in the shape of a date palm, with a cluster of small garnets for the dates. Otherwise her garb was restrained enough: a brown tweed suit of excellent quality, a cream-colored silk blouse with a frill at the neck, well-polished brown leather walking shoes, brown leather gloves, and a russet velvet toque such as the late Dowager Queen Mary had been wont to affect.

Mrs. Melloe had much that same regality of manner, she wasn't actually so much pushy as overwhelming. Dittany could see why someone as unassuming as Minerva would have had a hard time trying to tell such a personage to go peddle her papers. Dittany herself was not easily overwhelmed, she acknowledged the introduction with her usual brisk efficiency.

"How do you do, Mrs. Melloe. You don't look a bit like a Henbit. You wouldn't want to be connected with us anyway, we're totally devoid of class. Minerva, I need to talk to you. Excuse us, Mrs. Melloe."

Taking a grip on Minerva's arm, Dittany steered her out to the kitchen. "See, Minerva, you simply have to be polite but firm."

"Polite? Dittany, you were about as rude as you could have got."

"No, I wasn't. I could have been lots ruder if I'd really put my mind to it. People who barge around trying to muscle in on your ancestry just when you're ready to start supper aren't being all that dad-blanged polite either, in my considered opinion. I want you to look at this platinum print."

"What do you mean, platinum print? It's just a photo of some ratty-looking old coot with a team of—mules! Dittany, you can't mean—"

"Can't I, though? Read what's written on the back of the mount."

"Then hold the darned thing up to the light where I can see it. Hiram who? Dittany, am I reading this right?"

"You certainly are."

"I can't believe it! And there was I, thinking Zilla'd been nipping at the dandelion wine. Do you suppose she really did see Hiram Jellyby's ghost, or was she having some kind of present'ment, the way her grandmother used to?"

Dittany shrugged. "Your ghost is as good as mine.

Whatever she said, it was right about the treasure, though not in the way we expected."

She explained. Minerva goggled.

"But where did all those hundred-dollar bills come from?"

"That's what Sergeant MacVicar's over at Mountie headquarters for, trying to find out. Margaret's at our house now. She offered to mind the babies while Osbert and I went out to the community garden. It's beginning to look as if we might have to kidnap them back from her. Margaret and Zilla think the money might be the loot from a bank robbery that happened about eight years ago down around Windsor or somewhere. The bank president was kidnapped and murdered and his finger was sent to his wife. Do you remember anything about that?"

"No, but if Margaret says so, I'm willing to believe she's right. After having seen this picture, I'd believe pretty near anything. What are you going to do now?"

"Take the photograph back to Mr. Glunck, then go home and get supper."

"Zilla's not eating with you, is she?"

"Perish the thought. I told her we were out of tofu and she flounced off in a huff. She's hoping Hiram will show up again so she can ask him how he managed to transform his gold pieces into paper money. Oh, what I really came for was to ask you how you feel about taking the Thorbisher-Freep artifacts out of their display cases. Mr. Glunck's itching to show a collection of these platinum prints that Osbert's great-grandfather took around Lobelia Falls. Eliphalet Monk, his name was. Tell Mrs. Melloe, she may want to hang another leaf on her family tree."

"Now, Dittany, Mrs. Melloe's very sincere about her roots. Eliphalet Monk, eh? I'd have to look him up. As far as the photographs go, they'd certainly make a far more appropriate exhibit for the Architrave than that old theatrical junk. However, the condition of our acquiring the

Thorbisher-Freep Collection was that everything has to be kept on permanent display."

"That doesn't mean we have to keep it in the cases, though. We can stick a few of the best artifacts on the parlor whatnot and set out the rest on tables in the attic."

"What if people go up there and pinch them?"

"We should be so lucky. We might scrounge those old storm windows that the Boulangers have just had replaced, and lay them over the artifacts for protection."

Minerva was appeased. "Like cucumber frames. I don't see why that wouldn't work. All right then, tell Mr. Glunck I said go ahead. Look, I really must get back to Mrs. Melloe, though I have to say I'm about ancestored out for one day. After she leaves, if she ever does, I'll slip over to Zilla's and see if I can catch a glimpse of Hiram."

"Then I'll nip out the back door. Say good-bye to Mrs. Melloe for me. Maybe she'll take the hint."

Now to return Hiram's photograph. The Architrave would be closed by this time, but Dittany had her own key. She found Mr. Glunck in the kitchen of his small apartment on the first floor, meditating gently on the relative merits of vegetable and split pea soup. He was glad to get his artifact back, glad to hear of the trustees' unanimous approval. Dittany left him to his gloating and his soup, and went home to start supper.

CHAPTER

8

"*B*oo!" said Hiram Jel-
lyby.

"Oh, boo yourself, you old goat," replied Zilla Trott.
"Though I must admit I was sort of hoping you'd show up.
We've found your photograph and dug out your spring. At
least we think we have."

"Who's we? You an' your mules?"

"I told you last night we don't have any mules around
here these days. Though there were a few jackasses among
those present, now that you mention it," Zilla conceded.
"This afternoon we had a bunch of people over at Hunnikers' Field, if you remember where that is, getting the soil
ready to plant a community garden next year. We also had
a dowser trying to locate your spring, which he did. Unless
it's the wrong one."

"Dowser? You mean a water witch? With a forked
hazel twig that dips down an' shows you where to dig?"

"That's right, only this man used a fancy metal gadget
instead of a twig. He nailed the spring right on the button,
too."

"Did you find my gold?"

"Yes and no, as you might say. That's what I wanted

to talk to you about, Hiram. We did dig up a trunk that looked pretty much the way you described it, only this one had brass fitments instead of iron, and it was locked. When a young fellow picked the lock, we found the trunk full of paper money, all done up in waterproof packages. Now Hiram, I want you to tell me the truth, if you remember how. Was there really any chest of gold? And if there was, how the blue blazes did you manage to turn it into modern currency?"

"Yes, there was, an' no, I never. What would I want to change it for? Gold's gold, ain't it? An' paper's only paper, no matter what anybody says. An' furthermore, I ain't no magician. I'm just what's left of a damn good mule skinner. Where'd you get hold o' my photograph?"

"It was on file at the museum, which used to be the old Architrave house."

"Old, eh? Cripes, I hauled in most o' the lumber an' fittin's for that house when it was remodeled, me an' the mules. An' fought that cussed skinflint Henry Architrave for every penny o' the freight charges. God, Henry was mean! He was gettin' married an' wanted to gussy the place up for his bride, but he didn't want to pay for the work, no more'n he had to. Meanest bird I ever run acrost. When his own father died, he begrudged the two copper cent pieces to lay on the old man's eyes. An' that's no lie, Zilla. Henry claimed it was a heathen practice an' against religion, but what it boiled down to was that he just didn't want to waste them two cents. How come the Architraves ain't still livin' there?"

"Because there aren't any Architraves left. John was the last. I'm not sure whether he was Henry's son or his grandson, but anyway he must have been a chip off the old block. John would squeeze a nickel till the beaver bit him. Anyway, as I said, John was the tail end of the direct line. His wife was dead before him and they'd never had any children." Zilla sniffed. "Probably because John never got around to it, if he ran his private life the way he did the water department. Anyway, John left the house to the garden club for us to fix up and turn into a museum in memory of his wife, who'd been one of our presidents. So we did and it's real nice now. You ought to manifest yourself over there and have a look around once the curator puts your picture on display."

"I might, at that," Hiram conceded. "Be somethin' to do anyways. Say, it's comin' back to me about that photograph. By gorry, I remember it all, clear as a bell. Eliphalet Monk, that was his name. Kept me standin' in the road while he fiddled around up on a little stepladder with his head inside a red velvet bag stuck onto the back of his camera. Great big wooden box settin' up on three sticks, you'd o' thought it would topple over an' squoosh 'im, but it didn't. Don't s'pose there's any Monks left around here?"

"Oh yes, it was a Monk who jimmied open that trunk with the paper money in it. Osbert, his name is, he writes Western stories. His wife just had twins a couple of months ago, a boy and a girl. She was a Henbit, you probably remember the Henbits. Osbert's Aunt Arethusa lives here too, in the old Monk house. She writes romantic novels about dukes and earls."

"Cripes, don't neither of 'em do a lick of honest work?"

"Huh! Osbert and Arethusa each make enough money from their books every year to buy up half of Lobelia County, pretty near."

"You mean people get paid that good nowadays for lyin'? Mighty Jehu! When I think of all the lies I used to tell for nothin', I could bust out cryin' if I had anything left to cry with. But I wasn't stringin' you about that gold, Zilla, I swear I wasn't. If that box ain't there now, it's because some bugger went an' dug it up an' never told anybody. But I'm bettin' mine's still where I left it, irregardless. Wasn't nothin' in the Akashic Record about the gold bein' took away, an' they're usually pretty thorough when it comes to puttin' in the details."

"Then why don't I telephone Osbert and tell him we'd better go see if we can find that other box after he's finished his supper and helped Dittany put the twins to bed. Osbert's real good about helping with the babies, though he's no great shakes at chores, generally speaking. He means well, but he gets to thinking about mustangs on the mesas and buzzards over the buttes and forgets what he's holding the hammer for. I don't suppose you could come along with us, Hiram?"

"I don't see what'd stop me from tryin'. O' course I got no more personal interest in that gold, but it does seem a shame for nobody to be gettin' any good out of it. What I really ought to do is find them bones o' mine an' see to it they're buried decent so's I can get on with whatever I'm s'posed to be doin' next."

"If you don't care for the accommodations here, you're under no obligation to stay," Zilla replied somewhat huffily.

"Now ain't that just like a woman! I never said I didn't like it here, did I? But dang it, Zilla, a ha'nt's got to do what he's got to do."

"Seems to me I've heard that one before. Sit down, then, before you start thinning out. And try not to fall through the chair this time. Want a doughnut?"

"Oh, say them words again! I sure wouldn't mind feastin' my eyes on one, if I can't do no better. Used to be a woman down Hamilton way that made the best doughnuts I ever throwed a lip over. Jessie, her name was. Great big redhead with—um—don't s'pose you was plannin' to boil up a pot o' coffee to go with it?"

"I never drink coffee."

Nevertheless, Zilla went and got the ancestral percolator out of the pantry. "It just happens I bought some a while back when my cousin from Manitoba was here visiting. Lord knows what it'll do to you in your present condition."

"Only one way to find out."

Hiram settled himself without mishap this time, Zilla suspected he'd been in here practicing while she was off at the garden site. The coffee did smell good perking, she had to admit. Maybe it wouldn't hurt her to drink half a cupful too, just to fortify herself for what might turn into a hard night's work.

Having a man, even a not very solid one, sitting across the table did give a person an oddly cozy feeling despite the fact that Hiram was eyeing her plateful of tofu and bean sprout casserole with a mixture of contempt and puzzlement. Zilla herself was keeping a sharp lookout on that doughnut of Minerva's. Seeing the coffee gradually evaporate out of Hiram's cup didn't faze her much after last night's camomile tea episode, but watching a big, fluffy raised doughnut slowly deflate like a miniature inner tube with a slow leak was downright uncanny.

Eerier still was the effect this was having on Hiram Jellyby. He'd told her he could feast his eyes on the doughnut, and evidently he was doing exactly that. Zilla hadn't been particularly aware of the old gaffer's eyes before now. Like the rest of him they'd simply been, somehow, there. If she'd been asked what color they were, she'd have said, "I don't know. Sort of a washed-out blue, I guess." As the doughnut decreased in size, though, the eyes turned to a more and more intense turquoise color. They seemed to be lighted from within. By the time his coffee cup was empty and the doughnut but a shriveled ring on his plate, they were glowing like a pair of neon lamps.

What was even more remarkable was that the rest of him had begun to fade. Now she could see the back of his chair through his torso, yet those incandescent eyes gleamed on just as brightly, if not more so. Zilla found this somewhat disconcerting.

"Hiram, what's happening to you?"

"What do you mean, what's happenin' to me? I ain't never felt better in my afterlife. That coffee an' doughnut sure hit the spot. Made a new ha'nt o' me, by gorry. Don't I look it?"

"Well, you certainly look a lot perkier than you did last night. The thing I can't get over is that the rest of you's thinning out so fast you look like a wisp of leftover fog, but your eyes are glowing like a pair of bright blue buggy lamps."

Zilla didn't see any sense in mentioning automobile headlights. Hiram wouldn't know what she was talking about, most likely. Anyway, she was so down on internal combustion engines that she didn't even want to talk about them. Zilla regarded the ozone layer as a personal friend and hated to think what all those noxious emissions were doing to it. She was all set to give the former mule-teer a lecture on air pollution when Osbert arrived, shovel in hand, and she had to get up and let him in.

"Hello, Osbert, I figured it was about time you showed up. Park your shovel for a second and come meet Hiram Jellyby. Hiram, this is the Monk boy I was telling you about."

Seeing nothing but the remains of the tofu and bean sprout casserole, Osbert was momentarily nonplussed. Hiram spoke first, his voice low and soft as a prairie zephyr. Zilla heard him well enough but Osbert didn't, which was just as well. What he said was, "This the young squirt who tells lies for a livin'?"

Zilla, naturally, was not pleased. "Hiram, if you expect us to go digging all over Ontario for those bones of yours, you might be well advised to mind your manners. Speak up so Osbert can hear you, and remember you're in a civilized house. That's him across the table, Osbert, those two blue eyeballs."

"Oh, I'm sorry, I was looking in the wrong direction. How do you do, Mr. Jellyby."

"Hell's bells, can't you call me Hiram?" This time the voice came out clear enough. "Your great-great-grandfather took my picture oncet. That practic'ly makes us relatives, don't it? Yep, I knew Eliphalet Monk well. I used to bring in photography supplies that he ordered sent out from Toronto, me an' my mules. Split a jar with 'im now an' then too, not that Eliphalet was ever much of a drinker. Kind of a funny gink, took a bath every Saturday night reg'lar as clockwork, even in wintertime, an' changed 'is shirt three times a week. You kind o' favor Eliphalet, you know that, bub? Got that same wool-gatherin' expression, like a lost sheep on the mountain. Zilla tells me you married one o' the Henbit girls. Good-looker, is she?"

"I married the only Henbit girl available at the time, actually," said Osbert. "Dittany's an only child."

"Dittany, eh? Now that's a pretty name I never heard before. Makes me think o' me an' my mules singin' around the campfire, nights when the stars was hangin' overhead big as baked potaters."

"Doesn't it, though?" Osbert agreed. "I thought exactly the same thing the first time I heard it. And Dittany's as pretty as her name. Prettier. Lots prettier. You must drop over and see our twins next time you've got your ectoplasm on, Hiram. They're going to be three months old in a couple of days, we've been thinking we might have a little party for them. Very informal, of course, just animal crackers and cocoa to drink."

"No whiskey?"

Zilla snorted. "Don't you dare give that old buzzard whiskey, Osbert Monk. He lit up like a bagful of fireworks after one doughnut and a cup of coffee. Lord knows what a shot of red-eye would do to him. Come on then, we might as well get started. It would have made more sense for Hiram and me to meet you over by the footpath. You're closer to there than you are to here."

"I know, but Dittany and I didn't want you walking in the dark by yourself," Osbert replied. "We—er—weren't sure Hiram would be coming with you, and that Peeping

Tom's still hanging around. Ellie Bascom caught a glimpse of him last evening, Dittany says. Ellie claims he tinkled. She was terribly upset."

"As Ellie Bascom naturally would be. Huh! One peep at me and that'd be the last he ever peeped, I can tell you."

This was sheer bravado, Zilla remembered all too well how creepy she'd felt last night when she'd sensed that alien presence outside her own house. Funny, Hiram didn't make her feel uneasy, even now when there was nothing to be seen of him except those two gleaming blue eyeballs.

It was probably just as well, she thought, that everybody else in town was off to one or another of the evening's festivities. If they'd happened to meet a neighbor out walking the dog or stretching his legs, Hiram's optical manifestations might have been rather difficult to explain.

The eyeballs did come in handy, though, once the trio had left Lobelia Falls's none too abundant supply of streetlights behind them. Though the day had been reasonably salubrious, clouds had come in with the sunset. By now it was pitch dark, and walking on the dirt path could have been tricky. Osbert had brought along a flashlight but was loath to use it. Somebody running late to an engagement might notice the light bobbing along and spread a rumor that the treasure hunt was back on, with results that could only be conjectured.

As it turned out, however, Hiram's eyes, though casting no strong beams themselves, somehow managed to provide a kind of auxiliary illumination to each member of the party. They found their way to the spring with no trouble whatever. The water had cleared by now; Zilla dipped in her cupped hands, took a sip, and pronounced it real tasty.

Osbert drank too. Whether Hiram did was debatable. They saw no appreciable lowering of the water level, but that didn't mean anything. He'd have had to absorb a whole bucketful to produce any effect on a hole this size and didn't appear to be trying. Those sapphirine glitters were turning this way and that, surveying the landscape. After what seemed like a long while, and maybe was, the dead man gave his pronouncement.

"Yup, this is the place, eh. I could feel it in my bones if I knew where they was. Go ahead, Osbert, where you want to dig is right over here where Zilla's standin'. Move your number nines, woman, an' let the man work."

Zilla wasn't standing for that kind of nonsense. "Huh! I'd like to see the man who could outwork me. Hand over that shovel, Osbert."

Hiram was scandalized. "You goin' to let 'er, bub?"

"Why not?" said Osbert reasonably. "I found the last box. If Zilla wants a turn, why shouldn't she have one? Fair's fair."

"By gorry, ol' Eliphalet'll never be dead long as you're alive. I bet you're just like him, always changin' your shirt an' washin' your neck."

"Well, not always," Osbert admitted, "but frequently. When I was a kid my mother used to make me, and I just drifted into the habit. You know how it is. People do tend to wash more these days, what with indoor plumbing and all those soap commercials on television. In some circles it's considered more intellectual not to, I understand, but we Western writers aren't accustomed to thinking of ourselves as intellectuals. I don't, anyway. My Aunt Arethusa doesn't think I'm one either. But then I think she's a featherhead, so it evens out."

"Cripes, you're a cheeky young bugger. That's a fine way to talk about your own female relatives."

"Oh, it's not just me. Most people think Aunt Arethusa's a featherhead. Unless they've fallen in love with her, which happens to about forty percent of the men she meets, poor saps."

"How come?"

"I don't know. My wife calls it the moth and the flame

syndrome, they just take one close look and go up in smoke. Want me to spell you awhile, Zilla?"

"What for? I've only had time to scrape out about three spadefuls. It's not hard going here. I'm digging into the side, sort of. I figure Hiram's box is going to be down a ways. I'm making a mess of the water hole, but it'll settle again. Oops, I've—nope, just an old piece of rotten wood. It seems to be in the shape of a—well, I'll be hornswoggled. Hiram, would this by any chance be your grave marker? Careful, it's all punky and ready to fall apart."

"What of it?" grunted the late muleteer. "So'm I. Yep, this is my personal tribute to me. Not much left of it, but I'm all in 'cept the eyeballs, myself. Keep diggin', Zilla."

"I thought you didn't think digging was ladylike."

"Oh, hell, woman, I was just settin' a good example to this young sprout here. Tryin' to teach 'im a little decent respect for fair an' fragile femalehood, that's all."

"Hiram, I wish to heck you were substantial enough for me to give you a backhander with this shovel. Wait! I think I've really hit something this time."

Zilla was right. Half a minute's frantic digging revealed another small trunk, much the size of the first one but in somewhat worse condition. Between them, she and Osbert freed it from the friable soil and boosted it up on the ground. This lock didn't have to be jimmied. With hands that shook a little, Zilla threw back the lid.

"Gadzooks!" came a voice out of the darkness. "What are you doing with my great-grandmother's wedding china?"

CHAPTER
9

"*A*rethusa! Lord have mercy, you scared me out of a year's growth."

"Really, Zilla?" Arethusa was taking the matter lightly. "I should have thought any woman who consorts with my idiot nephew and a pair of floating eyeballs ought to be beyond scaring. To repeat my question, by what method have you come into possession of Great-granny's Chelseaware dinner set, which was clandestinely abstracted from her then not yet ancestral china cabinet during the honeymoon and never seen again?"

"If the china was never seen again," Zilla asked sensibly enough, "then how do you know this is it?"

"Intuition. Plus the fact that my esteemed great-grandfather beguiled those anxious last days prior to the nuptials taking still-life photographs of the wedding presents. After the china was stolen, he consoled his bride with a handsome platinum print of it as a memento to hang in the dining room, where in fact the print still hangs. I've been looking at that photograph all my life, and crying out in silent agony—crying inwardly would perhaps be a more succinct choice of words—because, as I thought, Great-granny's china would never be mine."

"But Arethusa, you already have lovely old china."

"Oh, yes, naturally Great-grandfather had to buy Great-grandmother another set, but nothing so magnificent. This one came over from England in a sailing ship ordered especially for the wedding."

"The ship?"

"Perhaps. I was, however, alluding primarily to the china. The set I inherited was just one that an itinerant peddler happened to have kicking around in his cart when he came through shortly after the honeymoon was so lamentably terminated. Well-nigh priceless by now, needless to say, but that's beside the point. How absurd, though, for someone to have gone to the bother of stealing these lovely dishes and then just bringing them out here and burying them. One thinks immediately of a jealous rival performing a final act of spite against the bride. Or against the groom, as the case might have been. Does one not?"

"One's more apt to think of some opportunist hoping to turn a dishonest buck once the heat was off," Zilla replied cynically. "This china must have been worth a pretty penny even in those days."

"In sooth," Arethusa agreed. "Perchance not a king's ransom, but belike a viscount's or a baronet's. I must say it was terribly decent of you to come and dig it up for me. Not to cavil, however, but one does wonder why you couldn't have waited for daylight, the chipping potential of fine porcelain being what it is even under optimum conditions and Osbert being such a ham-handed lout under any circumstances. Might one inquire what drove you to clandestine measures?"

"We weren't intending to dig up your stupid china at all," snarled the lout. "We didn't even know it was here. And as to being out roaming around in the dark, what brings you here?"

"Good question, i' faith. I know there was something.

What could it have been? Ah yes, I remember now, I was endeavoring to apprehend an ill-doer."

"An ill-doer?"

"In my personal opinion, yes. I consider it a resoundingly ill deed to trample all over a person's chrysanthemums for the purpose of peeking in at their windows. Old-maidish of me, perchance, but I took umbrage. So I slipped out the side door under cover of night's ebon mantle and gave chase."

"Arethusa Monk!" cried Zilla. "Are you saying you went after that Peeping Tom bare-handed?"

"Why? Is it a breach of etiquette to chase the creature without one's gloves on?"

"It's a breach of common sense for a woman your age to go after him at all. What if he'd turned and grabbed you by the throat?"

"I'd have pinked him with my rapier, naturally. Gadzooks, what sort of addlepated ninnyhammer dost think I am, eh? A dagger might have been the more appropriate weapon considering the hour and the nature of the errand, but I must confess that I felt no eagerness to grapple with the rogue hand to hand. Not that big a rogue, at any rate."

"How big a rogue was he?"

"Big enough, by my halidom! Had the rogue been smaller, I might have contented myself with a lesser weapon. Perhaps a golf club. Heroines in those mystery novels about boarding schools one used to read as a girl were always snatching up golf clubs in time of peril."

It was difficult to tell in the dark whether Osbert was sneering, but the tone of his voice indicated that he probably was. "Where the heck would you get a golf club, Aunt Arethusa? You don't play golf. All you play is the field."

"Precisely," his aunt agreed quite amicably, for her. "I should have had to request the loan of a mashie, a spoon, a cleek, or possibly a niblick from some golfer of my acquaintance. Archie, perchance."

"Archie's in Toronto, for Pete's sake."

"That did occur to me. In any event, I decided against the golf club, so the point is moot. The point of my rapier, on the other hand, is quite unmoot enough for practical purposes, such as stapping that runnagate through the vitals if I catch him clomping through my perennial borders again."

"You didn't really chase him all the way here with your rapier drawn, did you?"

"No. I chased him through Grandsire Coskoff's back yard and thence to some place or other where he had a bicycle hidden. Wherever that was, it was extremely dark. Not having thought to bring a linkboy or even a lanthorn with me, I was by then somewhat disoriented. The thing to do seemed to be just to keep walking, on the theory that I was bound to come out somewhere sooner or later. And, as you see, I did. Osbert, I am extremely fatigued. Will you kindly cease asking me silly questions and direct me to your car so that I can go and collapse in it while you and Zilla follow at a discreet pace, carrying the trunk very carefully between you and taking utmost pains not to joggle Great-granny's china?"

"I'm sorry, Aunt Arethusa, but we walked. We're over beyond the Enchanted Mountain, in that field we're planning to use for the community garden. I can run home and get the car if you want, but we do have a little unfinished business here."

"Such as what?"

"Well, as Zilla mentioned, Great-great-granny's wedding china wasn't what we came looking for. I don't know what sort of dumping ground this is," Osbert added somewhat pettishly. "First we dig up a boxful of money, then here's this priceless set of antique china, but when the heck are we going to get down to Hiram's gold pieces?"

"Never, if you just stand around yammerin'."

"Who spoke?" cried Arethusa. "Meseems I heard an alien voice."

"The hell you did," came the acerbic reply. "I'm just as Canadian as you are. At least I was once."

"Was where? Why? What? Whence? With whom am I having this conversation, if such it can be called? Zilla, whose eyeballs are those you brought with you?"

"Hiram Jellyby's. I guess you might call him my boarder. He used to be a mule skinner back in your great-grandparents' day."

"Oh. Then how do you do, Mr. Jellyby. Do I gather that you are an apparition, specter, wraith, shade, revenant, or earthbound spirit?"

"Catch on quick, don't you, sis? That's just what I am an' just what it looks like I'm goin' to go on bein' till you folks quit horsin' around with Miz Eliphalet's Sunday china an' find me them bones I left layin' around here someplace."

"Methought it was your gold you were after."

"Great Godfrey, no! What good would gold do me now? I was just usin' the gold as bait, so's to speak, eh. I figured if I showed somebody where to dig for it, they'd owe me a favor in return, see, an' I could haunt 'em till they stood an' delivered, as the stagecoach robbers used to say."

"Fie upon you, Mr. Jellyby. Have you no faith in the essential goodness of human nature?"

"Not much, if you want the truth. 'Tain't as if I hadn't been human once myself, you know. Knowin' me as I did then, I wouldn't o' trusted myself as far as I could throw a mule by the tail."

"Indeed?" said Arethusa. "One might have expected an entity in your situation to take a more spiritual point of view."

"Seems to me you're expectin' one hell of a lot from a thinned-out mule skinner," Hiram replied somewhat irascibly. "A person don't get no more spiritual just by cashin' in his chips. Don't think that for one minute, sis, 'cause that ain't how it works. What an entity's got to do is work up to goodness gradual, same as he had to back when he still had meat on his bones, providin' he ever got around to goin' in for self-improvement, which a surprisin' number o' people never do. Now take Zilla here, for instance. She ain't even dead yet an' I'll bet you any money that on the spiritual level, she's already up to somewheres around a sergeant-major's rank. An' here's me, deader'n a salt herrin' the past hundred years an' still no further along than a buck private. It's humblin', that's what it is."

"That so?" snapped Zilla. "I can't say I've noticed any sign of you slapping sackcloth and ashes on your head."

"There, see? Pickin' on me again. That's the trouble with you goody-goodies, you ain't got no fellow feelin' for us baddies. How you doin' there, bub? Hit my box yet?"

"No, but I'm still digging," grunted Osbert. "And finding it pretty warm work, now that I think of it. Here, Aunt Arethusa, want my jacket to rest your spavined bones on?"

"A veritable Sir Walter Raleigh, egad! Remind me to leave you my second-best bed. The one with the mouse in the mattress."

"Thanks, Auntie, but I've got my own bed. Which I'll be dad-blanged happy to lie in by the time we're finished out here. How far down did you find that gold, Hiram?"

"Not far, or I never would o' found it. I was just tryin' for enough water to fill my mules' gizzards an' boil me up a pot o' coffee. Too bad we didn't think to bring the coffeepot with us tonight, Zilla. We could o' lit us a little campfire an' sung around it, the way me an' the mules used to do back when I was me."

Hiram threw back his eyeballs and brayed. "Oh, Buffalo gals, ain't you comin' out tonight? Cripes, I'm in better voice now than I was when I had an Adam's apple to sing with. Don't I sound great, Zilla?"

"Not bad for somebody who took voice lessons from a team of mules," his temporary landlady conceded. "Yes, it's a shame we didn't think of the coffeepot. I could have used a hot drink myself about now. And we could have toasted marshmallows on the point of Arethusa's rapier. Want me to spell you awhile, Osbert?"

"No, I'm all right, if Hiram wouldn't mind juicing up his eyeballs a little and giving me more light down here. I think I've hit something but it doesn't feel like a box. Unless the box has fallen apart from the damp."

"Could of, I s'pose." Obligingly, Hiram raised his ocular candlepower. "This help any, bub?"

"Oh yes, thank you, that's much better. I have to go easy here. If that trunk's broken open, the gold pieces could be scattered all through the dirt. Take the shovel, will you, Zilla? I think what I'd better do is get down and feel around with my hands for whatever it was I—suffering shorthorns!"

"What is it, Osbert?" Zilla asked.

"Offhand, I'd say it's a piece of hip."

Hiram's eyeballs came whizzing past Osbert's shoulder. "Whose?" he yelped.

"I have no idea. It could be a sheep's, it's too big for a gopher and too small for a bison. I'm not much on anatomy. Here, Aunt Arethusa, hold this bone, will you?"

"Moi? You forget to whom you speak, jackanapes. Wait a minute, I seem to be wearing a petticoat. Literary tradition requires any heroine worthy of the name to sacrifice her petticoat in time of need. Turn your back, Hiram."

"Can't, I ain't got one."

"Oh, well." Arethusa shrugged, performed a series of dips and wiggles, and produced a dainty confection of silk and lace which she spread on the grass at the edge of her nephew's excavation. "There you are, you can lay the bones on this as you find them, so that they won't get mixed in with the thistles and ragweed."

"Good thinking, auntie. Here's another for the collection. A thigh bone, I think. The thigh bone's connected to the knee bone. That would be this little roundish thing, I expect. And the kneebone's connected to the leg bone, of which there seem to be two. Tibia and fibula, if my memory serves me. That means the shinbone and the other bone that comes with it, Aunt Arethusa. There ought to be some ankle bones around. Could these be they? I suppose they could, I can't think what else they'd be good for. You might try sorting them out, since you have nothing else to do."

"I have already donated my petticoat, I see no necessity to sacrifice my manicure. Dig on, varlet."

Osbert dug on, working outward and downward through the untidy jumble of ribs, vertebrae, radii, ulnae, a second tibia, a second fibula, a couple of humeri, another femur up among the collarbones and shoulder blades. This last seemed a most peculiar juxtaposition; Zilla advanced the theory that wolves or coyotes could have visited the burial site while yet there'd been reason to do so, and failed to tidy up after themselves. She took a keen interest in the bones, brushing off the dirt and arranging them in a logical pattern on Arethusa's petticoat as fast as Osbert dug them up.

As evidence collected, all the party became fairly certain that the bones must have belonged to a human being, probably an adult of average size and possibly a male. The pelvis, when Zilla had got it together, seemed to be a trifle narrower than the rib cage, whereas a woman's tends to be somewhat broader, as any experienced girl-watcher would have been willing to attest before intersexual ogling was outlawed by the antichauvinism movement.

"I wish those darned wolves hadn't gone off with the skull."

Osbert sounded fretful, and no wonder. It had taken him a good deal of excavating to accumulate a reasonably complete torso, and still not so much as a tooth of the head had shown up.

"Here, let me." Zilla was as weary of trying to match up vertebrae and ankle bones as Osbert was of groping around in damp sand. She took the spade from his no longer reluctant hand and tried to think herself into a coyote's frame of reference. "Let's see, seems to me I'd keep my nose pointing toward the spring, so that means I'd be kicking backward with my feet. Unless—oh, what the heck. Let's try over here for a change."

"Do," sighed Arethusa, who'd been trying to catch forty winks curled up on Osbert's jacket and not succeeding very well, even after it had occurred to her that she might be more comfortable if she removed her rapier from underneath.

The night must be far spent by now, though none of them could tell since there was no visible moon to go by, and nobody had thought to wear a watch. They were all, except presumably Hiram, feeling the effects of fatigue and exasperation. Yet Zilla dug doggedly on, and as always, it was dogged that did it.

"I've found a jaw!"

"Bully for you, ecod," Arethusa snarled drowsily.

"And a what-do-you call it? The round part."

"So that gives us a whole skull!" Osbert, who'd been sitting on the bank trying gamely not to shiver, sprung to his feet. "Let's see it. Thundering tumbleweeds, it's got three eye sockets!"

"Huh? Gimme a look."

With the speed of blue light, Hiram Jellyby was at Zilla's side. In a second flash, those two incandescent eyeballs were glittering out from inside the cranium. Spang in the middle and slightly above them was the neat, round hole that Osbert had taken for a third eye socket.

"Look at this, Zilla. Fits like a glove, bullet hole an' all."

"Yes, I see it does," Mrs. Trott agreed. "Well, Hiram, all I can say is, you've certainly changed a lot. So now it's

time for you to go on and do what you've got to do, is that
the program?"

"Hell, I wouldn't mind stickin' around for the funeral.
'Tain't every entity gets the chance to horn in on the
preachin'. What kind o' minister you got around here these
days? I'm warnin' you right here an' now, if he's the kind
that thumps the pulpit an' hollers about hellfire an' dam-
nation, I'm goin' to rise right up out o' my ol' pine box an'
tell 'im it ain't necessarily so."

"Then I sort of wish we did," said Zilla, "because it
would be something to see. But Mr. Pennyfeather's just a
nice, well-spoken man who'll talk about how you were
faithful to your duty and kind to your mules, as I gather
you must have been, what with digging them water holes
and singing around the campfire and all. That's true
enough, isn't it?"

"Hell, yes. Me an' my mules was always friends an'
buddies. I wisht I knew where they was buried. I wouldn't
mind havin' my bones in there with 'em."

"I'm afraid their bones must have been ground up to
make bonemeal," Osbert told Hiram as gently as possible.
"That was what usually happened, I believe. You might
think of them as fertilizing roses and other posies, like
Darling Clementine."

If a ghost could sniffle, then that was what Hiram
Jellyby was doing. As nobody liked to intrude on his grief,
they waited silently by in the dark until the muleteer himself spoke again.

"That was real nice o' you, bub. Made me feel warm
an' comforted. I don't s'pose you'd like to get up at the
funeral an' put in a good word for my ol' mules, would
you?"

"I'd be proud and honored." Osbert sounded a bit
choked up too. "As soon as we have a chance to sit down
and have a real heart-to-heart talk, you must tell me all
about them. Right now, we'd better get back to hunting

for that chestful of gold before Aunt Arethusa's rheumatics start kicking up. Can you suggest any place to dig that we haven't tried yet, Hiram? How about over on the south side?"

"Waste o' time. See, bub, it's come back to me that the place where I found the gold wasn't the same place where that bugger in the purple gaiters drilled me. So what it looks like to me is, we still ain't found the right water hole."

CHAPTER
10

"*O*h, for crying in the soup!" Dittany herself was close to sobbing. "You mean you went through all that work for nothing?"

"Not quite for nothing, darling," Osbert reminded his stricken wife gently. "We did find Hiram Jellyby's bones and Great-great-grandmother's wedding china. Hiram asked me to deliver a eulogy at his funeral."

"What are you going to say?"

"Well, what he mainly wants me to do is say something nice about his mules. They meant a lot to each other. Would you pass the marmalade, please, dear? I don't know why, but I'm still hungry."

"Poor, starved darling!" cried Dittany. "Shall I fry you a few more eggs and a buffalo steak?"

"Thanks, dear, but I'll just fill up on toast. It's not all that long till lunchtime, is it? I seem to have slept rather late."

"Why shouldn't you have? You didn't get home till half past three this morning, plumb beat to the socks. I practically had to undress you."

"That was kind of you, sweetheart. Remind me to do the same for you sometime soon."

"Osbert! Not in front of the twins. You're supposed to set an example."

"But I am, darling. I'm setting the example of a loving husband and father." Osbert proved his point with somewhat marmalady kisses all around. "What's happened to Ethel? Don't tell me she's quit nannying on us?"

"Perish the thought. She's just having her midmorning stroll, she'll be back. In fact she is, I'd better go see whom she's attacking out there. Oh, it's only Sergeant MacVicar. Ethel, quit licking his face, it's not respectful. Come in, Sergeant. Haul up and set. Want me to roast you a fatted calf?"

"And when was I e'er prodigal, Dittany lass? Except wi' unwanted advice, as my guid wife sometimes tells me. I wouldna say no to a cup of tea, if there's any left in the pot." Sergeant MacVicar cocked a quizzical eyebrow at Osbert's pajamas, which had little mustangs and cowboy hats printed all over them. "I trust you are not o'erfatigued from yesterday afternoon's labors, Deputy Monk?"

"No, he's plumb tuckered out from having spent the night digging up Hiram Jellyby's bones and Great-great-grandmother Monk's tea set while you were sleeping the sleep of the sarcastic," Dittany replied hotly. "What did you find out about the money?"

"Noo, lass, dinna fly off the handle. Would you care to eludicate, Deputy Monk?"

"What I'd really care to do is eat some more toast, if my beloved wife will give me any," Osbert confessed. "You first, please, Chief."

"Weel, then, pending further investigation, the hypothesis at RCMP headquarters is that yon trunkful of currency may be the loot from a remarkably daring robbery that took place eight years ago come Hallowe'en at a small but busy branch roughly halfway between Hamilton and Windsor. The remarkable part about it was that—"

Dittany knew it was rude to interrupt, but she also

knew what a Scotsman could be like when he'd got started on a good story. She had no time this morning for lengthy flights of rhetoric.

"That the thief carried off the money, then came back and got the banker and tried to hold him for ransom. But the banker's wife wouldn't pay because she thought it was some of the boys being funny, so the robber killed him and cut off his finger and sent it to her with a nasty note about ye of little faith," she encapsulated in a single breath before the sergeant could grab the floor again. "Zilla told me all about it while Margaret was watching the twins yesterday at teatime on account of the platinum print from the museum."

"Oh, aye?" The sergeant knew better than to start a new hare by inquiring about the platinum print. "Margaret didna tell me."

"Well, chances are you don't always tell her everything either. How much money was in the trunk?"

"Zilla did not impart yon piece of information?"

"She didn't know and don't be Scotch. We're all at sixes and sevens this morning and I haven't got time for argy-bargy. Haven't the Mounties counted it yet, for Pete's sake?"

"They had not by the time I left them, and it is quite likely they still haven't. They were going to fingerprint all the packages and perform other laboratory tests in the hope of tracking the miscreant. Or miscreants. The late bank watchman's testimony that only one robber was involved seems no less incredible now than it did at the time of the perpetration."

Osbert forgot the piece of toast he'd been about to steer mouthward. "The late bank watchman? When did he die?"

"Less than a week after the robbery, in a somewhat bizarre manner. He was trampled to death by a cow."

"A cow? You mean a steer?"

"No, a milch cow that the watchman, an elderly bachelor, had been accustomed to stable in his garage and put to graze in his back yard."

"But dairy cows don't trample people to death," Dittany protested.

"This one did, judging from the evidence. She was not, according to the sister who was living next door to the watchman at the time of his sudden demise, a contented cow. In fact the sister testified that there had been little sympathy between the cow and her brother for some time and that he had gone so far as to mention sending for the knacker within the cow's hearing. The sister felt that this rash move on the watchman's part might have precipitated the unwonted attack, but I pairsonally hae my doots."

"Well, of course you would, Chief," said Osbert. "Who wouldn't? Obviously it was the robber's accomplice who egged the cow on to trample the watchman, because the watchman knew who he was and was trying to blackmail him. The accomplice was probably the assistant manager, who'd agreed to help the robber because he wanted the banker's job."

"I'd be more inclined to think it was the head teller," said Dittany. "Head tellers get awfully fed up with having to dole out money all the time to other people and never getting to keep any for themselves. Zilla's mother's uncle used to be a head teller in a bank, but he finally got so tired of having to stay honest that he chucked up his job and turned to growing strawberries under glass for the fancy hotels and made a bundle, all of which he got to keep. Didn't the Mounties even investigate the head teller, Sergeant?"

"Yon head teller in this instance was a lady, Dittany lass. She and the assistant manager had gone directly from the bank at closing time on the afternoon of the robbery to the Presbyterian manse, where they were united in holy wedlock in the presence of various relatives and friends. The entire company then enjoyed a wedding supper at the home of the bride's aunt. At ten o'clock in the evening, the happy couple were seen off on the plane to Niagara Falls by the bridesmaid, the best man, and several of their co-workers, the aunt having stayed home to wash the dishes and count the silverware. It thus transpired that no member of the bank staff was without an ironclad alibi for the time of the robbery."

"How come the banker missed out on the wedding?"

"He had been invited. He had expressed regret that pressure of business would prevent his attending the ceremony, but had promised to join the supper party as soon as he could get away. When he failed to do so, his absence was noted but not gravely regretted. Merriment was by then running high and a superior officer's presence might, it was felt, have had a dampening effect, notwithstanding the president's having been on affable enough terms with his staff."

"Well, this is all very enigmatic," said Dittany, "but I have tiny garments to wash and molasses cookies to bake. You don't really want another slice of toast, do you, Osbert?"

"No, pet, I'd better go up and put some clothes on before we have any more callers. What happened to the watchman's sister after the alleged trampling, Chief?"

"I dinna ken, Deputy. Nor do I ken what happened to yon cow, though the logical outcome would nae doot hae been hamburger. Noo I must get back to the station. I will endeavor to ascertain the subsequent whereabouts of the sister and apprise you of any developments about the money. What are your plans for this afternoon?"

"Do we have any, Dittany?"

"We were going to take the twins to visit Grandsire Coskoff. Unless you'd rather work on your book?"

"No, I'll go with you. We might stop at Aunt Arethusa's and see what our chances are of getting Pollicot James to dowse us that other spring where the gold's supposed to be buried. He may not want to, now that he's already worked off his civic responsibility."

"What other spring?" demanded Sergeant MacVicar.

"Oh, that's right," said Osbert, "I didn't tell you. We have another enigma, Chief. We found what was left of the grave marker that Hiram whittled for himself in with the bones and the china. Whoever dug the hole to bury the china must have come across his bones, noticed the cross over in the field somewhere, and thrown it in out of superstition or general cussedness, not that it matters, I don't suppose. Hiram claims he was shot in a different place from where he'd left the trunkful of gold pieces."

"So that wad mean yon gold is still buried in Hunnikers' Field?"

"Or not, as the case may be. I can see why whoever shot Hiram might have buried the cross with his body to hide it so that nobody would go digging him up and find that bullet hole in his head and know he'd been shot. This wasn't exactly the Wild West, you know, even a hundred years ago. Hiram must have been a fairly well known character in the area. If they'd realized he'd been murdered, people might have taken umbrage and gone after the ornery rustler who killed him."

"On what grounds do you designate yon killer also a rustler, Deputy Monk?"

"Well, he'd have had to rustle Hiram's mules, wouldn't he? He couldn't just leave the critters wandering around by themselves singing 'Buffalo Gals.' Everybody would have known something had happened to Hiram and started organizing a necktie party."

"Of course they would," said Dittany. "So the killer must have taken the cross away from the place where the gold was buried, not knowing that the gold was in fact buried there. Unless the gold was really buried at that same water hole and the robber dug it up and took it away while he was burying Hiram and the china, assuming the same person did both. Which is possible, I suppose, because it was your great-great-grandmother's china and it was your great-great-grandfather who took Hiram's picture. Is it nice china, darling?"

"Grade A Number One, according to Aunt Arethusa. Chelseaware, I believe she said, imported from England specially for the wedding. And stolen while the bride and groom were on their honeymoon. Great-great-grandma must have been sick as a cat when she found out. Of course they got another set, but it wasn't the same. Naturally Aunt Arethusa snaffled the china right away. You don't mind, dear?"

"Oh, no," Dittany assured him. "It will come to Annie eventually anyway. We must pop in at Arethusa's and let her have a look at it, though I suppose it's a trifle early to be thinking of Annie's getting married and setting up housekeeping. Still, I can't help thinking how nicely it works out that you have a grandson just the right age, Sergeant MacVicar."

"Umph'a. It is, as you say, a wee bit airly to be posting the banns. But we never know, do we? Stranger things hae happened."

Sergeant MacVicar smiled into the basket at his potential granddaughter-in-law and let himself out. Osbert went upstairs to shower and dress. Dittany went down cellar to put in a load of wash, then came back to the kitchen and started her cookies. Ethel sat guarding the big pink-and-blue-padded clothes basket that still served as the twins' downstairs bassinet, though they'd be outgrowing it soon. "Oddly normal" seemed a contradiction in terms, but that was how the ancestral home felt to Dittany at that moment.

It did occur to her that she might call Zilla and ask whether Hiram Jellyby would mind having another look at the Akashic Record to determine whether the gold was still in its original hiding place, or whether it had been restolen at the time when his bones were interred with Great-great-grandmother Monk's wedding china. However, she wasn't sure whether Hiram might consider the request presumptuous, coming from a woman to whom he had not yet been introduced.

Furthermore, now that he was back here at the scene of his untimely demise, it might not be possible for Hiram to get to the records. From what little Dittany had been able to gather secondhand, Hiram himself was none too clear about how things worked on the astral plane; why risk causing him embarrassment? She was rolling out her cookie dough when she remembered what she'd been thinking a little while ago. Fortunately Osbert came downstairs as she was flouring the cutter, wearing his green and purple plaid flannel shirt and looking ready for anything, so she was able to share her thought.

"You know, Osbert, the person who buried that china most likely meant to dig it up again."

"That would be the logical assumption, precious."

"But he put Hiram's marker in the grave, or somebody did. And it seems just too much of a coincidence that one person would have buried Hiram and another person come along after him and buried the trunkful of china in practically the same spot, wouldn't you think? And the spring they were buried beside wouldn't be any help as a landmark because it was underground. So that being the case, how would the bad guy have known where to dig when he came back for the china? Unless," Dittany brought the old crinkle-edged tin cutter down on her dough with a small thump of satisfaction. "Unless he was a dowser, like Pollicot James?"

"A brilliant deduction, darling. So that's why you're so het up to see Grandsire Coskoff, eh? You want to ask him whether there were any dowsers living around here during the platinum-print era. Grandsire himself wouldn't have known such a person, I don't suppose, but his parents might have. And they'd have told him about the water witch because they seem to have told him every dad-blanged thing that ever happened in Lobelia Falls from the time they'd got here as settlers to the time they died at incredibly advanced ages. He's told me about fifty times, but I still can't remember whether it was the mother who died at ninety-seven and the father who lived to be a hundred and five, or vice versa. Do you suppose I'm growing senile, dearest?"

"No, darling. I think you automatically switch to brooding on distant mesas whenever the subject comes up, as people naturally tend to do when Grandsire gets started on the old folks' reminiscences. Speaking of families, did I happen to mention at suppertime last night that I'd met Mrs. Melloe at Minerva's house yesterday afternoon while I was polling the trustees about Hiram Jellyby's picture for Mr. Glunck? She wants to be a Henbit."

"Did you tell her she could?"

"Nope," Dittany confessed. "I was pretty sniffy to her, if you want the truth. Minerva said I was, anyway. It was Mrs. Melloe's own fault. She was being a pain in the neck, hanging around asking dumb questions when any fool could have seen Minerva was itching for the old pest to get the heck out of there so she could start her supper. But you know Minerva. She wouldn't so much as drop a hint even if she was in the last extremity of boredom. So I thought it would be an act of charity to give Mrs. Melloe the bum's rush."

Osbert gave her a kiss. "That's one of the things I love about you, dear, you're always doing something nice for somebody. Not to be hinting, but what time is lunch?"

"As soon as the cookies are baked. Another half or three quarters of an hour."

"Then you won't mind if I just nip in and see what's happening around the old corral?"

"Do."

Dittany smiled fondly as she heard the antique Remington galloping happily westward, and went on greasing her cookie sheets.

CHAPTER
11

Grandsire Coskoff's communication systems were functioning beautifully today. His hearing-aid batteries were all juiced up and raring to go, he caught Dittany's question first time around. "Hiram Jellyby, eh? My stars, I hadn't thought of Hiram Jellyby for years. Never met Hiram myself, of course, but Father used to talk about him when I was a boy. Something of a mystery man, Hiram was."

Grandsire was looking spruce and peppy as usual in his green velveteen smoking jacket and his red fez with the tassel cocked jauntily over his left ear. These garments were relics of the days when Turkish corners were in vogue, though they'd never been exactly rife in Lobelia Falls. It had been Grandsire's father, actually, who'd acquired the fez and jacket back in his salad days, when he'd done the Grand Tour all the way to Quebec City and back. He'd never got around to fixing up his own Turkish corner, and Grandsire had only taken to wearing the clothes during the past twenty years or so. Everybody knew he wore the fez mainly to cover his bald spot but it was generally conceded that, at the age of a hundred and one, a man might be pardoned his little vanities.

"Yes indeed," Grandsire went on."Hiram was a mule-teer, working mostly out of Scottsbeck. Scottsbeck was on the railroad by then, you know."

They did know, but listened patiently while he told them anyway, and tried to look adequately amazed when he described with fine dramatic flair how Hiram had driven off from Mountie headquarters into oblivion, tak-ing his mules with him. It was quite a while before Dittany managed to get in, "What about the man in the black frock coat and purple gaiters who was infesting these parts at that time? Wasn't he supposed to be a water witch or something?"

Grandsire shook his fez. "I'm afraid you've got me there, Dittany. I never heard of any such person. The only water witch I knew of in those days was your own Great-great-grandfather Henbit. Charlie, that was."

The old man chuckled. "Not that I'd have put it past Charlie Henbit to get himself up in a frock coat and purple gaiters if he'd taken a mind to. Charlie was a great one for acting, you know, always getting up shows and concerts. Folks made their own entertainment back then, none of this running off to the nickelodeon or the ice cream parlor the way kids do nowadays. Mainly because there wasn't one to run to, I expect, but anyway, that's how it was. Charlie was also one of the founders of the Male Archers' Target and Game Shooting Association, as of course I don't have to tell you. Yes indeed, he was a card, old Charlie Henbit."

Grandsire allowed himself a pause for chuckling, then went on. "But a good businessman, mind you. Charlie never let his family go in want no matter how tough the times were around here, nor anybody else who needed a handout, for that matter. Or who needed a well dug. He'd get out there with his hazel twig and find water every time, if there was any to find. People would send for Char-lie Henbit clear to Scottsbeck and Lammergen, not that

Lammergen was much of a place till the mincemeat factory started up."

"We know about the mincemeat factory," Dittany tried to interject, but Grandsire wasn't listening.

"Charlie started a little general store and trading post just about where Gumpert's store is now, and did well right from the start. After a while, he built on a big extension and took his sons Fred and Ditson, the one your own father was named for, as partners. They built another store or two and branched out into dry goods and notions. Then Fred died of the measles and Ditson's three sons went off to the war. Your grandfather was one of them."

Dittany decided they really had to hurry this visit along. The twins were starting to fidget and she herself was feeling a trifle twitchy about old Charlie and his hazel twig.

"That's right, Grandsire. Three went off but only Gramp came back, and he was half a leg short. He couldn't have stood on his stump all day to wait on customers even if he'd had the heart to run the store without his brothers. Besides, Scottsbeck was built up by then, people were beginning to have cars and drive over there to shop, so Gramp sold the store and started a real estate business in Scottsbeck. Daddy went to business college and went in with him and married Mum and had me. Then Daddy died and Gramp sold the real estate business and we lived on the money and his war pension. Then Grammy and Gramp died and Mum married Bert and that left just me. I married Osbert and we've had the twins and now I think we'd better get going. Thanks, Mrs. Coskoff, but we can't stay for tea. Arethusa's expecting us."

Left a widower a decade or two previously, Grandsire had, after a decent interval, married a much younger woman. The second Mrs. Coskoff was a mere seventy-nine, a pretty little dumpling with curly white hair, a cheery disposition, a dab hand at pastry, and some loss of hearing; the pair were blissfully happy together. She expressed regret that the Monks had to run off so soon, urged them to come again, reminded Dittany to be sure and keep the babies' feet warm because you never knew, and waved them off from behind the front-door window, which had little squares of colored glass set in around the edges as was a time-honored custom in Lobelia Falls.

"Well, Osbert," Dittany said when they got outside, "it looks as if there's an off chance you may be married to the great-great-granddaughter of a highwayman. Would you care for a divorce?"

"Perish the thought, darling. I've held up plenty of stagecoaches in my time too, you know."

"But only on paper," Dittany argued. "This holdup was the real McCoy, unless Hiram Jellyby remembered it wrong."

"Which he may well have done, darling. It didn't occur to him that I was digging at the wrong water hole until I'd rubbed half the skin off my best typing finger."

The tinge of rancor in Osbert's voice soon disappeared, for he was a happy soul by nature and eager to raise the pall of gloom that Grandsire Coskoff's words had engendered. "Furthermore, we don't know for sure that your great-great-grandfather ever actually did wear purple gaiters. Even if he did, why couldn't whoever killed Hiram have been somebody else dressed up in purple gaiters, pretending to be Charlie Henbit? In fact, it *would* have been somebody else, because Charlie would have had to stay and mind the store."

Osbert warmed to his theme. "Storekeepers in those days had a stern responsibility to their customers, you know, dear. If you'd driven old Nellie ten miles over a dirt road with ruts as deep as your buggy wheels to buy a pound of tea and a new pair of braces, you'd darn well expect the storekeeper to be there to wait on you and give you a free pickle out of the barrel and some Jujubes for the kids and pass the time of day and ask how the folks back home were making out. And if the storekeeper wasn't around, you'd sure as heck want to know why. And if the kid he'd left to guard the till told you the old man had taken the afternoon off to ride out to Hunnikers' Field and rob a mule skinner, it would be bound to cause talk and have a deleterious effect on customer relations. Grandsire said explicitly that Charlie Henbit was a good business-man, so it stands to reason he'd have been attending to his own affairs and not gone looking for trouble. You do see that, don't you, dearest?"

"Yes, darling. You're such a comfort. And when you come right down to it, we don't even know whether the man in the purple gaiters actually stole anything. Hiram may have been his first and last attempt at robbery, and he fluffed that one on account of the horsefly."

"True, dear. Perhaps the highwayman had a sick child at home and was just trying to rustle enough money to pay the doctor, though that raises the question of why he'd have been hanging around the saloon watching Hiram get bombed instead of home weeping by the sufferer's bed-side."

"It may have been the custom of the time," said Dittany. "Gram Henbit used to sing a song about a wee tot trudging back and forth to the gin mill trying to get her father to come home because the fire was out and little Willie was freezing in his mother's arms, but the old poop just stayed there lushing it up till Willie kicked the bucket. If I'd been that mother, I think I might quite easily have grabbed a hatchet and gone around busting up saloons like Carry Nation. After I'd straightened out the geezer I'd been dumb enough to marry, that is."

"You'd have been magnificent, darling." Osbert sighed. "It saddens me to think you may have missed a brilliant career as a saloon smasher by marrying a nonal-coholic. The trouble is, I tend to get hiccups after one glass of beer, as you know all too well. Are you quite sure you want to call on Aunt Arethusa?"

"Are you quite sure you want to go back and dig up that whole dad-blanged Hunniker meadow looking for a hypothetical second spring? We could wait for a sun shower, I suppose, and watch to see where the end of the rainbow hits."

Osbert sighed again, a little louder. "It's awfully late in the season for rainbows. We may as well bite the bullet and stop at Auntie's. I hope she doesn't come lunging at us with her rapier."

"Don't worry," Dittany consoled him. "She's probably forgotten where she put it."

Perhaps Arethusa had indeed forgotten. Anyway, she didn't have the rapier with her when she came to the door. Neither had she remembered to dress. She was still in her pink robe and bedroom slippers with her luxuriant raven tresses hanging halfway down her back, even though the morning was long spent and the afternoon half in the bag. Arethusa must have been abducting Lady Ermintrude today, Dittany decided. The authoress had kidnapped her ever-gullible heroine many times before, but it always took a lot out of her.

"No slavering suitors today, Auntie?" was Osbert's amiable greeting.

"Don't be disgusting, knave," was Arethusa's predictable reply. "Am I supping chez vous tonight?"

"I expect so. You generally do."

"Good. I had a vague though evidently mistaken notion that I was committed to dining with somebody or other at the inn."

"It wouldn't be Pollicot James, by any chance," Dittany suggested.

"No, it wouldn't. Of that fact I am positively, decidedly, definitely, and unequivocally certain. Pollicot and his mother have gone to Toronto for the ballet."

"What ballet?"

"Whatever ballet is there to be gone to, one assumes. Mrs. James does not take me into her confidence."

"Arethusa, was that a snippy remark?"

"Not at all, Dittany. I have no wish to be taken into Mrs. James's confidence. I do have a wish for a cup of tea and a currant scone, of which I still have a fair supply because Pollicot appeared not to be particularly hungry yesterday afternoon. May I offer you the hospitality of the kitchen table? And do the infants take cream or milk with their tea?"

"Oh, don't bother setting out cups for them. We have bottles with us if they start to howl."

"Chacun à son goût. The procedure I had in mind was to split the scones and toast them, thus restoring their pristine esculence. Does that meet with everyone's approval, or should one simply warm them in the oven?"

"I vote for splitting and toasting," said Osbert, knowing full well that his aunt could easily spend the rest of the afternoon debating the issue if somebody didn't settle it for her at the outset.

"So do I," added Dittany, thus clinching the majority vote. "Would you like me to split them?"

"By all means. Osbert can fill the kettle and put on the cups, plates, butter knives, and napkins. And I," Arethusa finished with a bravura flourish, "will get out the jam."

"Bully for you. When will the Jameses be back?"

"Next week, I believe. Or is it the week after? Or the week after that? Whenever the ballerinas get sick of having to be on their toes all the time, one assumes. It seems an odd way to make a living. But then," Arethusa added with a baleful glance at Osbert, who was trying to fold a napkin into the shape of a cactus, "so does rustling mongeese."

"They're mongooses," her nephew replied hotly, "and I've never rustled one in my life. It wouldn't be any use, they'd just sneak off between the horses' hooves before the rustlers could lasso them. And bite their fetlocks in passing, like as not. Mongooses are feisty little critters. Dangbust it, now where are we going to get another dowser in a hurry?"

"Stap my vitals! What would be the point in getting one now, churl? We've already excavated Great-grandmother's china, haven't we? Oh, and methinks I've uncovered the purloiner. Great-granny's diary contains some rather harsh words about an itinerant plasterer named Bulliver Spyte who'd pestered her with unwanted attentions even while he was plastering the walls of the nuptial chamber. At the very moment when she and Great-grandfather stepped forth from the church as man and wife, Spyte managed to hiss in her ear that she'd rue the day."

"And did she?" said Dittany.

"Never, not for one minute. But she did put quite a few question marks after Spyte's name when she got home from the honeymoon and found her lovely china gone. Come and see, Dittany, I've got it all washed and gloated over and set out on the dining room table. Whoever that rapscallion brigand was, one has to concede that he knew his trade. He appears to have purloined all Great-granny's embroidered napkins and bureau scarves to pack the dishes with; there's ne'er a crack nor chip. I've put the linens to soak in mild bleach, but I don't expect to salvage them all. They were badly yellowed and some have rotted in spots. Methought the usable ones might be put away for Annie's hope chest."

"Arethusa, what a lovely thought! Margaret will be so pleased."

"Margaret who, forsooth?"

"MacVicar, of course. We were thinking that Annie might be well advised to marry their youngest grandson, though of course we don't want to rush her into it. Come on, baby, we may as well begin stimulating your aesthetic sensibilities. Osbert, do you want to see the china or toast the scones?"

"I've already seen the china. Toasting scones is men's work. What do you say, Ren, want to help?"

Folding napkins into roughly the shape of cacti while toasting scones and riding herd on a somewhat squirmy infant required a high standard of hand-eye coordination and in fact didn't work quite the way Osbert had anticipated at first, but he and Rennie enjoyed a good laugh together and tried again. Meanwhile, the distaff side of the family were admiring the Eliphalet Monks' wedding china.

This was a full service for eight, including eight crescent-shaped dishes to hold the chop bones after they had been thoroughly gnawed and eight little round chips to set the tea cups on after the tea had been poured from the cups into the deep saucers from which it would have been drunk with genteel blowings and whiffings, according to the custom of the time. Arethusa had set it all out on her glass-topped dining table, which had gilded crocodiles forming the base. The Prince Regent had commissioned this table for Brighton Pavilion, but his friend Mrs. Fitzherbert had thought it a trifle outré so the maker had sold it to a rich Canadian lumber merchant in 1786. At least that was what the antique dealer had told her, and Arethusa was far too much of a lady to have doubted his word, particularly when he was offering a ten percent reduction in price for cash on the barrelhead or, more specifically, the crocodile head.

Wherever they'd come from, the gleaming saurians certainly set off the handsome chinaware in grand style. Dittany felt a twinge of envy and a moment's irritation that Osbert had yielded so easily to Arethusa's claim. Then she reflected that every one of those delicate hand-painted and lavishly curlicued pieces would have to be washed by hand every time they were used, and that therefore in her house they never would be. Here in Arethusa's stately home was clearly where the china belonged. When she got old enough, Annie would have to be sent over once a week for lessons in gracious living and high-class housekeeping. Rennie too, because times were changing and, as Mrs. Coskoff the second had so neatly put it, you never knew.

The appetizing odor of toasting scones soon drew them all back to the kitchen. Arethusa, who'd been rather shy of the twins up to now, snuggled Annie into the folds of her fuzzy pink robe. Annie responded by cooing up at her and snatching a handful of her long, dark hair. Dittany split another round of scones, Osbert toasted them. The grown-ups had another cup of tea apiece. Rennie requested a bottle, so then Annie decided she'd have one too.

Arethusa's elegant house was not generally thought of as a place to be cozy in, but cozy they undoubtedly were. Fully an hour passed, during which time Arethusa didn't once address Osbert as churl or knave and he made not a single slighting reference to her grammar or spelling. It was a jolt to them all when the clock struck five, and a far worse jolt to Arethusa when the doorbell rang and she remembered why.

"Stap my garters! That must be what's-his-name. It comes back to me now with a sickening thud. I promised to do something or other for some reason that seemed to make sense at the time. He said he'd come and escort me to wherever we're going. Stall the varlet off, Dittany, while I throw on a clothe or two. Here, take your moppet."

She handed Annie back to Dittany, who handed her over to Osbert and went to see what Arethusa had let herself in for this time. To her surprise, she was confronted by the new innkeeper, Hedrick Snarf, with a great bunch of assorted flowers and a vastly self-satisfied smirk.

"Would you kindly announce me to Miss Monk?"

Snarf didn't add the word *serf*, but serf was what he

obviously assumed Dittany to be. She chose not to disabuse him.

"Prithee step into the withdrawing room, sirrah, while I go get the silver tray to put your calling card on. Shall I relieve you of that shrubbery you're toting, or were you planning to strew it at Miss Monk's feet when she comes down?"

"Ah—will she be long?"

"Who knows? It depends on whether she gets to thinking about Sir Percy and Lady Ermintrude. Shall I run up and tell her not to think?"

"That might be helpful."

Nonplussed was as good a word as any, Dittany decided, to describe the facial expression that had by now replaced the new innkeeper's supercilious smirk. Total blankness could hardly be called an improvement, but at least it was a change. She gave Snarf an affable nod, left him juggling his mammoth bouquet from one arm to the other, and skipped up the rose-carpeted stairs to tap at Arethusa's bedroom door.

"His Innship awaits below, Moddom. Shall I unleash the wolfhounds?"

"Quit clowning and come in here, wench. This accursed zipper's got my hair all snarled up in its teeth."

"Gadzooks, we may have to amputate. Quit wiggling, can't you? What's that gazookus here for, anyway? He looks like an undertaker's assistant, coming to lay you out."

"I trust no lewd innuendo was meant by that remark. One gets enough purple-hued obliquity at romance writers' conventions. As I recall, Mr. whoever-he-is—"

"Snarf. Given name Hedrick, or so I've been given to understand."

"Thank you. Hedrick Snarf, eh? Too bad this gown hasn't a cuff, I could jot down a note for easy reference. To answer your question, this whatever it is started when

Archie and I were dining at the inn the last time he was here, whenever that was. Shortly after the boeuf bourguignon, I believe, or was it between the salad and the lemon soufflé? In any event, at some time during the meal, Mr. Snarf came loping up to our table and expressed the hope that everything was satisfactory."

"As innkeepers are wont to do."

"No doubt, but the point is that it was not. I explained to Mr. Snarf in some detail how the cuisine, the decor, the clientele, and the service had all been going to l'enfer in a handcart since Andrew McNaster left for Hollywood and Lemuel Pilchard became incapacitated. I recall having added with some acerbity that Mr. Snarf's policy of raising the prices did not in any way compensate for his lowering the tone, and that he'd jolly well better pull up his socks and straighten out the mess before Andrew came back and hurled him forth bodily into the exact center of the parking lot, as Andrew had been known to do on previous occasions when employees proved unsatisfactory. Are you quite through pulling my hair, wench?"

"Almost. Ah, there we are, all zipped. And this was the start of something beautiful?"

"Not precisely. Toss me a handful or two of pearls, prithee. This was the start of Mr. Snarf's pestering me with a spate of progress reports. By now, he avers, the inn has been totally regentrified and he has organized some kind of reception in my honor as a token of thanks for my solicitude on his behalf. A fallacious assumption on his part, since my solicitude was entirely directed toward maintaining a restaurant closer than Scottsbeck where one could rely on getting a halfway decent meal when a gentleman took one out."

"There's always the Kum-in Kafé and Live Bait Shop over in Lammergen," Dittany pointed out. "I don't think those pearls do much for this gown."

"Nor do I, on reflection." Arethusa was swirling her

jetty mane into a heavy chignon at the back of her neck. "Wouldst fetch the tourmaline brooch and the jeweled comb?"

"Sure I wouldst. Here, put on the bracelet that goes with it, and these droopy earrings that make you look like Mata Hari. There, now you're gentrified as all heck. Go ahead down and knock Snarf's eyeballs out."

"A splendid suggestion, forsooth."

Arethusa made sure the skirt of her claret-colored velvet dinner gown was hanging straight, adjusted her brooch, earrings, and bracelets, flung a long-fringed Spanish shawl about her, accepted without demur Dittany's suggestion that she also put on a pair of shoes, and sailed downstairs.

Dittany tagged along behind, partly to make sure Arethusa didn't trip over her long skirt and partly because she was curious to see whether Hedrick Snarf really did intend to strew the flowers. She could see the innkeeper through the double parlor doors, sitting in one of the needlepoint-covered Queen Anne chairs, twitching his lips and flicking his eyes back and forth from the doorway to the ormolu clock on the carved marble mantelpiece.

Snarf was not a prepossessing man, but he'd made the most of what he had. He'd had his dull brown hair blow-dried and fluffed out over his bald spot, he'd grown apologetic wisps of sideburns, and bought himself a high stiff collar, a black silk cravat and a black frock coat with a pinched-in waist. The gray striped trousers that accompanied his coat were not quite long enough in the leg. Dittany stopped short in the doorway and gasped. Along with the rest of his outmoded finery, Hedrick Snarf was wearing bright purple silk socks.

CHAPTER
12

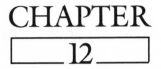

*D*ittany dumped the diaper bag next to the cellar door, laid Rennie on the kitchen table, and began to divest him of his outer wrappings. "You must admit, Osbert, that it's an odd coincidence. I'd like to see what the Akashic Record has to say about reincarnation."

"Perhaps there's a more scientific explanation," Osbert suggested. "There could be some gene in the Snarf family's DNA cycle that predisposes them toward frock coats and purple legwear. I can see why Snarf had to settle for purple socks because where the heck could a man find purple gaiters these days? What gets me is why that hombre thought he had to get himself up like a third cousin of Rhett Butler just to throw a wingding for Aunt Arethusa."

"And I further don't understand why he didn't invite any of Arethusa's family or friends," Dittany added with some acrimony. "Not that we'd have gone, needless to say, but it was pretty darned crass of Snarf not to ask us. I don't believe one soul here in Lobelia Falls even knew this brawl was going to happen. Surely we'd have heard if anybody we know got invited. Now I suppose the whole club will be down on Arethusa, they'll think she's trying to snoot them."

"No they won't, darling. They all know she's got pink marbles where her brains ought to be. Want me to light the campfire and open us a can of beans?"

"I'm not madly hungry after all those scones. Why don't you go rope a couple of mavericks while Ethel and I get the wee bairns fixed up? Then we'll decide what we feel like eating."

"Sure thing, Miz Dittany, ma'am. Would y'all care to meet me out by the doghouse when the moon comes over the mountain? I'm fixin' to throw you a little reception."

"Why, thank you kindly, Deputy Monk. You know I'm always receptive to your receptions. Now scat and earn us some daily bread. I'll let you know when the chuck wagon arrives."

Husband and wife buckled down to their respective tasks. An hour or so later, babies bedded and cayuses corralled, they met for a preprandial libation, an amusing little vintage out of a jug picked up more or less at random in the Scottsbeck supermarket.

"That casserole smells awfully good," Osbert remarked after a while in a hinting kind of way.

"It'll be ready in about three more minutes," Dittany assured him. "Think you can stand to wait?"

"I'll steel myself. What did you put in it?"

"Oh, a handful of this and a pinch of that. I can't remember."

"Those are always the best ones. Your instincts about casseroles are unerring. Which brings up another consideration." Osbert gave them each a modest dividend out of the jug. "You remember Grandsire Coskoff mentioned that your great-great-grandfather was a dowser?"

"Yes, and it shocked me to the core, if you want to know. Though now that I've seen Hedrick Snarf, I realize there are worse things Charlie Henbit could have been."

"Good for you, dear, that shows the power of positive thinking. But what I was getting at is, could the ability be hereditary? What if you've inherited old Charlie's water-witching gene? Have you ever tried to dowse?"

"No, frankly, the idea never occurred to me. I suppose I could give it a whirl, but where would I get a hazel twig? The only hazel I know of around town is Hazel Munson."

"It doesn't have to be a hazel rod," Osbert argued. "What about that metal contraption Pollicot James was using yesterday? We might rig something up with a bent coat hanger and a few brass buttons. Not tonight, because it's been a pretty busy day, but maybe tomorrow morning. Or what about using a pendulum? It seems to me I've read somewhere about somebody who used to dowse with a gold watch and chain."

"Did you really? Maybe that's how Great-great-grandfather used to do it. We've got his gold watch and chain upstairs, you know, in that little hidey-hole Gramp made where we keep the bankbooks and the rings Daddy gave to Mum that she gave to me when she married Bert and we're keeping for Annie."

"Are we?" said Osbert in some surprise.

"Of course we are. Rennie can have the watch to even up. It ought to be chock full of Great-great-grandfather's vibrations, unless they've all leaked out by now. I wouldn't mind giving that way a try. What's a person supposed to do?"

"Just wander around dangling the watch by its chain till it starts acting funny, I should think."

"But how would a person know what was funny? If I was walking along tripping over things, the watch would be bound to sway and jiggle anyway."

"You don't trip over things, sweetheart. At least not very often. Maybe you'd start feeling little electric shocks in your toes."

"I'm not altogether certain I'd care to feel little electric shocks in my toes," said Dittany. "What about that chart Hiram's supposed to have mailed to himself and we still haven't done anything about? Do you think there's any chance it could have survived?"

Osbert smiled. "I'd have said there was no chance for Hiram himself to have survived till I saw him last night with my own two eyes. At least I saw his two eyes with my two eyes. Unless I was really seeing with his eyes all the time. That was a dad-blanged odd experience, thinking back on it. Here were these two shiny blue eyes with no face around them. When I say shiny, I don't mean shining. They weren't emitting light the way a light bulb does, but they somehow made you able to see clearly in the dark. I can't explain how it was, dear, you'd have to experience it for yourself. Too bad Hiram isn't here to demonstrate."

"You lookin' for me, Bub?"

No part of the speaker was visible at the moment, but Zilla Trott was just coming through the back door, looking embarrassed and flustered. "I'm sorry to butt in on you just at mealtime," she fussed, "but this old goat insists you want to see him."

"We do," said Dittany. "I've been feeling slighted because Osbert got to meet Mr. Jellyby last night and I didn't. We were talking about him only a second ago, as a matter of fact. Come on, Zilla, sit down. I was about to take our supper out of the oven and you know I always make extra. It's just macaroni and cheese and a few other odds and ends. You can absorb that, can't you, Mr. Jellyby? Osbert, would you get the salad out of the fridge and bring a couple more plates? How about a sip of wine for starters? We were just having some."

"You wouldn't happen to have any homemade moonshine like your great-great-grampaw Charlie Henbit used to make, I don't s'pose?" came that wistful disembodied voice.

"I'm sorry, Mr. Jellyby, I'm afraid his recipe died with him."

"And a darned good thing it did, if you ask me," said Zilla. "I'll have a little wine, thanks, but don't you go giving Hiram anything alcoholic, eh. He got lit up like a Christmas tree last night on a cup of coffee and one of Minerva's doughnuts."

"Then for Pete's sake keep him away from that dandelion wine of yours," Dittany retorted.

Out of the everywhere came the kind of sinister heh-heh-heh noise that villains in the old melodramas are said to have gone around emitting. However, as none of the visible entities now present in the Henbit-Monk kitchen had ever been to a melodrama, except the one that they themselves had put on to benefit the Architrave,[*] they couldn't have said for sure. Zilla, however, knew at once what the snickering was all about.

"Hiram Jellyby! So that's the big attraction in my woodshed, is it? Don't tell me you've been sneaking drinks out of that big crock I've put my dandelions to ferment in? How in tarnation did you get the lid off?"

"I didn't have to get the lid off. I got mysterious powers."

"Like fun you have. There'd better not be any mysterious shrinkage inside that crock when I go to bottle my wine, or you'll find out who's got the powers around here, mister. My own great-grandfather was a medicine man. And a darned good one, from what I've heard tell of him."

"How about that?" cried Osbert. "Could he dowse for water?"

"I have no idea. Purification rites and dream interpretations were his specialties, I've been given to understand, though he also had quite a sideline curing hunting ponies of buffalo gores, These days, I suppose, he'd be called a psychiatrist. Back then, a medicine man had to pitch in wherever he was needed. But dowsing, no, I hardly think

* The Grub-and-Stakers Pinch a Poke

so. He wouldn't have had to go through any tomfoolery with a forked stick; every Indian worth his pemmican knew how to look for signs of underground water. Whatever made you ask, Osbert?"

"Because Pollicot James has gone to Toronto for an indefinite period and we still need to find that gold of Hiram's. Dittany's going to have a try tomorrow, we're hoping she may have inherited the ancestral knack. We called on Grandsire Coskoff this afternoon and he mentioned that her great-great-grandfather was a dowser. Did you actually know Charlie Henbit, Hiram?"

"Hell's fire, everybody knew Charlie Henbit. Charlie was a magician, you know. He could charm the birds right out o' the trees. I seen 'im do it more than once."

"What's so magic about that?" said Zilla. "I can charm birds myself. Some birds, anyway. All you need is a handful of birdseed and the knack of standing perfectly still. And remembering not to sneeze if a feather brushes too close to your nose."

"Charlie could bring 'em without the birdseed," Hiram insisted. "Birds just plain liked 'im, is what it was. Even birds that wouldn't o' guv the time o' day to no other livin' critter, they got on fine with Charlie. I seen Charlie Henbit call down a Swainson hawk an' a damn great mean-lookin' raven that would o' pecked a person's eyes out if they'd been anybody else's. Even a bald eagle. Mighty Jehu, Zilla, you ought to o' seen the talons on that critter! But all it done was wrapped 'em around the sleeve o' that ol' bearskin coat Charlie used to wear an' perched there on 'is arm cawm as a cucumber."

"Great-great-grandfather must have been awfully brave," said Dittany.

"Oh, Charlie Henbit wasn't afraid o' nothing. He'd get up before daylight an' go walkin' in the woods before it was time to open the store. I followed 'im a few times just for the fun of it, an' I never seen nothin' like what he could do. He'd hunker down on 'is knees an' talk to anything that come along. Weasels, skunks, squirrels, wasn't nothin' uppity about Charlie, he'd even talk to mice. Wildcats, elk, grizzly bears, nothin' fazed 'im, he just took 'em as they come an' they done the same by him. Might o' been partly the bearskin coat, I—Godfrey mighty! Here comes Charlie now, wearin' that same ratty ol' bearskin. Hey there, ol' pard! How's your feet an' ears? Still runnin' the store?"

As tactfully as possible, Dittany corrected Hiram's no doubt justified misapprehension. "Actually, this is Ethel. She's been upstairs minding the children. Here's your supper, Ethel. Come on, the rest of you, haul up and set. Hiram, you take this chair beside me. Zilla, you sit next to Osbert. Do you eat salad, Hiram?"

"I don't even know what it is. I might try a spoonful o' whatever's in that fancy bowl with the steam comin' out of it, just to see what happens. Don't gimme much, missus, I wouldn't know where to put it. Mind tellin' me how come you make the hired girl eat on the floor like a gol-durned dog?"

"Well, you see, Ethel is a dog. At least we think she is. Partly, anyway. Our neighbors got her from the dog pound and the town clerk makes us pay for a dog license every year, so we give her the benefit of the doubt. On the floor beside the stove is where Ethel prefers to eat and we're very fond of her so we just go along with whatever makes her happy."

"Just like how it used to be with me an' my mules. You don't s'pose Ethel might have a little mule in 'er somewheres?"

"I suppose it's possible; she can be pretty stubborn sometimes. Most people seem to think she's a cross between a black bear and a musk-ox. So birds and animals liked my great-great-grandfather, you say. How about people? Did they like him too?"

"I'll tell the cockeyed world they did. I can't remember one single soul in Lobelia Falls, nor Scottsbeck neither, even countin' his wife, that ever had a hard word for Charlie Henbit."

"You say he used to act out plays and things," Zilla prompted.

"That's right, Zilla. I tell you there was never a dull moment when Charlie was around. He plumb loved to dress up an' make the folks laugh, Charlie did."

"I don't suppose he ever dressed up in a black frock coat and purple gaiters?"

Dittany hadn't meant to ask that question, it just upped and asked itself. Hiram Jellyby took umbrage.

"You can quit thinkin' what you're thinkin', young woman, 'cause it ain't so. Whoever that geezer might o' been who followed me from the saloon, he sure wasn't Charlie Henbit, an' you can bet your bottom dollar on that. Hell, Charlie wouldn't even o' swatted the horsefly that kilt me. He'd o' just talked to it nice an' told it to go sting one o' them highbinders that come around with their medicine shows. Half a dollar for a bottle o' river water with a little port wine an' laudanum mixed in, an' a pinch o' cayenne pepper to give it a kick. I tell you they was highway robbers. Callin' themselves Dr. Cure-All or some damn thing an' claimin' that worthless muck they was peddlin' would fix anything from an ingrown toenail to a fractured skull! Should o' been strung up, the whole passel of 'em. Charlie was awful down on them patent medicines. He wouldn't even carry 'em in 'is store, 'cept for a few he knew was reliable. Mostly he'd tell you to bile up some tansy tea or put a mustard plaster on your chest, dependin' on what ailed you. An' it would work, because Charlie said it would."

"Thank you, Hiram, I just wanted to make sure. Actually Osbert and I have another candidate in mind, sort of. As it happened, we were just over visiting his Aunt Arethusa, whom you met last night, I understand, and in came this man wearing a black frock coat and bright purple socks."

"You don't say? What was the bugger callin' hisself?"

"Hedrick Snarf. He's the new innkeeper in town, or thinks he is. We couldn't help wondering if you happened to run across anything in the Akashic Record about reincarnation."

"Lemme think. Yup, seems to me I recollect a few entities lined up behind me lookin' to see who they was s'posed to be next time around, so's they'd know where to get theirselves born again once they'd taken the refresher course on teeth-cuttin' an' yellin' in the nighttime, all them things babies have to know. So what you're really wonderin' is whether this Snarf bird's the crook that done me in back when he used to be somebody else?"

"It did cross our minds. Mine, anyway. Osbert's more inclined to think those purple socks might have something to do with the DNA cycle, but it mightn't hurt to mosey on over to the inn and take a close look at Snarf, if you feel so inclined. Why, Hiram, I'm beginning to see you."

Whether it had been the strengthening essence of Dittany's casserole or just that the late muleteer was getting adjusted to his present surroundings, Hiram Jellyby had indeed begun to manifest himself. At first he resembled nothing more impressive than an underexposed black-and-white negative. Gradually, however, he assumed the three-dimensional appearance that Eliphalet Monk had captured so well in the platinum print, the only difference being that Hiram was now without his mules, which was probably just as well under the circumstances.

Dittany felt a surge of relief. She hadn't realized how much it took out of a person, trying to be a thoughtful hostess to a disembodied entity. Even in full ectoplasm, Hiram wasn't much to look at and that bullet hole he was now sporting in the middle of his forehead took a little getting used to. At least he was here, though, or seemed to be. Something was better than nothing.

"You weren't planning to go over to the inn right now, were you?" asked Zilla, knowing her hostess's propensity for not letting the grass grow under her feet.

"Oh no," Dittany reassured her. "We still have dessert. It's just applesauce and cookies; I finally got around to doing a little baking."

"What kind o' cookies?" asked Hiram.

"Big molasses ones with crinkles around the edges. They're Osbert's favorite."

"Mine too." Hiram Jellyby was one happy ghost, that was clear from the smile on his face, now that they could see it. "Used to be a woman over in Lammergen— Flossie, her name was—wonder what happened to Floss?"

"You might try looking up her phone number in the Akashic Record," Zilla told him rather nastily. "How come Arethusa isn't here, Dittany? Doesn't she usually have supper with you folks?"

"Unless she gets a better offer," said Dittany. "Tonight, Hedrick Snarf's throwing some kind of reception for her at the inn because she pinned his ears back about letting the place go to heck and told him Andy'd give him the heave-ho if he didn't straighten up and fly right. Which Andy certainly would do, as you well know. So Snarf's been pestering her for advice about fixing things up. I don't know whether he was afraid to spend Andy's money on calling in a professional consultant or if he's hoping to get his hooks into some of Arethusa's. Anyway, that's why she's not here."

Zilla was not satisfied. "Humph. What kind of reception?"

"I don't know."

"Why aren't you and Osbert there? Couldn't you have found somebody to sit with the twins?"

"We might have, I suppose, if we'd been invited."

"Not invited? Didn't Arethusa tell Snarf about you, for Pete's sake?"

"She forgot she herself was invited till Snarf arrived to pick her up."

"I must say, that's some way to run a reception. Who else is going?"

"Don't ask me. None of our friends, as far as I know. Surely we'd have heard."

"Well, this is one for the books! You're sure this reception's actually going to happen?"

"Now that you mention it, no. I'm not sure at all. Osbert, you don't suppose Arethusa's been abducted again?"

CHAPTER

13

Osbert attempted to calm his wife. "Simmer down, darling, she can't have been abducted."

"Why not?" Dittany rejoined somberly. "She was once before. You know perfectly well what a sink of iniquity that inn used to be before Andy McNaster got religion. Who's to say this Snarf bird hasn't sunk it again?"

"Since when did Andy McNaster get religion?" demanded Zilla.

"I was making a figurative allusion to Andy's pure and holy reverence for Arethusa, dag-nab it. Surely I don't have to remind you how fast he cleaned up his act once she started letting him ply her with champagne and steak dinners on the house."

"No, nor do you have to remind me that Andy's now down there in the Babylon of America, playing suave and sinister villains just the way he used to do when he was pulling sneaky deals right here in Lobelia Falls. Some reformation!" Having said her piece, Zilla essayed a bite of Dittany's casserole. "My stars, this is tasty. Could have used a pinch less sage, maybe, but I suppose you have to think of Osbert's profession."

"You're dern tootin', ma'am," Osbert agreed. "We riders of the purple sage have to keep our taste buds attuned to our work. I don't believe Hollywood's so iniquitous as it used to be, eh, now that it's become a suburb of Tokyo. And I'll tell you why I don't believe Aunt Arethusa's been abducted, Dittany. It's because Hedrick Snarf's only about half her size and weight."

"So what?" Dittany argued. "He's got henchpersons, hasn't he?"

"What henchpersons? According to my secret informants, namely Bob and Ray down at the police station, nary a one of the inn employees would give Hedrick Snarf the time of day, much less a helping hand in a nefarious enterprise."

"Snarf could have sent out for henchpersons, couldn't he? I don't care what anybody says, I think it's pretty darned skulduggerous that Hedrick Snarf hasn't invited one single, solitary person we know to that probably spurious shindig he's allegedly throwing tonight. I'd like to go down there and see for myself what's going on. But I suppose it wouldn't look right to barge in uninvited, now that I'm a mother."

Hiram Jellyby cleared his throat, or at least made the sort of noise people make who have throats to clear. "Ahem. If I was to dematerialize, I might sneak down there unbeknownst an' have a gander, assumin' I could remember what the lady looks like. I was so took up with findin' my bones last night, I didn't much notice nothin' else. You wouldn't happen to have a platinum print of her kickin' around, I don't s'pose?"

Dittany perked up. "That's a marvelous idea, Hiram. We do have lots of photographs of Arethusa. Osbert, would you mind bringing the album off the parlor table?"

"Sure thing, pardner."

Osbert galumphed parlorward and returned in a trice with a bunch of photographs taken the previous February, showing his aunt costumed for her role in Osbert's melo-drama. It was the one of Arethusa in her black Merry Widow corset and red silk skirt that caused the late mule skinner's eyes to flash emerald green with purple sparks.

"Oh gosh," fretted Dittany. "I hope his ectoplasm's not short-circuiting. Hiram, are you all right?"

"Hoo boy! I'll tell the cockeyed world I am. This dame sure as hell don't look like nobody's aunt to me."

"Well, you don't have to get profane about it," snapped Zilla.

She might perhaps have been feeling a trifle green-eyed herself. After all, Zilla was Hiram's closest friend, if one could be said to have formed any sort of meaningful relationship with a phantom. Dittany understood perfectly.

"He's right, Zilla. Arethusa isn't the auntliest person in the world, as I'm sure Osbert will be only too willing to testify. Would you like another cookie before you start out, Hiram?"

"Nope, thanks, I better get started. They'll be swillin' booze an' orgyin' around over there, I shouldn't be surprised." Hiram tried not to sound too hopeful, but he wasn't fooling a soul, particularly Zilla. "Am I fadin' yet?"

"You're beginning to thin out a little around the edges," Osbert told him encouragingly. "Maybe if the rest of us were to join hands and help you concentrate, it would help to speed up the dematerializing process."

"Wouldn't hurt none to try, I don't s'pose."

In fact it helped quite a lot. In a twinkling, Hiram was gone, all but the eyeballs. They were still shooting the odd purple gleam, although the emerald green had by now faded to a relatively unnoticeable teal blue. Like a good host, Osbert started to get up and open the door for the departing muleteer, but he needn't have bothered. Hiram had already oozed his way through the panels and was down the path, leaving a pretty sprinkling of pale lavender sparks in his wake.

"Those eyeballs of his had darned well better not be shooting sparks when he tries to crash that party," Zilla fussed. "Old fool!"

"I think Hiram's rather sweet," said Dittany. "I do hope we haven't landed him in a mess."

Though she didn't yet know it, Dittany needn't have worried about hired abductors. A reception, or a reasonable facsimile of one, was in fact taking place at the inn. Women in expensive and sometimes elegant gowns and men in well-pressed suits and ties, some of them even in dinner jackets, were passing to and fro from bar to buffet, stopping en route to exchange the vapidities that pass for conversation at such affairs. Hedrick Snarf was flitting around like a swallow over a swarm of mayflies, playing host with unabated fervor, herding all comers over to be presented to the guest of honor much as ancient Greeks might have presented their sacrifices before Aphrodite.

Arethusa herself was standing stock-still in front of a bank of potted palms rented for the occasion from one of Scottsbeck's swankiest funeral parlors. In her hand was a champagne glass, on her face was a vaguely Mona Lisa–ish smile. Her eyes were fathomless pools of inscrutability, her thoughts were elsewhere, as Arethusa's thoughts so often were. Even so, she was going through the motions with such finesse and savoir faire as only undertakers and reigning queens of roguish Regency romance are capable of displaying.

Whether Arethusa sensed an alien presence at her side was problematical. Whether she noticed that the level of the champagne in her glass was slowly being lowered without her having so much as touched her lips to the rim was doubtful. Arethusa wasn't even aware of the two points of light half a head below her own that showed first as a feeble glimmer, then brightened watt by watt and ohm by ohm into a pair of piercingly brilliant blue-green orbs shooting fuchsia-colored sparks that gathered around her jetty coiffure like an aureole and clashed almost audibly with the deep crimson of her gown.

Others were noticing, though. Glances were being cast, murmurs were being exchanged. When Hedrick Snarf spied Arethusa's empty glass and dispatched a waiter to fill it, and a disembodied male voice said to the waiter, "Don't mind if I do," the waiter, taken aback, sent a stream of champagne fizzing over Arethusa's velvet sleeve. When that same disembodied voice growled, "Watch it, bub," a sequined matron standing nearby squeaked like a startled mouse, which was about as close to manifesting extreme perturbation as Canadian matrons in polite company usually get.

But when the incandescent eyeballs, now the cynosure of every other eyeball in the ballroom, including at last Arethusa's, became surrounded by fuzzy gray whiskers, and when the whiskers attached themselves to a face, and when the amorphous gathering of fog below the face developed arms and legs and a sturdy though but rudely garbed torso, the squeak became a shriek, the shriek became a general outcry, and the revel, such as it had been, turned into a rout.

It was truly astonishing to see how many alleged stockbrokers, uncertified public accountants, speculators, and other presumed titans of industry became totally disoriented upon finding themselves in the presence of a genuine, grade-A specter. Even redoubtable females claiming to be real estate brokers lost their aplomb and demonstrated their willingness to leave the reception without even pausing to thank their host.

Champagne glasses fell from trembling hands, to be trampled by pounding feet that didn't seem to care whither they sped so long as they wound up somewhere else. Hedrick Snarf was well up in the pack, though he tried to save face by pretending he was there for the sole purpose of bringing order out of the rapidly accelerating chaos. Only Arethusa Monk remained beside the rented

palm trees, aloof and alone save for the ghostly figure that
had by now fully manifested itself as that of Hiram Jellyby.

"How very kind of you to appear," she said in her
most gracious manner. "Haven't we met before?"

"Yep," rejoined the muleteer. "Last night out by the
water hole where your nephew dug up my bones an' your
great-granny's weddin' china."

"Oh, yes, of course. I thought those eyeballs looked
familiar. You were the subject of Great-grandfather's platinum print. Would you care to sample the buffet with me?
I must confess to feeling a trifle peckish."

"Thanks, but I already et, or whatever it is I do, over
at your nephew's place. They sent me to find out if you'd
been abducted."

"No such luck, unfortunately, but it was kind of them
to think of me. Do try the caviar. It's quite tolerable though
not of the best quality."

Arethusa, happy now with a whole tableful of food to
herself and nobody trying to make conversation, was stuffing it in with a skill born of much practice and looking
around for a waiter because she couldn't recall having
drunk any of that champagne which had been poured for
her. Hiram, on the other hand, was eyeing the gussied-up
victuals askance and stepping well back from the buffet so
that he wouldn't inadvertently absorb anything he
couldn't recognize.

"Thanks, ma'am, but I ought to ooze myself back to
the house an' tell 'em you're still among those present
even if nobody else is. I kind o' hate to leave, though; I'm
hankerin' to get a closer look at that bugger with the
slicked-down hair an' the purple socks. He reminds me o'
that bird who shot me through the forehead."

"How interesting," Arethusa remarked through a
mouthful of curried shrimp. "It's a small world, isn't it? I
expect Mr. Snarf will be back sooner or later."

In fact, having run off his initial panic and brought

himself to a realization of his duties, Hedrick Snarf was even then reentering the ballroom. So were a few of the guests who'd managed to get hold of themselves and reflect on how much of that expensive food and drink they might still have a chance to consume. The more intrepid among the waiters and waitresses were beginning to sweep up the broken crystal and chill more champagne. Hiram, having effaced himself behind the potted palms, was doing his darnedest to demanifest, eyeballs and all.

Everybody was pretending that the apparition had been only a jolly jape and that they hadn't been fooled but were just going along with the joke. Everybody else was pretending to believe his fellow guests' protestations and was sneering at them behind their backs. The sangfroid and savoir faire with which the guest of honor was eating her way from one end of the buffet to the other did much to quell any lingering palpitations; the replenished supply of bubbly was soon effervescing in veins that had so recently run cold with terror of the unknown though not unseen.

The party, in short, was back on, louder and gayer than before since all those present except Arethusa were working so hard to convince each other that they weren't a bit scared and never had been. Bonhomie was rife, if not rampant, until all of a sudden, out of the figurative blue, the top plate from a stack of clean china that had been sitting unattended and unnoticed on a side table with not a soul anywhere near it rose straight into the air, sailed roughly four and a quarter meters of its own accord, and biffed Hedrick Snarf spang athwart the starboard ear.

As the startled innkeeper rubbed the assaulted and no doubt smarting organ, another plate soared Snarf-ward and caught him on the bridge of his nose. Arethusa, who had been leaning over to spear an oyster, drew herself up in haughty rebuke.

"Really, Mr. Snarf, it says very little for your managerial skills that you can't even control a stack of dessert plates."

"But I—ouch! Quit that."

Plates were flying thick and fast, Snarf was no longer the only one getting biffed. Titans and titanesses were eyeing each other with unfeigned suspicion and overt resentment. The champagne that had enlivened their spirits was now exciting their ire, they too began chucking china. When the available stock of crockery was depleted, they fell to throwing food. Hoarse guffaws and ribald remarks roared from an unseen throat but couched in the robust language of an old-time mule skinner who'd been in plenty of dance-hall fights in his day and knew how a first-rate brawl ought to be run spurred them on to ever more indecorous behavior. The inn that had become such a hotbed of gentilesse and politesse during the latter reign of Andrew McNaster was beginning to look like Bare Mountain on a really busy Walpurgisnacht.

There was only one thing left to do, Arethusa decided, and she appeared to be the only person in the room still competent to do it. Threading her way through the carnage much as a certain angel was said to have done during the Battle of Mons on August 23, 1914, she managed without scathe to reach the telephone.

"Sergeant MacVicar, I feel it my duty to inform you that a riot, debauch, fracas, melee, or affray is raging here at the inn, and that the incompetent Mr. Snarf is doing nothing whatsoever to quell it."

A loud crash, as of a chandelier being smashed to smithereens by somebody who'd essayed to swing on it, which later proved to have been the case, punctuated her statement in a way that no sergeant of police and most particularly Sergeant Donald MacVicar of the Lobelia Falls constabulary could have ignored. In a matter of perhaps three and a half minutes and two more broken windows, the full weight of the law, including Deputy Osbert

Monk, had invaded the premises and Sergeant MacVicar had spoken the awful words.

"Noo then, what's going on here?"

Arethusa did not wait to hear the answer, if indeed there was one. Her duty done, the buffet quite destroyed, the champagne bottles all empty and being used as weapons, she saw nothing to stay for. Nor did she feel any compulsion to take formal leave of Mr. Snarf. He had, in her estimation, behaved quite abominably. She entered the checkroom and searched out the Spanish shawl she had used for a wrap, the attendant appointed to perform such duties having refused to come out from under the counter and fetch it for her. She flung the great sweep of black silk and cabbage roses over her velvet gown with a cavalier's flourish, and sailed forth from the inn.

CHAPTER
14

Not until she had stepped out on the sidewalk and drawn a few deep breaths did Arethusa Monk become aware that she was not alone. Floating in the air at about the level of her tourmaline brooch were a pair of turquoise-colored orbs. Croaking in her ear was a disembodied voice, all but worn out from much hollering yet managing to utter words of genteel address.

"I figgered I better see you safe home, ma'am. Seems to me there's too damn many riffraffy buggers hangin' around this here gin mill tonight."

"How very gallant of you, Mr. Jellyby." Arethusa glanced down for an arm proffered for her to take. Seeing none and not wanting to embarrass her kind escort, she merely gave the eyeballs an affable nod. "One hates to be thought snobbish, but didn't you find that scurvy pack of tycoons and magnates Mr Snarf foisted upon us a trifle *infra dig*?"

"Hell, yes. Mangiest bunch o' flea-bitten coyotes I ever run into, an' that's sayin' some. Where was you plannin' to go, ma'am? If you'd like to hop along home an' loosen your corsets, I could manifest on over to Charlie Henbit's place an' pass the word that you ain't been abducted."

"Thank you, but why don't we go there together? Any fears about my wellbeing will be more quickly allayed if they see me in the flesh. Furthermore, we might talk Dittany into making us a pot of tea. With, perchance, cookies."

Spurred by the thought of cookies, Arethusa strode forward with verve and purpose. Hiram, of course, had no trouble keeping up with her since all he had to do was glide. He could have manifested himself a pair of feet but perhaps it hadn't seemed worth the bother. He probably figured Arethusa wouldn't notice one way or the other, as in fact she didn't. She was much too involved in planning the earful she intended to give Andrew McNaster on the subject of Hedrick Snarf the next time he telephoned from Hollywood to remind her that when he leered at some gorgeous movie actress in a suave and sinister fashion, his leer was really for her. It occurred to Arethusa that Andrew hadn't been calling lately with the same monotonous regularity as he'd done before he'd found so many other younger beauties to leer at. She wavered for a moment between a vague perturbation as to whether or not she'd heard from him this week and a somewhat less vague hope that one of these days he might quit calling altogether.

Which would not solve the problem of how to cope with the incompetent Snarf. She might even have to telephone Andrew herself, if she could remember where she'd put his telephone number. Perhaps it would be better to write a letter. The thought of writing led inevitably to musings upon Sir Percy and Lady Ermintrude. Hence it was from a deep rosy-brown study that Arethusa was aroused by a tumult reminiscent of that other tumult she'd so recently escaped from, except that here she could detect no sounds of smashing plates or squishing food. It was Hiram who made the inevitable inquiry.

"Great balls o' fire! What the jeezledy blankety-blank's goin' on over there?"

Arethusa cocked her head, listened with full attention for about half a minute, then gave the only reasonable explanation. "Offhand, I surmise that Ethel has cornered some creature of the night. A fruit-eating bat, perchance, or a stray lerot. Or are lerots diurnal?"

Without waiting for an answer, she upped the pace to a quick trot. When they got to the corner of Applewood Avenue, they could see that every light in Dittany and Osbert's house was blazing. Ethel was just inside the door, still emitting ungodly sounds. Zilla Trott was standing on the stoop brandishing, of all things, an old-fashioned wire carpet beater. She looked ready to go on the warpath but seemed nonplussed as to which warpath she should take.

"Gadzooks," panted Arethusa, "wherefor the tumult? Can't you shut that creature up? What's happened to Dittany?"

"Shut up, Ethel," said Zilla, taking first things first as was her wont.

Obliging animal that she was, Ethel shut. It being now possible to make oneself heard without screaming, Zilla explained. "Dittany's trying to get the twins quietened down. Ethel woke them up and scared them half to death, poor mites."

"But why? Methought Ethel was devoted to the twins."

"She is, that's why she was barking. She was trying to protect them from the Peeping Tom."

"Stap my garters!" cried Arethusa. "You mean he was here? Did you see him?"

Zilla shook her head. "I'm not sure. I saw something, at any rate. It was just after Sergeant MacVicar called about the riot. Osbert whizzed off and Dittany and I started picking up the supper dishes. Then we noticed this black form outside the big window over the kitchen table and Ethel started braying like the Bull of Bashan and the twins started yelling and Dittany ran up to stand guard over them. I grabbed the first weapon that came to hand—"

"Weapon? A carpet beater?"

"Well, sure, why not? I wasn't aiming to murder the rogue, I just wanted to get in a few licks and teach him some manners. But he got away, don't ask me how. I've always thought I was fairly spry on my pins."

Hiram Jellyby's floating eyeballs flashed brilliant scarlet. "Godfrey mighty, woman, don't you know no better? You could o' been kilt! Which way did the bugger go?"

"If I knew that," Zilla snorted, "do you think I'd still be standing here?"

"If you had a lick o' sense, you'd be home in your own kitchen where you belong. But that's a woman for you. Runnin' around like a hen with its head cut off, lookin' for some bugger that's hidin' in the bushes waitin' for you to come by so's he can stick a knife in you, like as not."

"Horsefeathers! I'd like to see him try."

"I sure as hell wouldn't. You two females get yourselves safe inside while I scout around a little. He won't see me in the dark."

"Like fun he won't. Your eyes are lit up like a pair of bicycle lamps."

"So he'll think I'm a pair o' bicycles. Who cares? Zilla, you better make Miz Arethusa here a cup o' tea. She's havin' a fit o' the weewaws."

"I am not!" Arethusa was quick to spurn the imputation that she was showing the white feather, though she remembered just in time to be gracious about it. "Thanks to your kind offices, sir, my mind is quite at ease. I should, however, relish a cup of tea since that Snarf creature reneged on his offer of dinner and I was forced to make a meager supper of leftover hors d'oeuvres. We might also think in terms of cookies, if Dittany can leave the infants long enough to set them out. One might further consider the soothing effect of a few doggie bones on Ethel. She's about to erupt again, and I must confess I find that Wagnerian woo-woo of hers somewhat grating on the nerves."

"Good thought. I'll get some."

Not stopping to read the ingredients on the package and get mad about the lack of essential vitamins and minerals, Zilla fetched forth a handful of dog biscuits. Taking this as a signal that her duty was done, Ethel graciously accepted the offering and began to munch. Hiram dimmed his eyeballs and set off on the hunt. Since there really didn't seem to be much else left to do, the two women went inside and put on the teakettle.

No sound of infant wails could be heard from above, it wasn't long before Dittany came down. Seeing that Arethusa had managed to find the cookies without aid, she got straight to the nitty-gritty.

"Who started the riot?"

Arethusa's reply was short and decisive. "Hedrick Snarf, of course."

"But what the heck for?"

"Because he's a blithering tomnoddy. Were these all the cookies you had?"

"Yes. Eat some bread and butter if you're still hungry. Come on, Arethusa, there must have been more to it than plain idiocy."

"Well, the caviar was not Beluga and the champagne was improperly chilled. Or else," Arethusa conceded after brief cogitation, "it might perchance have had something to do with Hiram Jellyby's eyeballs. They do have a way of shooting magenta sparks that some of the guests appeared to find a trifle disconcerting. As for myself, I found Mr. Jellyby quite the gentleman, as retired mule skinners go. He appointed himself my protector, a gesture I thought quite courageous in a man of such unreliable physique."

"For Pete's sake forget the manners and get on with the mayhem," Dittany sputtered. "What happened?"

"As I recall, first everybody ran out, then they all ran

back in, then they started throwing things and pounding each other with champagne bottles, at which point I went out to the reception desk and telephoned Sergeant MacVicar. And through it all, that purple-footed jacka-napes of a Snarf did nothing but whine and complain and bluster around. It was a source of deep and abiding satis-faction to me when Mr. Jellyby caught him so neatly on the nose with that first plate."

"What plate?"

"One of a stack that were, one gathers, intended for serving the dessert we never got." Arethusa did not hide her grief at the loss, as why should she? "Hiram started scaling them like Frisbees. At least I think he did. It was hard to tell since he was mostly invisible at the time. Or was he? He came and went, so to speak. In any event, upon reflection, I do see that it was somewhat on the ee-rie side to watch those plates apparently picking them-selves up and sailing across the room. Zounds, that man can throw!"

"No, he can't," Zilla protested. "He couldn't even have picked them up, they'd have passed right through his hands. He must have been using some kind of kinetic en-ergy."

"Then he's a poltergeist!" exclaimed Dittany. "That's what they do, you know. Just work themselves up to an inward simmer, then the umbrella stand starts shooting out canes and bumbershoots and Uncle Fred's picture hops off the whatnot and skims over to the mantelpiece."

"Well, he'd darn well better not simmer in my house, I'm not standing for any poltergeist nonsense. I'll just tell the old buzzard to pack up his ectoplasm and—oh, darn it! I think maybe I'd better get on home and put Michael's hand-painted shaving mug someplace safe, just in case. Michael set a lot of store by that mug."

"Now, Zilla, you're not walking home by yourself with that Peeping Tom on the loose. You just wait right here till Osbert comes home. Here, have another cookie to calm your nerves. Molasses is good for you, full of iron. Arethusa, have you any idea how long the riot's going to last?"

Dittany's aunt-in-law shrugged. "As long as it takes, one assumes. Not any great while, surely, they'd already smashed every one of the plates by the time I left. As riots go, quite frankly, I found this a woundily dull affair. Stap me, one might have thought even that lackwit Snarf could have put on a livelier mill. If it hadn't been for Mr. Jellyby's spirited exhortations, the whole melee would have been a miserable hum."

"Do you have to talk Regency all the time?" Zilla complained. "What do you mean, a hum?"

"A sham, a humbug, a paltry imitation of the real thing. Gadzooks, does nobody speak the king's English any more?"

"It has been quite a long time since we've had a king," Dittany pointed out. "What did Hiram say?"

"Very little that a gentlewoman would care to repeat. He hurled epithets and insults right and left, thus engendering a mass spirit of unfocused hostility. Nobody could make out who was insulting whom, so everybody took Mr. Jellyby's remarks personally, no doubt with sufficient reason. They were, in truth, an ill-conditioned assemblage. I cannot imagine where, or more importantly why, the Snarf creature dug them up."

"And there was nobody at all in the whole bunch whom you knew?"

"Nary a one, save for that scurvy knave who lured me into it. Not even the waiters looked familiar, now that I think of it. Snarf must have engineered a complete turnover of help, if such it could be called, though the minions did sweep up the broken glasses ably enough."

"How could they sweep," Dittany demanded, "if the riot was still going on?"

"Oh, the glassware was long smashed by then. That happened during phase one, after the woman disguised as a carp screamed."

Arethusa was well into her tale, or at least into a tale that might not have had much relevance to what had actually taken place but was at least interesting, when Osbert returned from the battle. He came not altogether unscathed, the left sleeve of his jacket was ripped from its armhole and his cheek was scratched, perhaps by the fingernails of some stalwart matron disguised as a carp. His mien, however, was jubilant.

"Leaping longhorns, what a brawl! Too bad you missed the party, Dittany. It would have warmed the cockles of your heart to watch Sergeant MacVicar arresting all those crooks."

"Crooks, darling? Were they really?"

"The crème de la crème of the underworld," Osbert confirmed. "All trying to pass themselves off as reputable dogcatchers, undertakers' assistants, and various other pillars of rectitude. Even those new waiters Snarf hired have records as long as your arm, we discovered. I'd like to know what kind of joint that hombre thinks he's running over there."

"The question is moot," said Arethusa, "since Snarf won't be running it much longer once I've dropped a flea into Andrew McNaster's aural orifice."

"Give 'em heck, Auntie. How did you know it was time to blow the whistle?"

"Woman's intuition, of course. Dost suppose I don't know a pack of caitiff knaves when I see them, jackanapes? Furthermore, with the buffet wrecked, the china in shards, and champagne squirted all over the furniture, there seemed nothing to stay for. One did, however, feel a need to make some parting gesture. Did you in fact apprehend the entire party?"

"Pretty much. Most of them were actively engaged in disturbing the peace, you know. Then there were a few who weren't actually doing anything at the moment but happened to have warrants outstanding on them. The

Scottsbeck police had to borrow Brown the Roofer's van
to help cart away the overflow. Remember Fred Churtle,*
Dittany? He sends you his regards."

"I hope you sent mine back, dear. How nice that you
got to see Fred again. I suppose it's no good asking him
and Mrs. Churtle over to Sunday night supper sometime,
she wouldn't want to leave her programs. This ought to be
a lucrative night for the bail bondsmen. Don't you feel a
warm glow, Arethusa, thinking of all the joy you've
spread?"

"In a word, no. I feel, if you really must know, a dash
of apprehension about that Peeping Tom who was lurking
around. What did he do, Dittany?"

"What do they always do? He peeped."

"Dittany!" exclaimed Osbert. "You don't mean the
Snooper's been here? When did you see him?"

"To the best of my recollection, about six and a half
minutes after you'd charged out the door."

"Great galloping garter snakes! I'll never dare let you
out of my sight again. I'd better call Sergeant MacVicar
first thing in the morning and tell him I'm on permanent
assignment as your bodyguard. Did that sidewinder
frighten the twins?"

"No, but Ethel did. She was only trying to protect
them, of course, not that any of us needed protecting. It
was nothing, really, just a glimpse of a dark figure out by
Ethel's doghouse, which you know she seldom uses anyway. Once she started raising the roof, he fled."

"Fled where?"

"I don't know, dear. Wherever Peeping Toms flee to.
He tinkled a little, that's all I can tell you. Zilla meant to
chase him with the carpet beater, but he'd got away before
I remembered where I put it. Hiram's gone looking for
him."

* The Grub-and-Stakers Quilt a Bee

"Mr. Jellyby is a veritable diamond in the rough," Arethusa interjected.

Zilla sniffed. "I'll grant you the rough, but I can't see the diamond. Being a hero's no strain on somebody who can't be killed because he's already been. Hiram can't even be hit, he just flies apart and comes back together."

"How do you know that, Zilla?"

"Because I've tried, darn it. That first night, he got me so exasperated I took a whack at him with the kitchen poker. Aggravating old bugger!"

"Ecod," remarked Arethusa, "meseems that's the first time I've heard you say bugger."

"That so? I must have picked it up from Hiram, he says it all the time. Anyway, bugger's not really a cussword unless you happen to be romantically involved with a sheep. I expect you folks would like me to get out of here, eh, so you can go to bed."

"Don't you want to wait till Hiram comes back?" said Dittany.

"What for? You know I like to get to bed at a reasonable hour, and there's no telling how long that old goat'll be floating around out there. 'Tisn't as if I'd have to get up and let him in, the way I would Nemea. I'd just as lief take the carpet beater with me, if you don't mind."

"Not at all," said Dittany, "but you're not walking back by yourself in the dark. Osbert's going to drive you home. Or I will, dear, if you're suffering from battle fatigue."

"No, you won't," Osbert replied stoutly. "What do you say, Aunt Arethusa, want me to drop you off on the way?"

"Meseems I distrust that ambiguous phraseology, varlet. Just hand me a brace of charged dueling pistols and I'll manage nicely by myself, thank you."

"I'm afraid we're out of charged dueling pistols at the moment," Dittany replied. "But we'd be happy to lend you the flyswatter."

CHAPTER
15

Osbert delivered Zilla and Arethusa to their respective abodes and returned without incident. For the rest of the night, peace reigned on Applewood Avenue, at least as far as the Monks were concerned. Ethel never woo-wooed once. The twins slept like angels. Nobody came thumping at the door to report a fresh calamity. As Dittany observed the following morning at breakfast, it almost seemed a trifle dull.

"Not that we can't use a spot of boredom, considering the way things have been going these last couple of days. Who the heck do you suppose that Peeping Tom can be? Surely he's nobody local."

"Why not, dear?" said Osbert through a mouthful of bacon.

"What would be the point? Everybody around here already knows all about everybody else, right down to the last safety pin in their undershirts. Speaking of which, you need some new underwear."

"Do I?" Osbert favored his wife with a dreamy smile and reached for the marmalade. "You're so perspicacious, dear. Does that mean I ought to go and buy some? I'll get around to it, sooner or later."

"A likely story, forsooth! What about that time before we were married when the billy goat ate your belt and you kept meaning to get a new one? I fully expected you to waltz yourself up to the altar with that old hunk of frayed clothesline still holding your pants up."

"And what if I had? A man's a man for a' that, as Sergeant MacVicar would be the first to tell you if I hadn't just beaten him to it. I tell you what, darling, why don't I drop a note to Santa Claus?"

"It's rather a long time till Christmas, dear," Dittany pointed out. "You'd be in rags by then. As an alternate suggestion why don't you write us a nice, fat check and take care of the twins for a couple of hours so that I can go shopping in Scottsbeck?"

"Would you really buy undies for me, sweetheart?"

"My devotion knows no bounds, darling. Besides, if I let you loose in the stores by yourself, you'd forget what you went for and come back with a stuffed emu."

Osbert nodded. "As a matter of fact, I've been thinking a stuffed emu might look rather fetching on the parlor mantelpiece."

"So it might," Dittany agreed. "We'd have to extend the mantel shelf out into the room about four feet and cut a hole in the ceiling for the neck to stick up through, but what the heck? Were you planning to scoff all that marmalade, or could you spare a dollop for a poor, tired mother of twins?"

"Oh, sorry, dear. Want me to help you slather it on?"

"Thanks, dear, but I daresay I can cope. I wonder whether Hiram ever got back to Zilla's."

Dittany spread marmalade on toast with an air of abstraction. "Osbert," she said after a bite or two, "does it strike you as being a trifle unusual that we've become so pally all of a sudden with a mule skinner who's been dead for over a hundred years?"

"I suppose some people might find it so, in a way," her

husband agreed after a moment's reflection. "Of course when you're used to having characters wander into your books before you've even had a chance to think them up, I suppose you adjust more easily to eating supper with a ghost than a certified public accountant or a geography teacher might, though you never know with geography teachers. As a matter of fact, I'm hoping some wayfaring stranger will mosey along to the old corral this morning. I can't think what to do with that mysterious trunk that's shown up in the chuck wagon where the case of canned peaches ought to be."

"You'll think of something, darling, you always do. Here's Ethel, back from her morning stroll. I'll get the twins dressed while you write the check."

Two hours later, Dittany was at the Scottsbeck Mall, dealing capably and efficiently with Osbert's underwear and various other matters. Unlike her mother, Dittany was not a compulsive shopper. Since she didn't get around to the stores all that often, however, it was close to noontime before she'd checked off everything on her list. She'd left the groceries till last because she didn't want to keep them sitting in a hot car, she felt the need of sustenance before tackling the supermarket. The Cozy Corner beckoned, she went in.

Dittany had barely picked up the menu and commenced an inner debate between the vitamin-packed Vegetarian Medley and the nitrite-laden Bratwurst Bow-Wow when a voice like the whine of a dentist's drill reverberated on her eardrums.

"Why, Mrs. Monk, how nice! May I join you?"

"Eh? Oh hello, Mrs. Melloe."

Dittany glanced around. Lunchers were swarming into the small restaurant; there wasn't a table left free. What could she decently say?

"Of course."

With a sigh of relief, Mrs. Melloe sat. The amateur

genealogist's relief was not, Dittany wisely surmised, at being granted permission to share the table. Mrs. Melloe would surely have sat down anyway, there'd have been no way to stop her short of physical violence or snatching the chair away. Mrs. Melloe was wearing pointy-toed pumps with two-inch heels, her relief was simply at getting the load off her feet.

"What a quaint little place! Do you come here often, Mrs. Monk?"

The Cozy Corner was about as quaint as several thousand others of its ilk scattered all across the North American continent, each contributing its share of uninspired decor and gastronomic outrage to the decline of the West. Dittany ignored the observation and addressed herself solely to the question.

"Not if I can help it. But I haven't finished my shopping and there's no place else handy."

"Well, the food here surely can't be any worse than it is at that inn of yours. I couldn't even get a halfway palatable breakfast this morning. The coffee was cold, the orange juice was lukewarm, and I don't even want to think about the omelet. Furthermore, the place looked like the morning after a barroom brawl. I tried to complain to the manager but the very snippy desk clerk informed me that he hadn't come in yet. Isn't anybody ever going to wait on us?"

Mrs. Melloe spoke those last words in loud and ringing tones. A harried waitress gave her a dirty look and trudged over to their table, dragging an order pad out of a quaintly ruffled apron pocket. "What'll you have?" she grunted.

Dittany decided Swiss cheese and lettuce would be the least apt to prove totally inedible. Mrs. Melloe opted for the soup of the day and a Blue Plate Special. She was all set to give a good many complicated instructions about how she wanted them served but the waitress didn't stick around to hear, for which Dittany didn't blame her a bit. Waiting on tables must, she thought, be about the third lousiest job in the world, particularly when you got customers like Mrs. Melloe.

But why had Mrs. Melloe said the inn's dining room *looked like* the morning after a brawl? Was it possible that she didn't know there'd actually been one?

Come to think of it, yes. Minerva had mentioned that Mrs. Melloe was going to Toronto yesterday. It was at least a two-hour drive. If the woman had had a lot to do and stayed to eat dinner, she might well not have got back to the inn till eleven or so. The riot had been over, the prisoners carted away, and Osbert safe home a little after ten. Most of the action had been in the ballroom. If Snarf had closed it off from the lobby, a late-returning guest wouldn't have seen whatever was left by then of the mess.

Regardless of the fact that there appeared to be only three waitresses handling this whole roomful of hungry people, and that only about two minutes had elapsed since her order was taken, Mrs. Melloe was already fretting because she hadn't yet got her soup. When the soup actually did arrive quite expeditiously, she didn't so much as glance at it, but let the bowl sit there cooling off while she went on unloading her woes to Dittany.

"I'm going to have to move out of the inn, that's all there is to it. I simply cannot endure slackness and inefficiency."

"So you're moving over here?" Dittany asked hopefully. "I'm told the Scottsbeck Arms is quite comfortable."

"But much too inconvenient for my research. I need to be right in the heart of Lobelia Falls. I've decided the only thing to do is rent a room in one of your lovely, spacious homes. Perhaps you might have some suggestions as to where I might look?" She smiled an arch smile and cocked an even archer eyebrow. "On Applewood Avenue, for instance? In the historic old Henbit house, perchance?"

"Which contains myself, my husband, who works at home and rattles the typewriter night and day, our twin babies, who plan to start teething in the near future, and our dog, who has operatic ambitions and likes to rehearse in the small hours of the morning. Our cleaning woman only shows up at the full of the moon, at which time her gums turn blue and her bite is death. If Mrs. Poppy took umbrage at having to clean up after a boarder, I couldn't answer for the consequences. Of course if you were willing to sign a waiver—"

"Oh, no, I hardly think we'd suit. What about your aunt?"

"She has the same cleaning woman."

"Would Mrs. Oakes consider taking a boarder?"

"For how long?" Dittany asked warily.

"That's hard to say. My genealogical research is taking longer than I'd anticipated. Some people just don't seem to want to cooperate."

"Well, you can hardly blame them," Dittany replied, knowing full well why Mrs. Melloe had spoken in just that astringent tone and with just that thin-lipped little smile. "Having a stranger in the house is a nuisance at the best of times, and some people might find it an imposition when a person they hardly know bursts in wanting them to dig out the family album and sit talking ancestors for hours on end just as they're about to put in a wash or start bottling their jelly."

Mrs. Melloe wasn't licked yet. "Then there are others who might be delighted at the opportunity to share their family history with a kinswoman who really cares. I've been deeply touched by the gracious welcome I've found almost everywhere I've gone. Though not quite." She gave Dittany another of those acid-tipped smiles and essayed a taste of her soup. "Ugh! Stone cold. Waitress! Waitress, this soup is cold."

"It was hot when I brought it." The weary servitor slammed Dittany's order down in front of her and went on to less obnoxiously importunate customers. Dittany concentrated on her sandwich, laid a two-dollar tip on the table, and wished Mrs. Melloe bon appetit.

"Good luck with your Blue Plate Special. I've got to run."

And warn Minerva Oakes not, under any circumstances, to let her spare bedroom to a pain in the neck like Tryphosa Melloe. Back when she'd needed the income, Minerva had shown a positive genius for saddling herself with boarders who'd ranged from the thoughtlessly inconsiderate to the truly gosh-awful. It was bad enough that Minerva's best buddy was harboring a bibulous apparition in her woodshed, though at least Hiram Jellyby didn't eat hamburgers in bed and ruin Zilla's good sheets with mustard stains as one of Minerva's early wrong guesses had been wont to do.

Watching that small helping of casserole wane while Hiram's eyeballs waxed had been an interesting experience, Dittany mused as she loaded her groceries and headed the car homeward. Now that she'd met the late mule skinner in person if not in the flesh, she was more inclined than before to credit his story of having been killed for a trunkful of gold in Hunnikers' Field. Whether the gold was still there remained to be dowsed.

One thing sure, a ghost who could play the *preux chevalier* to Arethusa Monk while terrorizing a roomful of assorted malefactors with only a stack of plates and a pair of spark-shooting eyeballs for weapons was not a wraith to be dismissed lightly. Besides, Hiram had been a friend of Charlie Henbit. It would be less than courteous for Charlie's great-great-granddaughter to go around assuming that her ancestor's old buddy was talking through his ectoplasmic hat.

Getting back to the subject of money in its various forms, Dittany wondered whether Sergeant MacVicar and the Mounties had yet been able to determine where that stash of legal tender had come from and how much it

counted up to. Perhaps Osbert had heard by now; she fed
the car a little extra gas, wondering whether he'd remembered the twins' bottles. Surely Ethel would have reminded him, Ethel had become almost obnoxiously
punctilious about her charges' mealtimes.

No, by golly, Ethel was not on the job. As Dittany
pulled into the driveway she spied a black mass that resembled a bearskin rug gone berserk galumphing up Cat
Alley with something long and flappy in its mouth. Something purple, moreover, and leglike.

"Ethel!" she cried. "Come here, old scout. What's that
you've found? Here, give it to me."

But Ethel didn't want to. The object was hers and
she planned to chew it. With jaws stubbornly clenched,
she retired into her doghouse, an imposing edifice with
stained-glass windows and wall-to-wall carpeting that
Henry Binkle had built back when he'd thought Ethel
was his dog and bestowed on the Monks as a wedding
present once she had made it clear that her heart was
elsewhere.

Normally Ethel ignored her doghouse. She preferred
to sprawl on the kitchen floor for her daytime siestas.
Come nightfall, her modus operandi was to drag Osbert's
bathrobe down on the floor at the foot of the connubial bed
and curl up on it with much grunting and complaining.
She only entered the doghouse for periods of philosophical
reflection or to masticate some interesting artifact that
her alleged mistress didn't want her to eat. These ill-
judged gourmandisings led to unfortunate results more
often than not, usually in the kitchen just as the Monks
were sitting down to a meal.

When Osbert came out to help with the groceries, Dittany told him, "I can manage the bundles. You'd better see
what Ethel's making herself sick on over there."

As Dittany began carrying her purchases into the
house, Osbert inserted his front half into the doghouse.
After a brief altercation with Ethel, he emerged trium-

phant, bearing a longish piece of heavy cloth, faded purple on the outside, bright purple on the inside.

"Tumultuous tumbleweeds, Dittany, look at this! See? Buttons!"

"Well, I'll be jiggered! Oh, where is Hiram Jellyby now that we need him?"

"Over at Zilla's, most likely getting pie-eyed on dandelion juice. Darling, do you see what this means?"

"It means we've acquired a gaiter. Now all we need is a century-old leg to fasten it on and Bob's your uncle. But, Osbert—"

"Yes, dear. You were about to observe that the man who killed Hiram Jellyby is unlikely to be still wearing his gaiters. Or more specifically, one gaiter."

"On the other hand," Dittany pointed out, "Hiram's still mooching around in his mule-skinner boots."

"True enough, pet. However, we do have to bear in mind that, when Hiram gets ready to demanifest, he doesn't take his boots off and park them on the hearth for Ethel to chew on."

"That did occur to me, sweetheart. I was thinking more along the lines of the bad guy's having perhaps left the gaiter as some kind of signal, perhaps in repentance for having killed Hiram. Although wouldn't it have been only involuntary manslaughter, with the horsefly as an accomplice?"

"If there'd been complicity between the shooter and the horsefly, the slaughter wouldn't have been involuntary," argued Osbert. "At least I don't think it would. You've raised an interesting legal quibble there, pet. If this gaiter had been lying out in Hunnikers' Field all these years, exposed to bad weather and marauding rodents, it seems to me there'd have been no sign of it left by now, except maybe the buttons."

"One of which is missing," Dittany pointed out gloomily. "Ethel's probably swallowed it. She'll be complaining of a bellyache once she gets over being cross with you for taking away her new toy. Anyway, this thing has to have come from somewhere, and I can't think of anyone in Lobelia Falls who goes in for purple gaiters. It was made for somebody with a fairly big leg. Look at this."

While she talked, Dittany had been fastening the buttons. The resulting shape was reminiscent of the way Toulouse Lautrec used to depict can-can girls' voluptuous limbs, only without the je ne sais quoi.

"You know," she mused, "I have a vague feeling that I've seen this gaiter before. Could it have been on one of the Traveling Thespians back when my mother was treading the boards?"

"Could it have been on your mother herself?"

"Of course not, goofus, it's miles too big for Mum."

"Mightn't it be something we've had kicking around the house and never noticed?"

Osbert himself was not much inclined to notice petty details, being so often preoccupied with buzzards over the buttes. Dittany, however, was an inspired housekeeper, which is to say that every so often she became inspired to turn out all the dresser drawers or sort through some long-forgotten boxful of artifacts that had been gathering dust in a closet for a decade or so. She shook her head.

"Dear, I've lived in this house all my life. Believe me, I'd have noticed. Mother's spare wigs and so forth are carefully stashed away in the cubbyhole under the eaves, with mothballs around them."

"Mothballs don't kill moths unless you succeed in beaning the critters with a fast pitch," Osbert pointed out.

"I know that, dear, but they do tend to discourage mice and squirrels."

"Oh, of course, silly of me. Do you think we might drop a line to the mothball factory and suggest they start marketing their product as mouseballs?"

"Mothballs also work pretty well against skunks and moles," said Dittany. "What about skunkballs, or moleballs? I'm rather inclined toward moleballs, myself. But then all the packages would have to have the old name scratched out and the new one written in, I doubt if the mothball magnates want to go to all that bother. You know what, Osbert? If you wouldn't mind putting the perishables in the fridge and riding herd on the wee bairns a little while longer, I'd like to take this gaiter over to Mr. Glunck and see whether perchance it's been snaffled out of the Thorbisher-Freep Collection."

"Itching iguanas!" cried Osbert, "you don't suppose Ethel's been robbing the Architrave?"

"Oh, no. I was thinking more along the lines that, since Mr. Glunck's been so avid to get his platinum prints into the Freep display cases, he might possibly have got a trifle absent-minded with some of the things he took out."

"You mean like mistaking a large-size purple gaiter for a handkerchief, wandering off with it trailing out of his coat pocket, and dropping it someplace where Ethel could get hold of it?"

"Something along those general lines," Dittany agreed. "I believe they're called Freudian slips, like forgetting to pick up your aunt at the airport because you didn't really want her to come home in the first place."

"But I feel that way even when I remember," Osbert protested. "Anyway, you always keep reminding me at twenty-minute intervals so how could I possibly forget?"

"Darling, I was speaking hypothetically. Mr. Glunck doesn't really have his heart in the Thorbisher-Freep collection, you know, for which I can't say I blame him. But he's far too conscientious not to have a complete inventory of everything that's in it, so may I please be excused?"

"Just so you don't stay away too long, precious. You know how it tears at my heartstrings when you're not here to fix lunch."

"Try to be brave, dear. Au revoir, then, and for Pete's sake don't go putting the eggs in the freezer with the ice cream this time."

CHAPTER
16

Mr. Glunck was affable as always but not much help. "This is surely a genuine Victorian gaiter, Mrs. Monk. Circa 1880, I'd say offhand. But it definitely didn't come from the Thorbisher-Freep collection or anywhere else that I know of. Nor, I may say, do we need any purple gaiters. As you know, we've had no dearth of donated clothing."

Dittany agreed somberly. An astonishing number of local residents had been only too happy to foist off ancestral Sunday-go-to-meetings on the Architrave; the big problem was how to display these garments in ways that wouldn't eat up too much space without making the donors feel slighted. But if Mr. Glunck said the museum possessed no purple gaiters, then it didn't and there was no point in belaboring the matter.

Which was not to say that Dittany was ready to quit. "They might have come out of the flea market stuff down cellar, Mr. Glunck. Though you wouldn't know much about that, would you?"

In those early weeks when the Grub-and-Stakers were trying to turn John Architrave's underfinanced legacy from a rundown old house into a bona fide museum, they'd been overwhelmed by a stream of donations ranging from carved coconuts to umbrella stands made of buffalo horns and alleged locks of Ivor Novello's hair. Therese Boulanger had got the bright idea of laying all the more obviously unsuitable artifacts out for sale on a table next to John's ancestral coal bin, on the theory that some people would buy absolutely anything if it was cheap enough and the proceeds would at least help to pay for cleaning supplies and brooms with which to knock down the cobwebs.

Now that they had a fully operative museum and a curator who wasn't afraid to refuse offerings of damaged bustles and whiskerless shaving brushes, people had quit thinking of the Architrave as a dumping ground for junk they hadn't the intestinal fortitude to throw away. The flea market had therefore been phased out, but chances were good that Therese Boulanger was still hanging on to the notebook in which she'd dutifully listed each and every contribution, along with the donor's name. It wouldn't hurt to ask.

Not now, of course. Therese would be just about to put the teabags into her pot, and Dittany ought by rights to be doing the same. She accelerated her pace and reached Applewood Avenue in a dead heat with Arethusa, somewhat to the latter's annoyance.

"Ods bodikins, wench, have you no sense of family responsibility? Who's fixing lunch?"

"Good question. How about you, for a change?"

Dittany didn't bother to wait for an answer. She opened the fridge and began setting the table with ham, cheese, salad makings, a loaf of bread, and a jar of mustard pickles, along with an assortment of plates and eating tools. "There you are, madam, feel free to browse at will. Come on, Osbert, belly up to the bar."

As to whether he'd remembered to feed the twins in her absence, Dittany didn't have to ask. The state of their faces left no room for doubt. She wiped them clean and tossed their bibs down the cellar stairs in the general direction of the washing machine, then took her own place and set about composing a sandwich. As was their wont, Osbert and Arethusa were holding a Mexican standoff over the topmost little onion in the pickle jar. Dittany ended the dispute by fishing out three onions and dealing out one apiece, not forgetting herself since, after all, it was she who'd made the pickles.

It might make sense henceforth to compound the pickles of nothing but onions. However, Gram Henbit had always used cucumber and cauliflower and Dittany was not one to fly in the face of tradition unless something occurred to steer her otherward. Like for instance that purple gaiter.

"Arethusa," she said once she'd dealt with a bite of sandwich, "you may be interested to learn that Ethel came home a while ago with a purple gaiter in her mouth."

The reigning queen of roguish Regency romance took the news calmly, being preoccupied with fishing out the biggest piece of cauliflower as a sop to her disappointment over there being no more little onions. "Not to shatter your apparent expectations, ecod, but the plain fact of the matter is that I find your information somewhat less than overwhelming. What, prithee, does a four-legged creature of undetermined species expect to accomplish with one single gaiter? Furthermore, I hardly think purple is Ethel's color. A bright scarlet, perhaps, with round black buttons—zounds! Are you intimating that this purple gaiter may perchance have graced the calf of that long-ago highwayman who erst effected the demise of the gallant chevalier who rescued me from the fell clutches of Hedrick Snarf and his brawling band of bibulous boors?"

Dittany nodded. "The possibility has to be considered, the gaiter's pretty faded. I did wonder if Ethel might have snitched it from the Architrave but Mr. Glunck says no. I'm going to call Therese later and find out whether she ever sold a pair through the flea market."

"Why not now, forsooth?"

"Oh, I couldn't, not till she's finished her tea and taken her little rest with the teabags squeezed out and laid on her eyelids. She claims it tones the system, though I can't think why."

"Are Therese's teabags germane to our present purpose?" asked Osbert.

"No, I suppose not, now that you mention it. Maybe what the teabags really do is tan the eyelids so they won't get wrinkles. Or maybe Therese just feels she ought to get all possible good out of them because everything costs so darned much these days."

"I should think Therese might forget her dad-blanged teabags for once in the interests of civic responsibility," Osbert fretted. "We can't just sit around here eating pickles with an important clue on our hands."

"Yes, darling," said Dittany. "Have some applesauce, it will calm your nerves. If you're all that itchy to telephone somebody, why don't you call up Sergeant MacVicar and ask if he's found out anything yet about that trunkful of money?"

"Splendid suggestion, darling."

Forgetting about the applesauce, Osbert sprinted for the instrument which still hung on the kitchen wall where Gramp Henbit as a young bridegroom had caused it to be put although one no longer cranked the box and asked Central to please get the number. A good many of Lobelia Falls's inhabitants still regretted not being able to crank the box.

Officer Ray was on the desk. He explained that Sergeant MacVicar had in fact returned from his visit to the RCMP but was at the moment eating cullen skink with Mrs. MacVicar and her cousin Matilda the mincemeat magnate, and could not be disturbed. Ray promised to pass along Osbert's message at the earliest opportunity. He would surely keep that promise; Ray's admiration for Deputy Monk knew few, if any, bounds.

Somewhat mollified, Osbert went back to the table and ate his applesauce. He was helping to clear the table and put the pickles away when Sergeant MacVicar returned his call. After a polite inquiry about Cousin Matilda, by whom Osbert had been briefly employed in a case of sabotage at the mincemeat factory,* he got to the nub.

"There's been an interesting new development in the case, Chief, that we're trying to get a line on here. In the meantime, we're wondering what you've found out about that money in the trunk."

"Oh, aye, Deputy Monk. Noo, there's another interesting development. The money has indeed been determined to have come from that robbery in which the banker was kidnapped and presumably murdered. His and one other's are the only fingerprints to have been found on the packages, as has been deduced from prints that were taken at the time of the robbery from sundry articles on his office desk and in his house. It is being theorized that the banker may have been forced to make up the bundles at the kidnappers' behest, after his abduction had been effected and before his finger was amputated."

"Then the banker would still have been alive when the kidnappers called his wife to ask for the ransom," said Osbert.

"Still alive and hard at work, on the strength of the evidence," the sergeant agreed.

"They might not have meant to kill him at all, unless he tried to make a run for it while they were telephoning. Or else they got plumb disgusted when his wife took his kidnapping as a joke."

"We may never know, Deputy Monk. Howsomever, yon interesting development to which I alluded is that the money in the trunk added up to less than we'd expected from the bills of large denomination that we were able to see through the plastic. The great bulk of the currency

*The Grub-and-Stakers Spin a Yarn

turned out to be of varying denominations, all in used bills such as would have been preferred by any bank robber conversant with the conventions of his trade. And what wad be this new development of yours?"

"A faded purple gaiter. You may recollect from Hiram Jellyby's narrative of his demise, Chief, that the man who held him up and accidentally shot him wore purple gaiters."

"Aye, and odd garb for a highwayman, in my opeenion."

"That's what Hiram thought, as do we all," Osbert concurred. "But anyhow, Ethel went for her usual stroll this morning and came home with this purple gaiter in her mouth."

"A man's gaiter?"

"Man-size, anyway. Dittany's first thought was that the gaiter must have come from the Thorbisher-Freep Collection. We checked with Mr. Glunck but he says not, unless it may have been sold through the flea market they were running before he took over as curator. We're going to ask Therese Boulanger about that as soon as she takes the teabags off her eyelids."

"M'phm."

Not a whit disconcerted by the teabags, Sergeant MacVicar asked Deputy Monk to report back on his findings and rang off, perhaps to go and eat some more cullen skink. Arethusa, who had been entertaining herself and the twins by tickling their knees with their bootie tassels, decided she ought to go home and get back to work before her cat, Rudolph, ate her latest chapter, as he was not at all unlikely to do if left long to his own devices. Like her vast reading public, Rudolph had a voracious appetite for Arethusa's works, though he could generally be distracted by a generous helping of *filet de poisson au vin blanc, rognons de veau flambé,* or any of the more expensive brands of cat food.

Left to themselves, Osbert and Dittany attended to the dishes, got the twins settled for their postprandial snooze, eyed the telephone as Rudolph might eye a *rôti de boeuf pôelé à la matignon* or a fresh batch of typescript, and finally succumbed.

Therese was gracious but brief. No, her records showed no acquisition or sale of purple gaiters either singly or as a pair. The only person she knew who owned any purple gaiters was Minerva Oakes and she was afraid she'd have to run now because her dryer was about to shut off.

Dittany hung up the phone. "Minerva Oakes! Can you beat that? Do you want to go see her, Osbert, or shall I?"

"You, dear. You'd better take the one Ethel found for purposes of comparison. You might also take Ethel while you're about it. When you're not around, she keeps pestering me to feed the twins even when they've just finished eating. Not that I begrudge the kids any time or task, as you well know, but I have all those elk to cope with and it does tend to break my train of thought when she grabs my pant leg and starts dragging me out to the kitchen."

"I understand, dear. Come on, Ethel, let's go for a walk. Minerva won't mind being barged in on, unless she's making elderberry jelly."

Minerva was not making elderberry jelly, as it turned out, and seemed quite pleased to be barged in on. "Well, this is nice. Just let me put the kettle on. Here, Ethel, I've been saving you this soup bone but you'll have to chew it outdoors. You don't mind her having it, Dittany?"

"Not at all, provided she chews like a lady. Don't make any tea for me, Minerva, we just got up from the table. What I came about was this."

Dittany opened the diaper bag she'd brought along from force of habit and took out the evidence. "Therese Boulanger says you own a pair of purple gaiters. I just wanted to make sure this isn't one of them."

Minerva put on her reading glasses and shook her head over the tooth marks. "It had better not be. Where did you find this?"

"I didn't. Ethel came home with it from her morning

walk. She usually wanders over toward the Enchanted Mountain and sometimes as far as Hunnikers' Field, so we couldn't help wondering. You know that story Hiram Jellyby told about how he happened to get shot."

"Why, yes, I—my stars and garters! Gaiters, I suppose I should have said. Come on upstairs, I've got the attic all straightened up for a change. I know exactly where to put my hand on Granny's gaiters. That was my Winona Pitcher grandmother, you know, the one who introduced archery to what was then the Grub-and-Stake Gardening Club. She wore those purple gaiters the day she won the Interprovincial Lady Archers' Roving Tournament, and they'd darned well better not be the ones Ethel's been dragging around. They're not just a family heirloom, they're a significant part of Lobelia Falls's historical heritage. I suppose by rights they ought to be on display at the Architrave, but I just don't have the heart to part with them."

"That's all right," said Dittany. "Mr. Glunck doesn't seem to think we're in urgent need of any more gaiters just now. Perhaps you could bequeath them to the museum in your will."

"Yes, so I could. Thank you for the suggestion. Watch your step here, I never could figure out why the carpenter put this funny kink in the attic stairway. It's a mercy I didn't break my neck the other day carrying all those boxes of trash down for the rubbish man to—Lord have mercy on us, will you look at this!"

The so recently tidied attic now looked as if it had been invaded by a posse of raccoons. Trunks, drawers, and boxes hung open, their contents strewn helter-skelter.

"Just day before yesterday I had this whole place clean as a whistle and neat as a pin," Minerva moaned, "and now—this is awful!"

"It's a mess, all right," Dittany agreed. "Can you tell if anything's missing? Where had you put those gaiters?"

"In that wicker trunk over there, under Granny's wedding petticoat. Here's the petticoat, down on the floor in a wad with a big smooch of dust across it. Doesn't this make you sick? All that lovely embroidery. Honestly, some people ought to be stuffed and mounted! Who in the world could have done such a thing?"

"Somebody who was in a desperate hurry to find something and didn't know where to look is the best I can think of. Can you tell what's missing?"

"I suppose so, once I get straightened out."

Minerva began picking things up and folding them away, Dittany gave what help she could. It wasn't so bad really, they found more mess than actual damage. What they did not find were Winona Pitcher's purple gaiters. Minerva sank into a rocking chair with one rocker missing and fanned herself with the lid of a broken shoebox that had contained a pair of elastic-sided boots once worn by Great-Grandfather Pitcher.

"I'm so mad I could spit! Not a blessed scrap missing except Granny's gaiters, the one thing above all that I really do treasure."

"Who besides yourself has been up here since you cleaned?" Dittany asked her.

"Nobody, or so I thought. Of course I haven't been home every minute of the day. You know how it is, you're popping in and out. But I always lock my door. Most always anyhow, unless I'm just running over to Zilla's or down to your place, or—well, you know."

"Sure. And sometimes you're gone for hours at a time. And when you do lock the door, you stick the key under the mat on the back doorstep."

"Well, naturally. I have to get back in, don't I? Why shouldn't I stay out if I feel like it? There's nothing special to keep me here, now that I've quit taking in boarders. Though Mrs. Melloe did mention that she's thinking about finding a quieter place to stay. She's fed up with the inn, which doesn't surprise me much considering the way Hedrick Snarf runs the place."

"Minerva Oakes, if you take that woman into your house you might as well book yourself a reservation at the booby hatch while you're about it. She'd drive you crazy in a week."

"Yes, but the poor soul—"

"Poor soul, my eyeball!" Dittany snarled. "Mrs. Melloe's got more gold clanking around her neck than most miners ever took out of the Klondike. Probably a darn sight more than Hiram Jellyby claims to have seen in that chest we haven't been able to find. Why can't she move over to Scottsbeck and rent a car to get back and forth?"

"She says she doesn't drive."

"Good, then maybe she won't come so often. Let her take a taxi, or hire a limousine and chauffeur. Or better still, go away and quit pestering us all to dig up her roots for her. Come on, Minerva, if we're through here we'd better let Sergeant MacVicar know what's happened. Too bad you cleaned so thoroughly, we might have found some footprints in the dust. I suppose he'll be mad at us for straightening up, but none of this stuff would have taken fingerprints very well and nowadays everybody knows enough to wear gloves anyway."

"And furthermore, I'm not keen on having it told around town what a slack-twisted housekeeper I am," Mrs. Oakes confessed. "Do we really have to call the sergeant?"

"I think he'd feel terribly slighted if we didn't," Dittany replied, knowing the best way to Minerva's heart. "And so would his wife, though of course Margaret wouldn't let on for fear of hurting your feelings. You know how careful Margaret MacVicar is about people's feelings."

"Yes, of course, I should have thought. Do you want to call the station, or shall I?"

"Well, it's your attic."

"And my gaiter, or was. You don't suppose Ethel's eaten the other one?"

"Gosh, I hope not. She'd be sick for a week. No, of course she didn't. Go ahead, Minerva."

"Donald MacVicar won't think I'm making a mountain out of a molehill?"

"Absolutely not," Dittany insisted.

"All right then, if you say so." Grudgingly, Minerva Oakes picked up the phone.

CHAPTER
17

"*A*nd you're certain this is your esteemed Granny's gaiter?" said the sergeant.

"As certain as I can be," Minerva replied in no uncertain tone. "I had the gaiters out to show Mrs. Melloe just yesterday afternoon. I'd come across them the day before when I was cleaning the attic and thought she'd be interested to see them because she's so red-hot on finding her roots. Her own great-grandmother was a Pitcher, she told me, though she hasn't yet figured out just how we're connected. Assuming we are, that is. I'm not altogether sure I want us to be, if you care to hear the plain truth. Any woman who keeps her gloves on while she's eating a buttered scone is just too cussed refined for my simple tastes."

"She didna!"

"I'll bet you she did," said Dittany, never one to hang back when she had a perfectly legitimate excuse to come forward. "She wore them this noontime at the Cozy Corner, eating soup. Though actually Mrs. Melloe wasn't so much eating her soup as complaining about it and waving her spoon at the waitress, who was in no mood to be spooned at, as who could blame her? Anyway, the gloves were navy blue to match her shoes, stockings, hat, and handbag. I couldn't see her slip. Mrs. Melloe does have lovely clothes, I must say. Today she had on a blue flowered shirtwaist with—oh, all right, Sergeant, you can quit glaring at me and get on with the grilling. I just thought Margaret would enjoy hearing about the outfit."

"Nae doot." Sergeant MacVicar's tone implied that Dittany was growing more like her mother every day, though this time he didn't come straight out and say so. "Noo then, Minerva Oakes, what did you do with yon gaiters after you'd shown them to Mrs. Melloe?"

"I took them back to the attic and put them in a wicker trunk with some other things of Granny Pitcher's, down at the bottom under her archery skirt and her wedding petticoat."

"And who knew you kept your granny's clothes in yon wicker trunk?"

"Why, nobody. I'd had them put away in different boxes and whatnot, but while I was straightening around up there, I got the bright idea of putting them all together in the wicker trunk. So I took everything else out of the trunk and repacked it with Granny's things and wrote out a list and stuck it inside the lid so that when the time comes to settle my estate, my children will know whose they were and not go tossing them out or selling them to an antique dealer. And I must say I'm none too happy about the way everything got slung around the floor, nor do I appreciate what happened to Granny's gaiter. Do you think there's any hope of finding the other one, Sergeant?"

"We can always hope, Minerva. Were you here all last evening?"

"Well no, as a matter of fact, I wasn't. I dropped over to Hazel Munson's for a few minutes to return a cake plate of hers that I'd been forgetting to take back, what with the excitement about the community garden and all. We got to talking, you know how you do. And it was a lovely night and Hazel's boys were out and Roger was down at the firehouse playing cribbage, so we thought we'd take a little stroll. We stopped for a while to listen to the madrigal singers rehearsing for the concert, which is going to be just lovely, then there was that big ruckus at the inn. What with one thing and another, I suppose I was gone a good part of the evening, though I hadn't meant to be."

"Did you lock your door as you left the house?"

"Come to think of it, I don't suppose I did. I'd only intended to be gone those few minutes, you see. And you know how it's been all these years, nobody ever thought to lock a door till Andy McNaster snatched the old Hendryx place and turned it into a honky-tonk. After Andy reformed, the inn got to be a really nice place, but since that Hedrick Snarf came along, it seems to be no more than a den of iniquity. Is it true that all those so-called swells last night were really a bunch of crooks?"

"Oh aye, we made quite a lucky haul." Sergeant MacVicar was trying to appear humble but he had so little to be humble about that he missed his mark by a long shot. "For a while it was standing room only at the Scottsbeck jail. And noo I must be off in search of your stolen property. By your leave, I'll take yon remaining gaiter with me so that my men will know what to look for."

"Yes, of course."

"And, Dittany, I think I must also borrow Deputy Monk and Ethel."

"You're taking Hiram Jellyby's story about the purple-gaitered highwayman seriously, then?"

"Let us say that I am taking seriously the suspeecion that somebody else is trying to make use of the late Mr. Jellyby's story for reasons that can thus far only be conjectured but must be looked into. Not wishing to disappoint either you or my wife, Dittany lass, I fear Margaret will not be available to mind yon wee bairns so that you can join the hunt."

"If you wanted to bring them over here—" Minerva offered with no great enthusiasm.

"Oh no, I wouldn't think of it," Dittany assured her.

"You'd better get out your slingshot and stand guard by the attic stairs in case that ornery coyote comes back for Winona's wedding petticoat. I expect Zilla would be glad to keep you company."

"I doubt it. Zilla's got her hands full shooing Hiram Jellyby away from the dandelion wine crock. A ghost in your woodshed's bad enough, but that pie-eyed old mule skinner's something else again. I told Zilla she'd better get Mr. Pennyfeather over to exorcise Hiram before he conjures up his mule team and has them stomping around out there with him, but she says she feels funny asking."

"You can hardly blame her for that," said Dittany. "Exorcism's not a very kind thing to do to a ghost who's just trying to be sociable."

"Oh, I suppose you're right. Frankly, I think Zilla kind of likes having Hiram around because he reminds her a little of Michael Trott. You're not old enough to have remembered Michael, Dittany, and I can't say you've missed much, though I hope you won't tell Zilla I said so. She's over at Hunnikers' Field just now. She figured there might be a few hopefuls out digging again and one of us had better show up, just in case. There's the gaiter, Sergeant. I'd be grateful if you'd keep it in this bag so that it won't get mauled around any worse than it's already been. Maybe I'm being foolish, but those gaiters mean a lot to me."

Sergeant MacVicar said he understood how Minerva felt, wrote her an official receipt on a leaf out of her grocery pad, and took his leave with the remaining artifact tucked under his arm. Dittany walked along beside him, oddly silent. Until Minerva mentioned digging just now, she'd entirely forgotten Hiram's tale about Charlie Henbit's having been a dowser and her own promise to try her hand at witching up that trunkful of gold pieces. Whatever had made her say she would? All she knew about dowsing was from watching Pollicot James walk back and forth with that little contraption of assorted metals held out in front of him.

One thing sure, Dittany Henbit Monk was not about to make a fool of herself in front of whoever might be out there now. She wondered whether Hiram's eyeballs were up to another after-dark treasure hunt. She'd like to ask Osbert, but it didn't look as though she was going to get the chance since Sergeant MacVicar was coming in with her.

Osbert greeted them both like a pair of long-lost cousins. "Swiveling sidewinders, am I glad you've shown up! I've had an epiphany."

"Really?" said Dittany. "Where did you put it?"

"Nowhere, yet, but I'm—well, the thing of it is, I've been referring to the females in the herd that's getting poached by the bad guys as lady elk. 'Female' sounds too coldly biological and 'she-elk' a trifle peremptory, don't you think? But then 'lady elk' began to strike me as too drawing-roomish for a split-hooved ruminant who's married to a galloping hat rack. So then it occurred to me that 'cow elk' might be the appropriate term. As in 'cow moose,' you know. And then all of a sudden it struck me about the cow."

"As it naturally would." Dittany was not unused to Osbert's epiphanies. "When you say 'the cow,' are you referring to cows in general, cows as the significant others of bulls, or one specific cow?"

"That's what I love about you, dear, you're so brilliantly logical. The specific cow I have in mind is the cow who trampled the bank clerk to death in an unexplained fit of pique."

"Oh, of course. Silly of me not to have realized. What about that cow, darling?"

"Well, as you know, dairy cows aren't precisely my field. But I couldn't recall Zane Grey's ever mentioning anything about a cow trampling its milker to death for what was apparently no good reason, so I got to thinking about that bank guard's cow. And the more I thought, the odder it got. So what I'm getting at is, how would you feel about calling up the RCMP, Chief, and asking them if they know what happened to that cow, and whether they ever found out what made her turn so belligerent all of a sudden?"

"M'ph. I was about to ask you, Deputy Monk, to assist in a hunt for that purple gaiter of which Mrs. Oakes was robbed last night. Howsomever, if you feel strongly that the late bank clerk's cow is in any way germane to the problem at hand, I will authorize you to make the call yourself whilst I round up a posse."

"Ormerod Burlson's better than I am at finding things."

"Officer Burlson lacks your quickness of perception. Pairchance you may care to join the hunt once your curiosity about yon cow is satisfied?"

"Oh, yes, sure. Thanks, Chief. Would you know the RCMP's phone number offhand?"

It went without saying that Sergeant MacVicar did. He suggested that Osbert ask to be connected with Constable Alexander MacVicar, Corporal Andrew MacVicar, or Sergeant Archibald MacVicar, depending on which of his three sons might be available at the moment, and explain to them that the matter was urgent. He would leave it to Deputy Monk to think of a reasonable excuse for chasing down information about an animal that had probably been transmigrated into dog food eight years ago.

Sergeant MacVicar didn't add this last thought aloud because he'd learned through experience to respect Deputy Monk's hunches even when they popped up at inconvenient times. He went off to assemble his posse, Osbert rushed to the telephone. Dittany, left alone with her dilemma, decided she might as well wash a load of diapers. She'd barely got the detergent measured out when Osbert stuck his head down the cellar stairway.

"I'm off, dear. Charlie Evans is flying me down to Kingston in the crop-dusting plane and Andrew MacVicar's arranged for a police car to meet me at the airport. I should be home by suppertime."

"*Hasta la vista.*"

What else could she say? Time was when Dittany would have crowded happily into that small and smelly airplane and flown into the blue with her husband. Now she could only wait and hope the cow had seen the error of its ways. The beast must still be alive, at any rate, or Osbert wouldn't be dashing off like this. Darn it, why did men have all the epiphanies and women get stuck with the laundry?

As Dittany added the softening agent that was supposed to be kinder to infant bums than any other leading softening agent, her eye drifted to the heavy overhead beams. Gramp Henbit had been a great one for driving nails into those beams and hanging things on them, such as bunches of rusty keys that didn't unlock anything and strange little gadgets for doing things that probably didn't need doing and wouldn't have got done even if a person ever found out what they were intended to do. Dittany felt about Gramp's artifacts much as Minerva Oakes felt about Winona Pitcher's purple gaiters: they weren't good for much but she wouldn't part with them for the world. Though she would, she promised herself, dust down some of the cobwebs they'd collected. As soon as she got around to it.

And why not now? Dittany nipped up the stairs to check on the twins, they seemed happy enough in their basket. She pinned an old towel around the kitchen broom, another around her hair, and went back to antagonize the current generation of spiders.

It was rather fun swiping along the beams, being careful of Gramp's gadgets, thinking fond thoughts of the old man and of the hours he and his small granddaughter had spent down here together. Every one of these nails had a story dangling from it, Dittany must try to remember them all and tell them again when the twins were old enough to understand. Now what in the world was this old thing? It looked like a giant wishbone, she took it down from its nail and burst out laughing.

The object was indeed a wishbone, taken from the biggest turkey ever raised in Lobelia Falls and served years ago at the town's centennial celebration. There hadn't been an oven big enough to hold a bird that size; they'd had to dig a fire pit lined with hot stones and bake the huge turkey for many hours before it could be dug up and served. Gramp had been given the honor of carving, he'd got enough meat off the carcass to feed everybody in town except himself. Not to be left out, he'd carefully saved the wishbone, dried and gilded it, and hung it on his front door at Christmastime with a sprig of holly and a red ribbon bow. After using it thus for a few years, he'd begun to worry about what the elements might be doing to the historic bone and left it hanging in the cellar.

Perhaps it should be over at the Architrave, Dittany thought fleetingly, she wondered how Mr. Glunck would react to a turkey wishbone over a foot long and big around as a broom handle. She took it down and blew the dust off. The gilding Gramp had put on still showed, in spots. On impulse, she took the two ends in her hands and held the bone out in front of her the way Pollicot James had held his divining rod. After its long drying out, the bone wasn't so heavy as she'd expected; somehow it had a right feel to it. She washed it off under the faucet in the soapstone laundry sink and carried it upstairs.

There was plenty of gold in the house. Besides Dittany's own wedding ring, there were the rings Daddy had given Mum that she was keeping for Annie. There were cuff links and collar studs, bar pins and stickpins, Gramp Henbit's gold watch on a heavy gold chain with a gold nugget on it that was all the gold Gramp's father had ever got out of a gold mine he'd bought shares in. Having cleaned and polished the wishbone as best she could, Dittany selected a pair of gold filigree cuff links and lashed them securely to the tip of the wishbone with heavy button thread. Now all she could do was try her luck and hope for the best. If only Osbert would get home in time to mind the kids, and if only Hiram Jellyby would lend her his eyeballs!

CHAPTER
18

"*M*y brother never really understood Mossy."

The sister of the late bank clerk was a shortish, roundish woman with an abundance of curly gray hair and a motherly expression. Her name was Mildred Orser and she was very glad to see Deputy Monk because she felt it was high time somebody listened to Mossy's side of the story.

"Mossy's a lovely cow, but she doesn't like to be hurried. You can't blame a cow for wanting to march to the drummer she hears, is how I look at it. But Wilberforce couldn't see that, he'd just march out to the barn with his pink plastic bucket and expect her to stand and deliver. That's no way to treat a cow. What I do is, I sing to Mossy awhile and tell her what pretty eyes she has, and maybe give her a carrot or an apple. Just a little extra something to show her I really care, you know. These things count, with a cow."

"I'm sure they do," said Osbert, although he wasn't sure at all and didn't much care for the way Mossy was switching her tail and pawing the ground.

"And of course I'm always careful to rub a little Bag

Balm into my hands before I start to milk, and to keep my nails well manicured. Can you imagine a more off-putting thing for a cow than having to entrust her udder to rough, ill-tended hands? I'm afraid Wilberforce wasn't always so considerate in that respect as he might have been."

"On the other hand, Mossy wasn't all that considerate of Wilberforce," Osbert pointed out. "Or so I gather from the coroner's report."

"Oh, that horrid coroner's report!" Mildred Orser shook her gray curls in righteous indignation. "I did think of suing for slander on Mossy's behalf, but my lawyer advised against it. After all, as he pointed out, our great goal had already been achieved; I'd managed to save her life. Do you know, those beastly policemen were all set to gun Mossy down as if she'd been some great big vicious monster? I just flung myself in front of her and told them straight out, 'If you're going to shoot Mossy,' I said, 'you'll have to shoot me first. This cow,' I said, 'is the innocent victim of some evildoer's foul machination.' And I was right!"

"How so, Mrs. Orser?"

"Well, not to be blowing my own horn, but what I did was, I made the policemen grant Mossy a reprieve until we could get the vet to come and look her over. As I'd already suspected, and as the vet's examination confirmed, the inside of her poor mouth was all blistered and her breath smelled funny. So that got Mossy another reprieve until the next morning at milking time when, sure enough, her milk turned out to be positively reeking with horse liniment."

"Holy cow!" cried Osbert, "you mean your brother had been dumb enough to—oh, sorry. I shouldn't speak disrespectfully of the stomped."

"Oh, that's quite all right, Deputy Monk. I must confess that I was pretty miffed with Wilberforce at the time, myself, mangled though he was. But then I got to thinking, out there alone in the barn all night with poor, dear Mossy. I didn't dare leave her alone for a second, you know, I was so afraid those bloodthirsty policemen would sneak back and effect her demise with a dart gun or some other nefarious device. They'd been quite sniffy with me, you know, they'd thought I was acting like a hysterical old kook. It was a triumphant moment for me, I can tell you, when that liniment turned up in the milk. After that, of course, they hadn't a leg to stand on and they knew it. I assumed legal custody of Mossy and we've been the best of pals ever since. Haven't we, Mossy Possy."

"But whatever possessed your brother to feed horse liniment to a cow? Aside from the fact that it wasn't very appropriate, didn't he know such embrocations are intended for external use only?"

"Precisely my point, Deputy Monk. That's what I asked myself, that awful night alone in the barn with Mossy, feeding her ice cubes to ease the pain of the blisters in her mouth. Yes, Wilberforce did know that liniment isn't to be taken internally. He'd been an athlete in his youth—in fact he'd held the county egg-and-spoon championship two years in succession—and these things take their toll later on in life. You know how it is. Or perhaps you don't, since you're still young enough to think it won't happen to you, which I certainly hope it won't."

"Thank you, Mrs. Orser."

"Not at all, Mr. Monk. Anyway, Wilberforce used to apply liniment to his trick knee every night, regular as clockwork, before going to bed. But his was people liniment, not like the horse liniment that had been given to Mossy."

"This was established as a solid fact?"

"Oh yes. Aside from the vet's report, the bottle turned up in the trash after I'd forced those silly policemen to see the error of their ways, not that I ever got any thanks for putting them straight. But there was no way to prove it hadn't been Wilberforce himself who'd given Mossy the liniment, thus bringing about his own demise. It was all water over the dam by then anyway, so I just had to let the whole thing drop. I couldn't save my brother, but at least I was able to rescue Mossy, and frankly I find her the more congenial of the two. Wilberforce was inclined to be testy, you know."

"Actually, I hadn't known," said Osbert. "Do you think your brother's testiness contributed to his fatal misunderstanding with Mossy?"

"Oh, no doubt whatsoever, in my mind. Wilberforce never stopped to consider that there might be two sides to any question. It was his way or no way, and of course that's not how to approach a cow with a sensitive nature. I'm sure Mossy didn't mean to stomp so hard, but what was a poor cow to do when she had a mouthful of horrible blisters and goodness knows how many more down in her tum-tum? Cows have four stomachs, you know. Can you picture yourself stuck with four awful tummyaches, all at the same time?"

"Well, not easily," Osbert admitted, "but I can see what you mean. That must have been a terrible position for Mossy to be in."

"There, Mossy, you see? Deputy Monk understands, even if silly old Wilberforce didn't."

Mildred Orser rubbed her cheek against the cow's glossy brown neck. Mossy reciprocated the caress by wiping her nose on Mrs. Orser's pink-and-white gingham blouse. At least it looked to Osbert as if she was wiping her nose, but perhaps Mossy had some loftier purpose in mind. He cleared his throat.

"I don't like to be reopening old wounds, Mrs. Orser, but do you think we could get a clearer picture of what actually happened that night? You hadn't happened to see anybody hanging around the barn during the afternoon?"

"No, not a soul. But then I wouldn't have, you see; it

was my day to volunteer at the fish farm. I was up to my ears in baby trout till about four o'clock, then I had to do a little grocery shopping on the way home and then, you know how it is, I just wanted to get into something comfortable and put my feet up."

"You didn't stop to say hello to Mossy?"

"Oh no, I never did, not around milking time. She was still Wilberforce's cow then, you see, he didn't take kindly to what he looked upon as interference. I had to be very circumspect."

"So you don't know who fed her the liniment. But you're quite sure Wilberforce wouldn't have done so? Even if somebody had told him that was the right thing to do?"

"Oh, yes, I'm sure. To begin with, Mossy hadn't been sick, so he'd have had no occasion to give her any medication. Furthermore, Wilberforce wouldn't have taken advice from anybody, not even Queen Elizabeth, although he did think very highly of Her Majesty, as do we all. I suppose if Her Majesty had supplied the liniment herself, free of charge, he might have been willing to give it a go, but she'd have known better in the first place, being a sensible woman and fond of animals. Furthermore, she's far too busy with affairs of state to have bothered herself with the crotchets of Wilberforce Woodiwiss. Though I'm sure she'd enjoy meeting Mossy, should the occasion ever arise."

"One never knows," said Osbert. "Now, just to make sure I've got everything clear in my mind, you live in this house here, which is to say the blue one. Your brother lived in that house over there, namely the green one, with the barn in between."

"Yes, that's right. Wilberforce never married. He lived with Mother in the green house, which is the house we both grew up in, until she died, then he bought Mossy because he'd always wanted a cow and Mother had been against his having one. After Frank—my husband—and I got married, we lived in Kingston for a while. Frank worked at a miniature golf course, but there didn't seem to be much future in it, so he got this wonderful job as a tour guide on a tramp steamer that takes people on cruises to faraway places with strange-sounding names. Of course this means he has to be away a lot; he decided it would be better if I lived near my family, so I took over the blue house, which had been my aunt Bertha's while we were growing up. Aunt Bertha was always fond of Frank. He's very popular with the passengers and also plays the flageolet quite capably. He's going to come ashore and settle down, though, now that we've inherited Mossy, because a cow needs a cowherd. Anyhow, there it is."

There what was? Osbert was still feeling a communication gap, he tried a direct question. "So in fact you were in your own house relaxing at the time Mossy attacked your brother?"

"I prefer not to use the word *attacked*, Deputy Monk. As I see it, Wilberforce merely happened to be standing in the way when Mossy, goaded to desperation by the pain in her blistered mouth and the effect of the liniment on her intricate digestive system, reared up and began flailing about with her hooves."

"How do you know she reared and flailed, Mrs. Orser? Could you see her from where you were?"

"I was alerted by wild outcries, some of them Mossy's and some, I believe, Wilberforce's. It was hard to tell which were whose. By the time I'd zipped up my housecoat and rushed over to the barn, Wilberforce was on the floor with his head smashed in and this little gold whistle lying beside him. It's ruined, I'm afraid, Mossy must have trampled it. She was still rearing and flailing, but not all that vigorously. Even then she was no heifer, you know; she tired rather quickly. I got her into her stall and phoned the police, little knowing what a stupid fuss they were going to make. But we've been through all that."

"Yes, now, about this gold whistle, were you surprised to see it there?"

"Not particularly. I assumed Wilberforce had meant to blow it in an attempt to summon help."

"Did he usually blow on his gold whistle when he needed help?"

"I really have no way to answer that. It was so unlike Wilberforce to admit being in a situation he couldn't cope with by himself."

"But this was his whistle?"

"Whose else could it have been? Keep it if you want it. I haven't the heart to throw it out, but it reminds me too much of poor Mossy's terrible suffering. And Wilberforce's too, of course," she added as an afterthought.

Osbert thanked her and pocketed the mangled artifact. "Where do you think the horse liniment came from?"

"Why, I suppose somebody must have brought it. Somebody who owned a horse, wouldn't you think?"

"But why bring horse liniment to a cow barn?"

"You know, Deputy Monk, that's a very good question. Perhaps because they couldn't find any cow liniment, at least I've never seen any. Or perhaps because they knew horse liniment would disagree with a cow, as indeed it did. But what has all this to do with Wilberforce's gold whistle? If it was in fact his, now that I think about it. I can see Wilberforce wanting to own a gold whistle, but I can't see him going out and buying one."

"Then isn't it possible that the whistle was dropped by the person who fed Mossy the liniment? Would you happen to know of anybody else who carried a gold whistle?"

"Do you mean anybody now living?"

"Well, I suppose so." This was a question Osbert hadn't expected. "Anybody who was living at the time of your brother's—ah—misfortune, anyway."

"Oh, too bad!" cried Mrs. Orser. "If you'd said anybody who'd been living until slightly less than a week before my brother's sad demise, I'd have had the answer right on the tip of my tongue. As it is, I'm afraid I'll just have to say no."

"But if you'd been able to say yes, whom would you have named?"

"Why, Mr. Cottle, of course."

"Mr. Cottle being—"

"My brother's late employer. The bank president who, as you may recall, was so regrettably kidnapped and murdered."

"Mr. Cottle had owned a gold whistle? This couldn't have been the one you found after Mossy—uh—"

"Oh, no. Mr. Cottle was a nice enough man, but he wouldn't have given away his gold whistle. With him it wasn't just the whistle, you see, it was gold everything. Mr. Cottle had a positive passion for gold jewelry and trinkets. All perfectly suited to a man in his position, of course. He had this lovely gold watch about the size of a turnip, on a very striking gold watch chain strung across his tummy with various objects hanging from it, all pure gold. Besides the gold whistle, there were a couple of big round seals, Mr. Cottle called them, and a gold toothpick in a little gold case that had been his great-grandfather's, and a timberwolf's tooth with a gold filling and a ring in the top. To hang it from the chain you know. And a gold nugget carved into the shape of a beetle, and a gold pencil and a gold cigar cutter that had a steel nipper because of course gold won't cut anything."

"That must have bothered him a little," said Osbert.

"Oh, I suppose it did, but he never let on. Wilberforce said Mr. Cottle had never been one to complain about little things, which is more than could be said for Wilberforce, poor fellow. Did I mention the twenty-dollar gold piece? Wilberforce said they could always tell when Mr. Cottle was coming because they could hear him tinkling. The tellers used to sing 'Jingle Bells' under their breath."

"Did he have a snowy white beard?" Osbert asked hopefully.

Mrs. Orser giggled. "No, isn't it a pity? As a matter of fact, Mr. Cottle was practically hairless. I used to see him occasionally myself. At the bank, you know, Frank and I had our account there. Of course we switched over after the tragedy because Frank didn't like me going into a bank where people got tied up and lugged away and had their fingers cut off. Frank is quite ferociously protective of me when he can find the time. He brought me the cutest little Malay kris on his last trip home, and he's promised me some poisoned arrows to keep in a jar on the mantelpiece because one never knows. But getting back to Mr. Cottle, he did have rather attractive eyebrows but his head was completely bald except for a little gray fuzz behind the ears and his skin was as pink as a baby's. He looked as if he'd never had to shave in his life."

"Lucky him."

Osbert ran a fingertip over his own by now somewhat raspy chin and wondered if Charlie Evans happened to keep a spare razor in the crop-dusting plane. It would be a shame to spoil the family reunion to which he was eagerly looking forward by having his loved ones break out into howls of anguish when he tried to kiss them. Not that they ever had so far, but a responsible husband and father had to consider these things.

As Osbert considered, Mrs. Orser resumed her inventory. Mr. Cottle had been what might be called a portly man, he'd always left his suit coat unbuttoned so that his watch chain could be shown off to best effect. He'd affected an old-fashioned gold pince nez on a thin gold chain attached to a gold button pinned to his left lapel. He'd worn a heavy gold wedding band and a gold signet ring set with a big garnet, and a gold stickpin with a smaller garnet in his tie. Mrs. Orser rather thought Mr. Cottle had had a few gold fillings in his teeth but could not be certain about that as he and she hadn't been on sufficiently familiar terms.

"Oh, and his watch chain also had a little gold penknife on it that he used to sharpen pencils with, Wilberforce said. Not that he ever used a wooden pencil because he had his gold one. Wilberforce thought Mr. Cottle just enjoyed sharpening pencils so that he could show off his gold knife. Wilberforce could be catty sometimes. I know it's women who are supposed to be catty, but I'm sure that if you went around counting, you'd find there are quite as many he-cats as she-cats. If not more."

"Truer words were never spoken, Mrs. Orser. Well, this has been extremely helpful and I thank you for giving me your time. Nice meeting you, Mossy."

Osbert half expected Mossy to offer him her hoof but she didn't, so he said good-bye and got back into the police car with the constable who'd been inconspicuously taking notes of the conversation, with special reference to the enigmatic trinket Mrs. Orser had found in the barn after her brother's tragic and still not wholly explained death. It was interesting about that whistle. Interesting too about the kidnapped banker's multipurpose watch chain. That jingling adornment made Osbert think of something, something he'd heard about quite recently but couldn't pin down at the moment. It would come to him, like as not, sooner or later.

CHAPTER
19

"*D*arling, you're home!"

"Yes, dear. I did say I would be, you know." Osbert gave his wife a few extra kisses to make sure she got the message loud and clear. "Too bad you weren't along on the ride, you'd have enjoyed meeting Mossy. She's the cow who inadvertently effected the demise of the bank watchman, as you may recall. Her current owner made it clear that Mossy was more sinned against than sinning."

"I'm glad to hear it," said Dittany. "Have you had anything to eat?"

"Nope. Charlie Evans did suggest that as we passed over Oshawa we might parachute down for a pizza, but I was anxious to get home. Charlie's writing an epic poem about crop-dusting, you'll be interested to know, though right now he's stuck on a rhyme for insectivora."

"Couldn't he switch to 'bugs'?"

"I did raise the suggestion, as a matter of fact, but Charlie didn't seem to feel 'bugs' was epical enough. How about if I pour us each a modest tot of sherry to cut the phlegm?"

"Why not? After all, I have miles to go before I sleep."

"You do?" Osbert's eyes narrowed. This was not the homecoming he had envisioned. "How many miles?"

"As many as it takes, my love. You do remember that tonight's the night I dowse for the gold. I've got my divining rod all shined up and ready to dip. Want to see?"

"But of course, my beauty of the buttes." Osbert leaned forward with polite interest, then reared back like a spooked mustang. "Great galloping garter snakes, is that a divining rod?"

"This is it," Dittany confirmed. "Rather impressive, don't you think?"

"Impressive is hardly the word. Where the heck did you get that mass of ossification? Off a pterodactyl?"

"It's just a turkey wishbone, silly. Formerly the property, I grant you, of a very large turkey. Those are the cuff links you inherited from your great-uncle Bedivere, the one your mother never liked. You don't mind using them, do you?"

"Nope. Us old cowhands don't go in much for gold cuff links out here on the range, where men are men and women are treasured for their ability to lug a fifty-pound wishbone around for hours on end without buckling at the knees. When were you planning to dowse?"

"I suppose that will have to depend on how long it takes Hiram Jellyby to get his eyeballs charged up. So many things seem to depend on Hiram lately. It's strange what a difference he's made in the aura around here. Do you suppose we'll ever get back to normal?"

Osbert removed the bedizened wishbone from his wife's grasp and took both her hands firmly in his own. "Darling, do you recall the day we first met?"

"Of course," said Dittany. "It was at the bake sale, when the billygoat got up on the bandstand and ate your belt. That was right after John Architrave got murdered and we were trying to save the Enchanted Mountain for the spotted pipsissewa."*

"My point precisely. Normal is simply not an appli-

* The Grub-and-Stakers Move a Mountain

cable word in Lobelia Falls. Most people, according to the late Ralph Waldo Emerson, live lives of quiet desperation. Show me one inhabitant of this town who's living a life of quiet desperation and I'll show you the UFO he flew in on."

"I see the force of your argument, dear. Never having lived anywhere else, I have no real basis for comparison, but I suppose we do tend to have rather more things going on here at any given moment than they have in Scottsbeck or Lammergen. Or Toronto or Montreal or New York or London or any of those other quaint backwaters. Will you mind staying with the children while I dowse?"

"What?" yowled Osbert. "Me sit here sucking my thumb and nursing my gout while you brave the impenetrable wilderness with nothing but an oversized turkey bone and a pair of disembodied eyeballs for protection?"

"I expect Zilla wouldn't mind coming along to keep Hiram company," Dittany temporized.

"Zilla is not your lawfully wedded husband, madam!"

"You're quite right, dear, she isn't," Dittany agreed willingly enough. "Nor, I must say, is it at all likely that she ever would have been or have wished to be. However, you have to admit that Zilla could be a formidable adversary if we should happen to be attacked by gold rustlers, assuming there's actually any gold out there to be rustled, which we should know fairly soon unless this wishbone lets us down. Dearest, you've had a long and smelly trip in that poky little plane of Charlie's, and interviewed the cow and all; don't you think you should just settle down quietly here at home with the children and catch up on your bonding?"

"In a word, dear, no. Why can't we just bundle the tads into their carriage and trundle them along to the scene of the action?"

"And expose their delicate little lungs to the night air?"

Rennie, perhaps feeling left out of the conversation, chose that moment to demonstrate what a pair of delicate little lungs could do when called upon for a bravura performance. Annie was quick to follow suit. Dittany began to think perhaps she'd been a trifle overprotective of the twins. They did own a large supply of assorted carriage robes and buntings, not to mention the multitude of booties, bonnets, leggings, sweaters, and other tiny garments that hadn't even been worn yet and would soon be outgrown if they didn't get cracking; perhaps it was time for the wee ones to begin enjoying the local night life. She pacified them with infant food of a suitable nature, finished her sherry, and was preparing to fortify the inner woman for the evening's adventure when who should show up but Zilla and a misty something with a faint, far-off flavor of ancient mule that could only be Hiram Jellyby.

"Well, the very people we were hoping to see," Dittany said, although in fact Hiram was so far more a state of mind than a viewable object. "What can I get you, Mr. Jellyby?"

"What you drinkin'?"

"Sherry, actually. Want some?"

"I dunno. It don't have none o' them vitamin things in it that Zilla's always gassin' about?"

"No, none at all. Sherry's just plain grape squeezings fortified with a little brandy."

"Oh. Well then, hell. Go ahead, slide the bottle over this way an' gimme a shot at the emanations. An' don't you go glarin' at me like that, Zilla. Cripes, Miz Monk, I never seen such a woman for glarin', her an' that she-cougar she's got helpin' her run the place. Them two, they'll set there lashin' their tails an' glarin' at me as if I was a rabbit they was fixin' to have for supper. If I had any nerves left, I'd be twitchin' like a toad eatin' lightnin'."

"And if you had any brains left," snapped Zilla, "you'd keep your cussed old beak out of that sherry bottle. You've already been sniffing half the day at my dandelion wine crock, and don't think I don't know it. You've got one eye bright orange and the other one striped like the Union Jack."

"Ain't every ha'nt could o' done it," Hiram replied complacently. "Gimme another sniff o' that sherry, Miz Monk, an' I'll show you fireworks like you never seen before."

"Just call me Dittany, everybody else does. You'd better hold back on the voltage, though, Hiram. We may need some extra illumination out at Hunnikers' Field tonight. I'm counting on you to help me catch Charlie Henbit's emanations when I try to dowse."

"Ain't never let you down yet, have I?"

"No, but this is the first time I've had occasion to ask you for a favor. Not that you wouldn't have granted it willingly, I'm sure."

"I ain't so dang-fired certain of that."

Maybe sherry was not Hiram's tipple. It seemed to be putting him in a mood that some of Osbert's characters, adhering to the tradition of the sagebrush intelligentsia, would unhesitatingly have described as ornery. He spurned the supper Dittany offered him, claiming that he could see vitamins crawling all over the plate and giving the others an uneasy feeling that maybe he was right. He took exception to including the babies in the expedition, even though nobody wanted to stay home and babysit them so there was really nothing the Monks could do except take them along. He claimed he didn't like the way Ethel was staring at him and threatened to put a hex on her if she didn't cut it out, although he obviously had not the faintest notion of how to go about hexing any creature great or small.

Under heavy grilling from Zilla, whose shamanistic ancestry naturally gave her the edge, Hiram was forced to admit that he'd probably have failed of his purpose anyway since nothing about hexes had been listed against his name in the Akashic Record. Having to knuckle under didn't make the phantom's temper any sweeter. All in all, it was a grumpy little troupe who finally set out for Hunnikers' Field with Osbert pushing the twin-filled pram, Ethel clutching the diaper bag in her teeth, Dittany toting her as yet untried divining rod, and Zilla carrying a grudge against Hiram.

Letting a deceased mule skinner make free with the sherry bottle had been a terrible mistake, Dittany could see that now. Hiram had sniffed up so many emanations that he couldn't even glide straight. He kept reeling into first one, then another member of the party. Not that any of them felt anything more than a coolish, dampish whiff like the momentary opening of a refrigerator door, but all the same it was disconcerting. Furthermore, those variegated eyeballs, which they'd hoped to depend on for illumination, kept flickering off and on, changing color, and spinning around like pinwheels.

This was not, Dittany couldn't help feeling, the most auspicious way to be embarking on her potential new career as a dowser. She wished they'd thought to bring a kerosene lantern. Charlie Henbit would almost certainly have brought along a kerosene lantern, assuming he ever went out dowsing after dark. Maybe she'd been silly to feel self-conscious about making her debut in the daytime. What would it have mattered if she'd gathered an audience of snickering onlookers? At least she wouldn't now be running the risk of falling into one or another of those gaping tiger pits with which Hunnikers' Field was now pretty copiously pocked.

But here they were and the moment of truth was at hand. Osbert parked the baby carriage well away from any of the pits and made sure the safety brake was truly and duly applied. Ethel took up her Noble Dog stance beside the carriage with the diaper bag set squarely between her front paws, ready to be snatched up and put to use should an emergency occur, as it almost certainly would if that bedizened wishbone didn't produce results quite soon. All was prepared; there was no longer any room for procrastination. Dittany took the two ends of her improvised divining rod in her hands and looked around.

"Where shall I start?"

"Let the bone tell you," said Zilla.

"It doesn't seem to want to."

"Then just begin. Start walking. Hiram, for Pete's sake can't you tag along and give her some light without falling all over yourself?"

"Nope."

Hiram proved his point by disappearing into one of the deeper pits and beginning to sing "Buffalo Gals." Dittany shrugged, looked up at the rather wan and puny moon that appeared to be all the help she was going to get, and stepped forward.

It wasn't so bad once she got going. The air was cool and fresh, her eyes were accustomed to the darkness by now, the moon kindly refrained from ducking behind any of the wisps of cloud that were skittering overhead. After a few minutes, Dittany began to feel as if the bone was gently pulling her along in some occult way. She also began to sense a presence hereabout that she couldn't account for, maybe even more than one. It was hard to sort out the emanations with Hiram emitting his raucous outcries from the bottom of the pit, Osbert sprinting back and forth between his wife and his babies at a little less than the speed of light to make sure none of them was in immediate need of succor, Ethel growling at Osbert to quit being so dithery, and Zilla gliding stealthily from one alder bush to another, guarding the periphery with her hatchet at the ready.

Dittany had not realized Zilla was bringing her hatchet. She must have parked it outside the door when she and Hiram dropped over to the Monks' and picked it up when they left for the field. Well, why not? A hatchet was not an inappropriate weapon out here, it shouldn't jar the vibrations too badly. The neophyte dowser strode on, trying to emulate the steady rhythm Pollicot James had set for himself, striving to keep the business end of the wishbone level in relation to the terrain, which was not easy as the turkey who'd originally owned the bone had been a curvaceous fowl and the bone had probably warped a little more in the long drying-out process.

Osbert's mother's uncle's cuff links kept making a gentle tinkling sound. They reminded Dittany of the description Osbert had passed on from Mrs. Orser of the late bank president's melodious watch chain, and also of the way Tryphosa Melloe's various accoutrements had clanked together when she'd beckoned imperiously to that poor, overworked waitress at the Cozy Corner Café.

Dittany wished she hadn't thought of the demised bank president. She couldn't help wondering whether those vague emanations she was feeling might be Mr. Cottle's revenant spirit, out hunting for the finger that his cruel kidnappers had lopped off. She hoped not, she would much prefer to think he'd managed to find out where his wife had had the amputated digit interred, climbed in with it, and was by now resting in peace under the expensive tombstone that Mrs. Cottle had no doubt caused to be erected.

Her wrists were starting to ache from her efforts to control the bone, she paused in her stride to ease them for a moment. By rights, the cuff links' jingle ought to have stopped as soon as she did. Nevertheless, Dittany could have sworn that she still heard tinkling, faint as the fairy chimes she'd been wont as a tot to imagine at the bottom of the garden.

No, this was no imagining, that was a different tinkle. She could feel the fine hairs on the back of her neck beginning to prickle, she'd better not stand here mooning or she'd scare herself into a fit. She strode out with all the bravery she could muster, which wasn't much. And the bone dipped!

"Osbert, come quick! It's doing it!"

"It's what?" Osbert came galloping across the field faster than a startled elk. "What happened?"

"It did it! It's tugging, it won't straighten up. Feel."

"Hobbled horntoads, you're right! I've got the shovel, just let me—could you scooch over just a—there, I've got the point into the ground. Now I think the bone will let you stand aside, darling. Hiram, could you levitate yourself out of that hole and shine your eyes this way? I think we may have found your gold."

By this time, Hiram had sung himself free of his sulks and got his eyeballs under reasonable control, though the light they emitted was an unappealing mustard color with faint streaks of red. He rose from the hole with no more than a reasonable amount of cussing and complaining, and glided in a fairly straight line to the spot where Osbert had begun to dig.

"Ayup. I can feel the spring bubblin' through where the soles o' my feet would be if they was. This is the place, all right. Keep diggin', bub."

Was it more fairies at the bottom of the garden, or had Dittany really heard an intake of breath somewhere off among the tiger pits? "Osbert," she whispered, "I think there's somebody out here."

"Yes dear. You, me, Zilla, the children, Hiram. And Ethel, of course. Ethel, what's the matter? What are you growling about?"

For growling Ethel undoubtedly was. She was up on her feet, still straddling the diaper bag, her teeth bared in as ominous a snarl as could be achieved by an animal designed along the general lines of a giant bath mat. Her eyes were shooting green fire, her paws scrabbling at the ground as if revving up for a takeoff. Her head was darting from side to side, her ears flapping across her face with every dart and causing added annoyance, as if she weren't annoyed enough already. Osbert was about to go over and see what was eating her when his shovel struck something. Something roughly the size and shape of a crate of canned peaches, covered with ancient waxed canvas.

"I—I think—" Frantically he scraped away the sand. Opening the top was no chore at all, the lock was gone, the rusted-through hinges crumbled at a touch. The contents were as bright and shiny as on the day Hiram Jellyby had found them and reburied them.

"Here's your gold, Hiram!"

"Danged if it ain't! Good shovelin', bub."

"Good dowsing, you mean," Osbert demurred. "It's Dittany who deserves the credit."

"It was really the turkey bone," Dittany was murmuring when all at once they found themselves invaded. The intruder was a bearded man dressed in an old-fashioned frock coat with purple socks pulled up over his pant legs as if to simulate a pair of purple gaiters that he'd meant to wear and couldn't find at the crucial moment. He was steering a bicycle one-handed and flourishing a six-shooter.

Ten feet from the group, he leaped off the bicycle, flung it from him, and pointed his gun at Hiram. This was a reasonable mistake, Hiram stood beside the trunkful of gold pieces, fully manifested now in his mule skinner clothes, apparently solid and strong as the Pre-Cambrian Shield.

"Stand and deliver," roared the brigand bicycler.

Hiram just gave him a look. "By gorry, mister, I seen you before! I'd know them squinchy little eyes anywhere."

"How kind of you to remember," the bearded one replied urbanely. "Now, sir, I'll thank you to load all that gold into these nice, new canvas saddlebags I've brought with me and strap them to my bicycle carrier."

"Sorry, mister. 'Fraid I can't oblige."

"I've got six bullets in here that say you can. Come on, old-timer, I mean business. Jump!"

The gun went off. A bullet buried itself in the turf about an inch and a half from Hiram's left boot. He gazed down at the small hole it made with an expression of mild amusement.

"Hell, I seen better shootin' than that from a ten-year-old kid with a bunged-up ol' horse pistol. Try again a little harder, mister."

"Damn you! Do you think I won't?"

The highwayman was rattled, Dittany sensed. He'd thought this holdup was going to be a piece of cake, with only a weaponless old gaffer, a young couple, and a brace of babies standing between him and the gold. Apparently he was unaware of Zilla Trott, even now sneaking up on him from behind with her hatchet at the ready. Dittany did hope Zilla wouldn't attempt any drastic cleavage in front of the twins, she didn't want them collecting subliminal memories of gore and bloodshed at so tender an age.

The highwayman, if that was what he deemed himself to be, was preparing to take a shot at Hiram's other boot. At the gun went off, Hiram, with every appearance of enjoyment, bounced about three feet off the ground and came back to roost smack on top of the gold. This further infuriated the shooter, one of whose purple socks had by now slipped down and was bunched untidily around his ankle.

As Hiram was unkindly pointing this out, Osbert took advantage of the diversion to slip over and help Ethel guard the babies, he signaled for Dittany to join them. Perhaps he had some thought of barricading his family behind the perambulator and shooting it out with the holdup man, though that seemed unlikely unless he was planning to improvise a bow and arrows from alder twigs.

Or perhaps Osbert was thinking in terms of a slingshot. It occurred to Dittany that she was still holding the wishbone. With that and the elastic top of her panty hose, much might be accomplished if she could only wiggle out of the garment without attracting that madman's notice. Now he was aiming straight for Hiram's midsection, shooting to kill, or so he erroneously assumed. Hiram was egging the ruffian on, flitting about like a veritable Tyl Eulenspiegel, making him waste his ammunition.

Five shots had been fired by now. If that weapon was in fact a six-shooter and the highwayman was no more adept at reloading than he was at trying to pick off a victim who was, had he but known, proof against the fastest bullet, this performance was not going to last much longer. The highwayman raised his gun again, and aimed deliberately at Hiram's chest. Hiram took the bullet without batting an eye.

"Oh, a bulletproof vest, eh? Think you're damned smart, don't you?" The gunman whirled, grabbed Dittany, who'd been trying to reach Osbert and the babies, and clamped his hands around her throat.

"All right, joker, this is it. Pack up that gold and bring it here or I strangle the girl!"

This was too much for Osbert and Ethel. Together, they launched themselves like rockets against the highwayman. Emitting a wild war whoop, Zilla slammed the flat side of her hatchet down on his head. Ethel grabbed his wrist in her teeth. Having landed a lusty right to the midriff, Osbert, with great presence of mind, then tied the winded rogue's shoelaces together in a hard knot so that he couldn't run away, even assuming he'd be able to wiggle out from under his various assailants.

"You know what?" said Zilla as she checked over her weapon for possible damage, "I'll bet you a nickel this bozo is the Peeping Tom. Two or three people have mentioned hearing a little tinkling noise when he was sneaking around the neighborhood. I heard it myself just now, when I felled him."

Strictly speaking, the felling had been a joint effort,

but Osbert was not about to quibble. His mind was already speeding in a new direction. "A tinkling noise, eh? Hiram, shine your eyes this way, can you?"

By now, the late muleteer's eyes were a brilliant, clear canary yellow and working just fine. It was as Osbert had deduced. He unbuttoned the fallen would-be murderer's frock coat to reveal a splendid gold watch chain replete with sundry equally auriferous accoutrements including a gold pencil, a gold penknife, a twenty-dollar gold piece, a gold nugget carved in the shape of a beetle, a gold toothpick in a gold case, a gold cigar cutter with a steel blade, and a timberwolf's tooth with a gold filling in it.

CHAPTER
20

As they gazed in wonderment upon the telltale watch chain, a bright red sports car with lots of chrome trimming pulled to a stop at the edge of the field. A man got out carrying a large electric lantern and held the door open for two women. One, easily recognized in the lantern's light, was Arethusa Monk wearing her Spanish shawl. The other, Dittany deduced, must be Mrs. Pollicot James, less quickly indentifiable because she wasn't carrying her dulcimer.

"Is everybody all right here?" cried Pollicot James, for of course no other could be driving such a car and escorting such passengers. "Mother and I came back early. We were out for a little spin to celebrate our reunion with darling Arethusa when we heard shots being fired."

"As well you might," Dittany shouted back. "This gazookus was trying to shoot Hiram Jellyby."

"Hiram Jellyby?" Darling Arethusa's voice conveyed only gentle amusement. "Stap my garters, what an exercise in futility. Or was it? You're not leaking ectoplasm anywhere, are you, Mr. Jellyby?"

"Nope. Sound as a bell, far's I can make out."

The voice came from just below the bright yellow eyes,

which were now the only visible evidence that Hiram was still among those present. Mrs. Pollicot James seemed nonplussed, as well she might.

"This—er—gazookus you mention, Mrs. Monk. I'm afraid I don't quite see—"

"He's the body on the ground," Dittany explained. "Zilla—that is to say, Mrs. Trott—you met her that day at the garden club wingding—beaned him with her hatchet. Then my husband tied his shoelaces together, showing commendable presence of mind if I do say so. The gazookus is really a crooked banker. He's also the rotter who made the security guard's cow drink horse liniment, which was a perfectly awful thing to do and whatever punishment he gets, it serves him right. I expect all that face fungus he's wearing peels off easily enough. Osbert darling, would you mind giving it a tug?"

"Not at all, darling. I've been thinking myself that there's something a trifle spurious—ah, yes. Sorry about the tugging. I'm afraid you overdid the spirit gum a bit, Mr. Cottle."

"Cottle!" shrieked Mrs. James. "Pollicot, give me that lantern."

"M'ff." The man on the ground sounded indignant, but as he was trying to articulate through a mouthful of crepe hair, his wrath did not come out strong and clear, which was probably just as well.

"Shine your lantern a little closer, Mrs. James," Osbert suggested.

The strong light brought out golden glints from the watch chain, the penknife, the pencil, the gold piece, the cigar cutter, the nugget carved into a beetle, and the goldfilled wolf's tooth. Osbert had got the beard all off now, revealing a large, smooth, pink face with a reasonably adequate pair of eyebrows but little else to distinguish it from many other bland, pink faces of either sex.

"James!" cried the mother.

"Father!" cried the son.

"Stap my garters!" cried Arethusa, not to be left out of the conversation. "It was my impression, Mrs. James, that you were a widow."

"It was my impression also," the elder woman assured her with considerable heat. "James, explain yourself."

"Go fry your ears, Penelope," snarled the renegade. "What the hell was the idea, refusing to pay my ransom? Fine wife you turned out to be! A man goes to all the pain and bother of chopping off his own pinkie finger at great personal inconvenience, not to mention the nuisance of wrapping it up and sending it off and having to wear gloves all the time forever after with tissue paper stuffed in the left-hand baby finger, and where does it get him? I know all about that phoney memorial service you put on, Penelope. Swanking around in a black designer-model outfit and a widow's veil, forsooth!"

"Did you say forsooth, Mr. Cottle?" Arethusa inquired with professional interest.

"I sure as heck did, Tootsie, and I'll say it again, all I want to. Forsooth! Forsooth! Forsooth! Put that in your pipe and smoke it, Penelope. As for that mollycoddle son of yours, he can go out and find himself a job peddling shoelaces, for all of me. I'm cutting him out of my will as soon as I can find myself a sufficiently unscrupulous lawyer. And furthermore, Penelope, I'm filing for divorce on the grounds of mental cruelty. Refusing to ransom your mutilated husband! Calling yourself Mrs. Pollicot James! What was wrong with Mrs. James Cottle, pray tell? For the information of all present, I want it made publicly known that this woman was no more born a Pollicot than the man in the moon. Her old man's name was plain Bill Bugglesby. At the time of her birth, Bill was working on the railroad as a spikeman."

"A spikeman?" inquired Osbert, always ready to broaden his horizons.

"That's just what he was, bub. Old Bill's duty was to

walk the tracks with a bottle of spike polish at the ready, shining up the tips of the spikes as soon as they got the least bit dull and grungy-looking. His division foreman had been butler to one of those stately home dukes or earls or whatever in England. When he came to Canada to seek his fortune, he brought with him a lot of high standards and lofty ideals which, as I'm sure we all agree, helped our fair Commonwealth to become what she is today."

"He's talking nonsense," insisted Mrs. Cottle, as she must now be known, though perhaps only temporarily. "My father was a steel magnate."

"I'm not saying he wasn't, Penelope. What happened was," Cottle had his audience in the palm of his hand now and was making the most of the situation, "Bill Bugglesby got into a poker game with a gink who owned a small railroad-spike foundry. I'm not saying Bill played with marked cards, mind you; I'm only saying that by the end of that game, Bill owned the deed to the foundry. The business wasn't much when he took it over, the plain fact of the matter was that the gink hadn't been any too adept at forging railroad spikes. But Bill knew spikes from the ground up, needless to say, so he just forged ahead until he'd cornered the spike market for most of the western provinces, which just goes to show what diligence, perseverance, and a few extra aces up your sleeve can accomplish."

"Very interesting," snapped Dittany. "Now tell us why you fed poor Mossy that bottle of horse liniment, causing her to become distracted with pain and trample an innocent security guard to death?"

"Wilberforce Woodiwiss innocent?" snarled the renegade banker. "Back up and come again, girlie. Woodiwiss lied to the cops about me carrying myself on my back, didn't he? Furthermore, he helped me get that trunkful of money wrapped up and packed. Added to which, he took one end when I took the other and we lugged it together out to my car. As per our agreement, which I carried out faithfully, I paid him the stipulated sum before I tied him up. In stolen money, I grant you. I had to bring the loot out here and bury it by myself, of course, but that was no great problem. I'm a rugged outdoorsman type, as anybody could tell you who wasn't planning to defame my character the second she opens her mouth again, which Penelope has always been far too prone to do."

"Rugged, indeed!" Mrs. Cottle sniffed one of her more contemptuous sniffs. "What's this nonsense about feeding liniment to a cow? I had no idea you were so versatile, James. Wasn't it rather careless of you to kill your henchperson by so messy a method?"

"Look, you do what you can with what you've got. Woodiwiss was an idiot for trying to keep a cow anyway. What does a bank security guard know about cows? Took him six months to figure out how to get the milk, he thought he was supposed to use the beast's tail as a pump handle. That's the kind of incompetence a person has to work with nowadays, not worth the powder to blow 'em to Detroit. Come on, you good-for-nothing young squirt, untie my shoelaces and let me get out of here with my gold."

"That's not your gold," Osbert replied, quite unperturbed.

"What do you mean, it's not my gold? I held you up according to accepted protocol, didn't I? Was there any flaw in my technique from start to finish?"

"Well, you'd laid the groundwork thoroughly enough by creeping around and listening under people's windows for what information you could pick up that might be useful in your attempt to resteal the bank money. You did slip a bit there, however, in failing to muffle your watch chain adequately. Tinkles were reported by various residents who naturally assumed you were just a dirty-minded old voyeur."

"That was what I wanted them to think, it was part of

my disguise. I'll be more careful about the watch chain next time." Cottle was trying to wheedle himself into his captors' good graces. "And I'm really sorry about the purple gaiters. I'd stolen them from—perhaps I shouldn't mention where."

"You stole them from Minerva Oakes's attic in your guise as Tryphosa Melloe the root lady," said Dittany. "It was a caddish and contemptible thing to do, and furthermore those gaiters are of great historical significance to the town of Lobelia Falls, having been worn by no less a figure than Winona Pitcher, about whom you must surely have gleaned a vast amount of information during your Peeping Tom and Melloe phases. You'd better be able to produce the gaiter that's still missing if you don't want another fifty years or so tacked on to your sentence."

"What sentence? You can't pin anything on me."

"Oh, yes, we can. You stole Hedrick Snarf's purple silk socks, too. You must have broken into his room at the inn. Why didn't you steal a horse while you were about it, instead of an unpicturesque bicycle?"

"Because I didn't want a horse, damn it! Oh, sorry, Mrs. Monk I didn't mean to use language unbecoming a gentleman, but you can be pretty exasperating, you know. Anyway, the truth is that I'm scared of horses. They blow in your ear when you're trying to get the saddle on. I can't stand having my ear blown into by a great big slobbering creature with iron toenails. Bicycles, now, you know where you are with a bicycle. They don't have offensive habits, they don't keep wanting bagfuls of oats all the time, and they don't bite your leg when you try to climb onto them. Furthermore, they're easy to steal. Where was I going to rustle a horse in a hurry? Give me a good old two-wheeler any day and to blazes with authenticity. I figured you small-town hicks wouldn't notice the difference in the dark anyway. Little did I reck that I was going to be up against a pair of neon eyeballs and a bulletproof vest."

"That wasn't a bulletproof vest," Osbert explained. "Your bullets went through Hiram without making any impression because he happens to be a ghost."

"What? Are you crazy? How could he be a ghost? I saw him plain as day. Plainer. You don't think I believed all that garbage people were dishing out about that old mule skinner who got shot to death out here leaving a trunkful of gold he was expecting you to dig up. I wasn't born yesterday, you know."

"But Mr. Cottle, if you were so sure the dead mule skinner's tale was a lot of horse feathers, why were you so eager to rob us of the gold?"

"As things turned out, that became the only option open to me, so I thought I might as well give it a go. You see, what I did when I robbed my own bank was, I retained a sackful of cash for my immediate expenses and got Woodiwiss to help me pack up the leftovers in waterproof bundles which neatly fitted into a small trunk with a lot of brass trimming on it that I thought would be easy to locate in the fullness of time by divining, at which I'm supremely adept."

"Why did you bury the trunk out here?" barked Zilla, who thus far had been standing guard in stern silence with her hatchet at the ready.

"Oh, this just looked to me like a nice, godforsaken place in the middle of nowhere. I was getting a little worried about trundling the money around in my car, which of course was a new one that I'd bought under an assumed name with falsified identification papers as any practical man of business engaged in major embezzlement would naturally remember to do. Once I got the trunk stashed away, I was footloose and fancy-free to go whither I listed and do as I pleased without Penelope yammering at me to take her someplace cultural when I lusted to wallow in the fleshpots. Which, I may say with a good deal of satisfaction, is precisely what I've been doing ever since my unfortunate demise."

"I always knew you were essentially a lout, James," the ex-widow said with a good deal of bitterness.

"And how right you were, Penelope," replied the errant spouse. "Not for me the two-string dulcimer, kiddo. You can keep your waly-waly, I'll stick to my hot-cha-cha."

"Philistine!" snarled Pollicot, casting an anxious glance at Arethusa.

His father nodded as best he could since Ethel was still refusing him permission to sit up and none of the other seemed interested in calling her off.

"You hit the nail on the head, my boy, if indeed you are the fruit of my loins, which I've sometimes wondered about because I've never been able to figure out how any son of a red-hot papa like me could have turned out to be such a cold fish. Anyway, I'd been flinging the moolah high, wide, and handsome until I happened to notice a month or so ago that I was just about at the bottom of the sack. It then occurred to me that I might be wise to re-plenish my supply before I found myself flat broke with my stash of cash buried under the winter snows out here where the wind comes whistling up the pant legs and the grizzly bears come prowling o'er the plains."

"They don't, actually," said Dittany.

"Oh yeah? Then what's this thing sitting here growl-ing at me?"

"We're not quite sure, but her name is Ethel and she's pretty darned sore at you just now so I'd suggest you quit thrashing around like that. You were saying that you'd decided to come back here and dig up the leftover money you'd stolen from the bank."

"Embezzled, if you please, Mrs. Monk. Okay, I stole it, but *embezzled* is a more courteous term to use when chat-ting with a larcenous bank president, as Penelope here would be the first to tell you if she weren't so preoccupied just now in trying to figure out some way of putting a good face on the social dilemma that she's going to find herself in when I get carted off to the steel chateau."

Mr. Cottle was smiling a mean and sinister smile. "Hard lines, Penelope, old girl. But you did take me for better or worse, you know. You simply didn't realize how much worse I could be. I've enjoyed many a quiet chuckle thinking about what you'd say if you ever found out what really happened to me. That memorial service which you organized and I attended in my guise as Tryphosa Melloe was one of the high points. The lies people tell in the interests of propriety!"

"What guise?" scoffed the by now totally exasperated Mrs. Cottle. "Surely, James, you don't think you could have fooled your own wife?"

"Of course I do, and can, and have. And will again if I can manage to break away from this pack of yahoos. You wouldn't care to pick up that hatchet of Mrs. Trott's and brain this snarling behemoth before it takes a hunk out of me?"

"You're quite right, James, I should not care to brain this snarling behemoth. I should, on the other hand, be quite pleased to watch it take a hunk out of you. If I knew the proper form of address, I should assure the creature that it needn't hang back on my account. I trust you realize that you have in fact put me in an impossible position, and probably ruined what would have been a highly suitable marriage between your son and Miss Arethusa Monk, who happens to be the reigning queen of roguish Regency romance."

"With a queenly income to match, I trust," sneered the incorrigible Cottle. "Sorry to queer your pitch, son, but some day your princess will come, assuming your mother doesn't head her off at the pass. You don't really suppose old clutchy-claws Penelope will ever let you off the leash, do you, Billy-boy?"

"Is that his real name?" Dittany asked.

"Oh, yes, William Bugglesby Cottle, named for his grandpa the railroad spike magnate. I don't know where this Pollicot nonsense came from. Now, people, not to be rashly importunate, but do you suppose I could sit up and pick the knots out of my shoelaces? It's damp lying here and I'm subject to rheumatic twinges. Look, how about if we work out a little deal?"

"What sort of deal?" Osbert asked him.

"A pecunarily viable one, shall we say? The gist of it is, as I've been frank to reveal, I am at the moment in an unfortunate position fiscally as well as physically. As you know, that trunkful of stolen pelf, not to put it too crassly, was accidentally dowsed by Billy here, not that I hold it against him because he didn't know any better, poor simp. According to information gained from my nocturnal researches around the neighborhood, the loot which I'd meant to be the prop and mainstay of my twilight years is now in the far too capable hands of the RCMP. Can you corroborate this, Mr. Monk?"

"Oh, yes, you're quite right."

"Of all sad words of tongue or pen, the saddest are these: it might have been. This was a disappointment to me, naturally, but not necessarily a catastrophe, since I was also hearing rumors of a chest of gold that had been buried out here by an old mule skinner. And almost but not quite retrieved by an ancestor of mine, interestingly enough. Mrs. Oakes might like to know that in my quest for my imaginary roots while disguised as Mrs. Melloe— which I've enjoyed very much, by the way—I discovered that I am in fact descended from a delightful fellow who was known to his fellow bandits and mule rustlers as Fancylegs Ford—Ford being an alias, of course—because of his penchant for wearing a pair of purple gaiters that he'd acquired from some Eastern dude during a train robbery. Great-Uncle Fancylegs had had the misfortune to shoot the mule skinner dead while trying to intimidate him into revealing the whereabouts of the gold."

"Got me spang between the eyes," confirmed a voice from the dark. "What did the bugger do with my mules?

He better o' treated 'em right, or I'll look 'im up in the Akashic Record an'—"

"Take it easy, old scout. According to my researches, Fancylegs was dreadfully upset at having killed you, he hadn't meant to do more than scare you into giving up the gold. He buried you as best he could, not very efficiently, I'm afraid, because he wasn't used to manual labor. Then he tied his horse behind your wagon and drove off with the mule team. As it happened, he knew of a railroad baron who'd once been a mule driver himself and still hankered after a team of his own. Your mules being apparently somewhat outstanding specimens of the breed—"

"Best dern mules in all Canada, an' I'll lick the ha'nt that says they wasn't."

"Well, I expect they must have been, because the railroad baron built them a palatial stable with solid silver drinking troughs and all modern conveniences—modern for the times, that is. He also had your wagon gilded. He used to hitch it up to the team and drive across the prairies singing 'Buffalo Gals.' There was a story around that the mules used to sing along with the driver, but one suspects that may have been some drunken newspaperman's flight of fancy."

CHAPTER
21

"*T*hat ain't no flight o' fancy, dag-nab it!" Hiram Jellyby was beside himself with anger, his eyeballs a flaming vermilion. "I learnt them mules to sing 'Buffalo Gals' myself, nights around the campfire after we was fed an' watered an' felt like havin' a little hooraw before we turned in." His temper softened. "But you say they done all right for theirselves after I was kilt?"

"Couldn't have done better, by all accounts. Every one of them lived to a ripe old age and was buried with solemn rites, including a beanhole barbecue and massed singing of 'Buffalo Gals' by mixed choirs imported all the way from Ottawa. Those mules used to get written up in the papers every so often, I've seen stories myself. My Uncle James, for whom I was named, kept a scrapbook. The man who bought the mules was the same railroad baron for whom Bill Bugglesby used to polish spikes. I rather think it may indirectly have been he and his mules who drew me to Penelope. I can't think what else could have caused me to succumb to her charms, except possibly the size of the fortune Bill was willing to settle on his only child."

"By gorry! My ol' buddies writ up in the papers."

Hiram was sniffling a bit, and who could have blamed him? Osbert and Dittany exchanged compassionate glances; Zilla and Arethusa beamed at Hiram with genuine affection. For all but the Cottles, this was a tender moment in what had thus far been a singularly untender evening. Dittany made a mental note to tell Mr. Glunck about the newspaper stories so that he could hunt them up and put copies on display with the platinum prints. Osbert began mentally recasting the eulogy he meant to deliver at the interment of Hiram's bones, which had been set for the following morning. As they stood there, each with his own thoughts, James Cottle now upright but with his shoelaces still in a hard knot, a voice came out of the darkness.

"Noo then, what's going on here?"

"Sergeant MacVicar," shouted Osbert. "Howdy, Chief, you're just the man we want to see. Here's your Peeping Tom, who also happens to be both the bank robber and the murderer who killed the bank guard by feeding liniment to his cow."

"Not to mention the sneak thief who swiped Winona Pitcher's purple gaiters out of Minerva Oakes's attic while impersonating a respectable woman in search of her roots," Zilla Trott prompted.

"Hoots toots, a veritable one-man crime wave. Wad you happen to hae found oot yon arch-villain's real name?"

"It's Cottle," said Dittany. "Plain old James Cottle. And Mrs. allegedly Pollicot James here is really Mrs. James Cottle and her son is William Bugglesby Cottle, named for his rich grandfather the spike-polisher."

"I see. You couldna hae made the situation clearer, lass. Have you charged him, Deputy Monk?"

"No, Chief. To tell you the truth, I'm a bit nonplussed, not to say buffaloed, about the protocol. Mr. Cottle's admitted in front of me and all these other witnesses that he robbed his own bank and cut off his own finger and tried to extort ransom from his wife. He carried part of the loot away in a sack and he's pretty steamed at you for giving the Mounties that other trunkful of money he'd buried out here, which he'd planned to toss away in riotous living as he's already done with the other half. He's a thoroughgoing bad hat, Chief, I didn't know whether the bank robbery charge or the manslaughter by cow ought to take precedence."

"Aye, Deputy Monk, an interesting legal point to consider. Cottle's fingerprints being on the money wrappings, there can be nae doot of his guilt in yon matter of the bank robbery. As to the manslaughter charge, I fear we should have to find the liniment bottle in order to make it stick."

"Ha! Ha!" crowed the one-man crime wave. "I deny the liniment. You can't pin Wilberforce Woodiwiss's death on me, you haven't a shred of evidence."

"Want to bet?" Osbert retorted smugly. "What about the golden whistle that was found on the floor of the cow garage and identified by Mildred Orser, sister of Wilberforce Woodiwiss and present owner of the cow, whose name happens to be Mossy, as having come from that very watch chain you've got strung across your ugly paunch right now?"

"A golden whistle!" Avid greed was written large now on the banker's normally bland pink countenance. "Where is it? Let me see, quick!"

"Here it is."

From his pocket Osbert extracted a small cardboard box lined with cotton that had originally contained a bracelet made from slices of kiwi fruit embedded in clear plastic which Dittany's mother had mistakenly thought her daughter would like for a birthday present. Now lying on the cotton was the little golden whistle Mrs. Orser had given him, still bravely shining despite its battered and trodden-upon condition. The banker moaned.

"Damn that cow! Why couldn't she have watched where she put her stupid feet?"

That did it. Sergeant MacVicar rose up in the full majesty of the law, read James Cottle his rights in a resounding Presbyterian tone, and arrested him with a verve and panache that none of the onlookers would ever forget.

Awesome was the moment when the sergeant snapped on the handcuffs. Held were several breaths as Osbert knelt to slash away the knotted shoelaces. The laces would of course have had to be removed anyway when Cottle got to the jail, so that he wouldn't try to hang himself with them. Nothing, however, seemed further from the prisoner's mind than suicide; he was already talking boastfully of getting a flexible-minded lawyer and beating the rap.

"Nonsense, James," his wife retorted sharply. "You are now a jailbird and I am going to initiate divorce proceedings tomorrow morning."

This statement, regrettably, elevated Cottle's spirits to a new high. He was singing "Buffalo Gals" at the top of his untuneful voice when they loaded him into Lobelia Falls's official and only police car. Hiram Jellyby remarked scathingly that his mules had sung it better, and was quite likely right.

The box of gold pieces that Cottle had hoped to steal to make up for his confiscated bank loot was loaded into the back of the police car. Cottle had clamored to sit beside the gold but Sergeant MacVicar wouldn't let him and it served him right, as Penelope Bugglesby Cottle was the first to remind him.

"Pollicot," she went on, "take me home. I am totally prostrate."

She neither looked nor sounded even moderately prostrate. Her son glanced uneasily from his mother to Arethusa and back again. "Ah—er—mother—"

"Now, Pollicot!"

The son cast one last, yearning look at the lady of his heart and helped his mother into the red sports car. Arethusa didn't even notice.

"Well," said Zilla, absentmindedly polishing the blade of her trusty hatchet on the hem of her skirt, "I guess that's it for tonight. Might as well mosey along home."

"Drop by the house in a while for a cup of camomile tea if you'd like to," said Dittany. "We've got to get the kids to bed first. They've been out too late, the little rounders. Now what did I do with Gramp's wishbone?"

"Here it is, dear," said Osbert.

"But where are the gold cuff links I'd tied on to the tip? That ornery sidewinder Cottle must have pinched them from force of habit."

"A knave of the first water," remarked Arethusa. "One can hardly admire so thoroughgoing a scoundrel, but one does have to feel a certain grudging respect for his audacity. Have I mislaid an escort around here somewhere? Meseems I came with some chap driving a red car."

"William Bugglesby Cottle," Dittany reminded her. "Previously known to us all as Pollicot James, for reasons that may never be fully explained. And his mother, who claims to be totally prostrated. I have a feeling you won't be seeing much more of that twosome, Arethusa. You weren't really planning to marry him, were you?"

"Marry whom, prithee? What was that you were saying about tea?"

"Come on, Dittany," said Osbert. "Climb in with the kids and I'll give you a ride home."

"Thank you darling, but somebody has to carry the turkey bone. Oh well, those cuff links were ugly anyway. Then we'll see you later, Zilla?"

"No, I don't think so, thanks. I'm not trusting Hiram with that sherry bottle of yours a second time. What do you think will become of the gold? Do you suppose we'll ever find out where it came from?"

"I shouldn't be surprised," said Osbert. "Sergeant MacVicar will get his sons working on it. Look at that moon up there. Doesn't it make you want to sing?"

It did. They all joined in on "Buffalo Gals": Dittany, Zilla, Arethusa, Hiram, Annie, Rennie, and Ethel. It was a merry party that walked home from Hunnikers' Field that night.

And it was a record crowd that met the following morning to hear Mr. Pennyfeather preach his memorial sermon over the aged and eroded bones of the late Hiram Jellyby. Hiram's mortal remains were gathered into a nice mahogany box that Michael Trott had made in manual training class when he was a boy. Zilla and Minerva had lined it elegantly with the remains of a silk-covered down comforter that had been purchased by Minerva's mother in 1927. Mr. Glunck had lent the platinum print to be displayed in front of the box during the service. Hiram was deeply moved by this public show of concern and compassion. He was attending the service but did not plan to materialize in front of the congregation because he didn't think it would be quite the thing for the ghost to hog the show away from the bones. Zilla didn't think so either.

It was, as everybody later agreed, a lovely service even though Mr. Pennyfeather had drawn the line at "Buffalo Gals" and substituted "Shall We Gather at the River," which was appropriate enough in its way. Osbert delivered his eulogy with grace, brevity, and a touch of humor. When he mentioned the faithful mules and their meaningful relationship with their devoted driver, a few heartfelt sniffles came from what appeared to be an empty space in the front pew, but nobody noticed those because so many others were sniffling too.

A light collation in the vestry after the bones had been reverently interred in the graveyard beside the church gave people a chance to recruit their inner persons on lemonade and brownies, tell each other how nice it had been of them to come, and speculate about what was going to happen to all that gold.

On that question, rumors were rife, Grandsire Coskoff's being the rifest. He remembered his father telling about a miner who'd staggered into Lobelia Falls broke to the wide and desperately sick with fever. Kind townsfolk had nursed him back to health and given him a grubstake. Some years later, the miner had struck it rich, remembered his benefactors, and shipped them a chestful of gold with which to build a shelter for the needy and helpless of the area, but the chest was hijacked along the way. If this claim could be proved, and Mr. Glunck was rooting through the archives in high hopes of producing the required evidence, the gold might legally be applied to the old people's housing project to which many descendants of those same townspeople were already committed. There was a good deal of disparity as to how this project should be carried out, but a general feeling that there was no sense in starting to argue about the blueprints until they knew for sure who was going to get the gold.

All in all it was a well-satisfied group that eventually finished the brownies, sorted out who owned the various cake plates and cookie tins, and dispersed. Minerva asked Zilla if she'd like to stop over for a sandwich and a cup of tea but Zilla said she didn't think she'd better. She had things to do back home.

In fact, Zilla had almost nothing to do back home. Nemea was out in the garden, twitching the tip end of her tail back and forth while keeping a steady surveillance on a certain spot under a pea vine. She barely rolled an eye when Zilla came around the side of the house and let herself in at the kitchen door.

Once inside, Zilla stood aimlessly beside the sink, feeling more alone than she had for years. Even her usually perceptive cat hadn't noticed how solitary Zilla felt. Nemea would saunter in when she took the notion, she'd be friendly enough, but did Nemea really care? What did Zilla Trott actually mean to her cat? A well-filled food dish? A warm lap to sleep on when Nemea took the notion? A leg to rub against, an ear to purr into, a clean kitty box when cold weather came and going outdoors for practical purposes ceased to appeal?

Was this all Zilla Trott's future was to be?

For a little while—too short a while—there had been another human voice in the house, sometimes also another face: bearded, weather-worn, not always clearly manifested, frequently showing the effects of spirits other than the ectoplasmic kind, never what a person could call a handsome face, yet somehow not unattractive. A lone widow learned to take what she got and be grateful, Hiram's companionship had been at least a change. Even a pleasant one, some of the time.

But now that old mule skinner's bones had been dug up from where his murderer had hidden them and decently laid to rest in consecrated ground. Hiram Jellyby's last mission on this earth was accomplished. He'd said it himself: a haunt has to do what he has to do. The old coot must be back where he'd come from by now, checking over the Akashic Record to find out what was next on his agenda.

Well, she supposed it had been fun of a sort while it lasted. Zilla picked up the teakettle, filled it with water enough for two cups—habits were so quickly learned, so hard to put aside—and spooned dried camomile flowers into her teapot. The water boiled, she made the tea and poured herself a cup.

One solitary cup. Zilla dumped herself down in the wooden chair where she always sat and gazed bleakly into the cup. The camomile tea was bright yellow, as yellow as Hiram's eyes had been last night out at Hunnikers' Field. Why had she bothered to make tea she didn't want? Where was the comfort of drinking alone? She lifted her hand to set the cup and saucer aside.

"Boo!"

For a stunned moment, Zilla sat paralyzed, then she

let him have it. "Boo yourself, you old reprobate! Why aren't you up there somewhere studying the Akashic Record? Weren't you spouting off a while back about how a haunt's got to do what he's got to do?"

"Oh hell, Zilla, I'm in no all-fired hurry. Ain't no such thing as time anyways, that's just somethin' the smart alecks in the front office thunk up to keep the clockmakers in business. What's that muck you're drinkin'? Can't you find a decent cup o' coffee an' maybe a spare doughnut around here someplace?"

Zilla Trott pushed back her chair, picked up the cup she'd set aside, and dumped her camomile tea in the sink. "All right, you darned old slave-driver, I'll put the coffee-pot on. I'm not going begging to Minerva for any more doughnuts, though, just when we thought we'd got you safely planted. How about if I open us a can of beans?"